Praise for

CANYONS OF NIGHT

"Jayne Castle has delivered another captivating romance in *Canyons of Night*, the conclusion to the addictive Looking Glass Trilogy. No matter who she's writing as, whether it's as Castle, Jayne Ann Krentz, or Amanda Quick, this is one author who never, ever disappoints . . . [A] spectacular read that'll have you reading nonstop for hours only to lament the end when you turn your final page."   —*Fresh Fiction*

"Writing as Castle, romance supernova Jayne Ann Krentz delivers another irresistible addition to her Harmony books while, at the same time, cleverly freshening the series up by setting things in the new locale of Rainshadow. With its danger-infused, passion-rich plot; captivatingly wrought characters; and sharp humor, *Canyons of Night* is both a must-read for Harmony addicts and also an excellent introduction for newbies to Castle's unique brand of romance."
—*Booklist* (starred review)

"Complex, bold, funny, and hot, this darkly tantalizing tale, uplifted by dust bunny antics and zingy dialogue, masterfully concludes the captivating Looking Glass Trilogy. It lays the groundwork for Castle's new Rainshadow series, which will explore the remote island's mysterious Preserve and promises to be one of her most intriguing projects to date."
—*Library Journal*

"I really enjoyed the romantic chemistry between the hero and heroine . . . Several action scenes keep the story interesting and the description of the inside of the Preserve includes some creative delights."   —*Romance Book Scene*

continued . . .

Praise for

MIDNIGHT CRYSTAL

"Castle delivers another captivating futuristic romance that has all the sexy chemistry, sharply addictive wit, and fast-paced intrigue her readers expect." —*Chicago Tribune*

"In the latest flawlessly written addition to her futuristic romantic-suspense series, Castle cleverly clicks the final pieces of her Dreamlight Trilogy into place, creating a fast-paced, sexy, and witty treat." —*Booklist*

"With her classic, sassy flair, Castle brings this engrossing trilogy to a satisfying and thoroughly delightful conclusion, putting the old Winters/Jones feud to rest in a most romantic way." —*Library Journal*

"It is always lovely to visit Harmony again. The plot has plenty of excitement, danger, and hot steamy sex to go around." —*Fresh Fiction*

"A terrific entry that fans of the author will relish. The story line is fast paced and action packed . . . This is a winning stand-alone, but the brilliance of the author comes across by reading and comparing the trilogy." —*Midwest Book Review*

"Plenty of sensual tension and some quirky characters as well." —*The Romance Readers Connection*

"With her usual talent, the author weaves what should be way too many components together into a story that keeps you glued to the pages . . . a spectacular read . . . I was disappointed when I finally set the book down, and still have burning questions about the dust bunnies. Can I hope for more stories set on Harmony? One can always hope." —*Night Owl Reviews*

The LOST NIGHT

A RAINSHADOW NOVEL

JAYNE CASTLE

JOVE BOOKS, NEW YORK

THE BERKLEY PUBLISHING GROUP
Published by the Penguin Group
Penguin Group (USA) Inc.
375 Hudson Street, New York, New York 10014, USA
Penguin Group (Canada), 90 Eglinton Avenue East, Suite 700, Toronto, Ontario M4P 2Y3, Canada
(a division of Pearson Penguin Canada Inc.) • Penguin Books Ltd., 80 Strand, London WC2R 0RL,
England • Penguin Group Ireland, 25 St. Stephen's Green, Dublin 2, Ireland (a division of Penguin
Books Ltd.) • Penguin Group (Australia), 250 Camberwell Road, Camberwell, Victoria 3124, Australia
(a division of Pearson Australia Group Pty. Ltd.) • Penguin Books India Pvt. Ltd., 11 Community
Centre, Panchsheel Park, New Delhi—110 017, India • Penguin Group (NZ), 67 Apollo Drive,
Rosedale, Auckland 0632, New Zealand (a division of Pearson New Zealand Ltd.) • Penguin Books
(South Africa) (Pty.) Ltd., 24 Sturdee Avenue, Rosebank, Johannesburg 2196, South Africa

Penguin Books Ltd., Registered Offices: 80 Strand, London WC2R 0RL, England

THE LOST NIGHT

A Jove Book / published by arrangement with the author

ISBN: 978-1-62090-420-6

JOVE®
Jove Books are published by The Berkley Publishing Group,
a division of Penguin Group (USA) Inc.,
375 Hudson Street, New York, New York 10014.
JOVE® is a registered trademark of Penguin Group (USA) Inc.
The "J" design is a trademark of Penguin Group (USA) Inc.

PRINTED IN THE UNITED STATES OF AMERICA

For Darwina, who knows a great role model when she sees one. Amberella rules!

A Note from Jayne

Welcome to Rainshadow Island on the world of Harmony.

In the Rainshadow novels you will meet the passionate men and women who are drawn to this remote island in the Amber Sea. You will also get to know their friends and neighbors in the small town of Shadow Bay.

Everyone on Rainshadow has a past; everyone has secrets. But none of those secrets is as dangerous as the ancient mystery concealed inside the paranormal fence that guards the forbidden portion of the island known as the Preserve.

The secrets of the Preserve have been locked away for centuries. But now something dangerous is stirring. . . .

I hope you will enjoy the Rainshadow novels.

Sincerely,
Jayne

Chapter 1

"YOU BELONG TO ME," THE VAMPIRE SAID. "SOON YOU will understand that you are meant to be my bride. No matter what happens to me in this place, I will escape and I will come for you."

Marcus Lancaster's voice was rich, compelling, and resonant, the voice of an opera singer or the ultimate con man. He accompanied the words with a sly whisper of compelling energy that shivered with promise. *I can fulfill your deepest desires.*

Rachel Blake did not doubt for a moment that he truly did want her, but she was certain it was not because he had fallen in love with her. Lancaster was one of the monsters. That crowd didn't have the capacity to love. They were inclined, however, to be obsessive in their desires and, therefore, quite dangerous.

"I knew this was a waste of time." Rachel gathered up her notepad and pen and got to her feet. The silvery charms attached to her bracelet shivered and clashed lightly.

"You cannot run from me, my beloved," Lancaster said. He reached up with one well-manicured hand and touched the ear stud in his left ear. The small item of jewelry was made of black metal and set with a stone that was the color of rain.

The gesture was casual; made in an absent manner, as if Lancaster was not aware of what he was doing. But the hair on the back of Rachel's neck stirred. A chill of intuition raised goose bumps on her arms. Her palms went cold.

Lancaster wore another piece of jewelry, too, a discreet signet ring engraved with the image of a mythical Old World beast, a griffin.

She had shut down her senses so she wouldn't have to view Lancaster's aura, but there were traces of his energy on the table and everything else that he had touched in the room. She could not abide the way he was watching her. She had to get out of there.

She looked at the one-way window set into the wall as she went toward the door and raised her voice a little to make sure her unseen audience could hear her.

"That's it, Dr. Oakford. I'm finished here. There's nothing I can do with this one."

She did not have to see the faces of Dr. Ian Oakford and the other members of the clinic staff who were observing the therapy session to know that they were all reacting with shock and outrage. Ditching a patient the way she had just done was extremely unprofessional. But she no longer cared. She'd had enough of Oakford and his team, enough of their research, enough of trying to fit in to the mainstream world of clinical para-psychology.

A woman—at least one who had been raised in a Harmonic Enlightenment community—could take only so much. Her parents and her instructors at the Academy were right. She was not cut out for mainstream life.

Most people would not have known Lancaster for what he was. Tall, blond, blue-eyed, and handsome in a slick, distinguished way, he was a natural-born predator that moved easily among his prey. But the dark side of her talent for aura healing was the ability to see the monsters and recognize them for what they were.

Lancaster had made a tidy fortune in the financial world. But a few days ago he had shocked his associates and his clients when he had voluntarily committed himself to the Chapman Clinic. He claimed to be plagued with severe para-psych trauma induced by the death of his wife several months earlier. His symptoms consisted of nightmares and dangerous delusions—precisely the severe symptoms required to be admitted to Dr. Oakford's new research program at the clinic.

She opened the door, stepped out into the hall, and signaled to the waiting orderly.

"You can take Mr. Lancaster back to his room, Carl," she said. "We're finished."

"Yes, ma'am."

Carl moved into the therapy room.

"Time to go, Mr. Lancaster," he said in the soothing, upbeat tone he used with all of the patients.

Lancaster chuckled. "I think I make Miss Blake nervous, Carl."

He got to his feet with leisurely grace, as though he were still dressed in the elegant silver gray suit and white tie that he had been wearing when he had walked into the clinic. Credit where credit was due, Rachel thought. Lancaster managed to make the baggy shirt and trousers that were standard issue for all patients look like resort-casual attire.

"Do you think she's afraid of me, Carl?" Lancaster infused his mellifluous words with just the right tincture of regret. "The last thing I want to do is frighten her."

"No, Mr. Lancaster, I'm sure Rachel isn't afraid of you," Carl said. "She has no reason to be afraid of you, now does she?"

"An excellent question, Carl. One that only Rachel can answer."

Rachel ignored both of them. The tiny stones set into her charms were starting to brighten. That was not a good sign because she was not consciously heating the crystals. They were reacting to her anxiety, a strong indication that her current state of psychical awareness and control was anything but harmonically tuned.

This was it, she thought. Lancaster was the last straw. She was going to hand in her resignation. The money was good at the clinic and the work provided the illusion that, in spite of what everyone back home said, she could make a place for herself in the mainstream world. But she had not signed on to deal with monsters like Marcus Lancaster. Nor was he the only one enrolled in the research trial. There was a very good reason why the patients in Oakford's project were housed in a locked ward.

She was an aura healer. She needed to use her talents in a positive way.

According to mainstream theories of para-psychology, energy-sucking psychic vampires were a myth; the stuff of horror novels and scary movies. But Rachel had met a few in her time and she knew the truth. The monsters were real. The good news was that most of them were relatively weak. They tended to pursue careers as con men, cult leaders, and politicians. They preyed on the emotionally vulnerable and the gullible.

Nobody denied that such low-level human predators existed, but few thought of them as vampires or monsters. Psychology textbooks, therapists, and clinicians had invented more politically correct terms to describe them. The diagnostic descriptions often involved the phrase *personality disorder* or *para-sociopath*. But the ancients back on the Old World had gotten it right, Rachel thought. So had the philosophers who had founded the Harmonic Enlightenment movement and established the Principles of Harmonic Enlightenment. The correct description for the Marcus Lancasters of the world was *evil*. When that particular attribute was coupled with some paranormal talent, you got psychic vampire.

The question that was worrying her the most was why Lancaster was attracted to her. She knew it was not love or even simple lust that had made him fixate on her out of all the members of the clinic staff. She had learned at the Academy that it was the prospect of controlling others that fascinated the monsters. By the nature of her own psychic ability and training she possessed a high degree of immunity to their talents. But she suspected her immunity was the very quality that had drawn Lancaster's attention. She was a challenge to him. Seducing and controlling her would affirm his own power.

The problem for the creeps was that they were incapable of achieving any degree of inner harmony. They spent their lives trying to fill the dead-zones on their spectrums. No ponzi scheme was ever lucrative enough, no cult was ever large enough, no business empire was ever sufficiently profitable, no position on the academic or political ladder was imbued with enough power to content a vampire.

And for the subset of vicious monsters who were drawn to death and violence, no amount of torture and killing could satisfy the bloodlust.

But monsters had dreams, too, Rachel thought. Evidently Marcus Lancaster had concluded that controlling her would fulfill some of his own dark fantasies.

Ian Oakford was waiting for her at the end of the hall. Last month when she had met him she had done a little fantasizing of her own. Ian was an intelligent, good-looking man with a very buff build and a lot of stylishly cut brown hair. He was endowed with the strong-jawed, trust-me-I'm-a-doctor presence that the patients and most of his female staff found appealing. Rachel was convinced that he could have had a lucrative second career as an actor playing a doctor in pharmaceutical commercials.

Not that Ian wasn't already doing very well for himself. He was still young by the standards of the profession, but his talent for para-psychology, combined with a lot of drive and ambition, had taken him far. Six months ago he had been appointed director of the new research wing of the Chapman Clinic. The funding from drug companies had quickly followed. He had several clinical trials in various stages of progress.

At that moment, however, Ian did not exhibit the kind, reassuring air that people liked in those engaged in the healing profession. Behind the lenses of his designer glasses his gray eyes glittered with anger. His square jaw was rigid.

"What do you think you're doing, walking out of a therapy session like that?" he demanded.

His voice was tight but controlled. Ian prided himself on never expressing extremes of emotions of any kind. He viewed such displays as a symptom of instability in the aura. He was right, of course, at least according to the Principles, and she had admired him for his self-mastery. But she did not need her talent to tell her that he was furious. She didn't blame him. He had taken a huge risk bringing her onto his research team. Her professional failings reflected badly on his judgment.

She braced herself for the inevitable. This was it, the end of her first really good job in the mainstream world. Her parents would breathe a sigh of relief. They had warned her about the difficulties she would encounter when she left the Academy and the Community.

"Marcus Lancaster is not experiencing severe para-trauma, Dr. Oakford," she said quietly. "He's faking it. He's incapable of feeling any sense of loss unless it affects his bottom line or threatens his personal safety. A dead wife wouldn't cut it, trust me, not unless her death cost him financially, which, according to what I found online, was not the case. Just the opposite. He inherited a lot of money when she died."

"You're wrong. No one could fake those night sweats and hallucinations."

"He is," she said simply. "And you and the others here at the clinic are buying his act."

"Why would a man in Lancaster's position pretend to have such a severe mental illness? It could destroy him financially and socially. No one in his right mind would voluntarily commit himself for treatment in a para-psych hospital the way Lancaster did unless he truly feared for his sanity."

"I have no idea why he committed himself volun-tarily," Rachel said. "You could ask him, but I can tell you right now he'll lie through his fangs."

"Fangs?"

"Sorry, teeth. As I was saying, I don't have any idea why he went to so much trouble to get into your research project, but if I were you, I'd watch out for a lawsuit somewhere down the road."

"Lawsuit?"

"I suspect that Lancaster has a long history of financial cons and schemes," she said. "Maybe he's got a plan for proving that he was a victim of unethical research practices. Who knows? I can't begin to guess his objectives but I can promise you that there is nothing you or I or modern para-pharmaceuticals can do for him. We can't fix the monsters."

"I have warned you before that we do not use terms like *monsters* and *vampires* in this clinic. I realize you're not a professional, Miss Blake, but that is no excuse for unprofessional language."

"Yes, Doctor."

"There are no such things as human monsters. How many times do I have to explain to you that Lancaster suffers from para-psych trauma complicated by an underlying instability of his para-senses?" Ian must have realized that his voice was rising. He regained control immediately. "I did not hire you to diagnose my patients. Your sole responsibility is to identify the erratic currents in their auras so that their disorders can be treated by a qualified therapist and appropriate prescriptions can be written."

"I understand," she said.

Behind Ian, Helen Nelson and Adrian Evans, the two members of the staff who had been observing the session with Oakford, walked quietly away in the opposite direction. They knew what was going to happen next, Rachel thought. They were on their way to spread the gossip.

Just before the pair turned the corner, Helen glanced back and gave Rachel a sympathetic look. Rachel managed a wan smile in return. She was keenly aware that most of the professional staff at the clinic viewed her with disapproval and, in some cases, outright hostility. Helen had been one of the kinder people on the research team. She had gone so far as to invite Rachel to join her for lunch in the company cafeteria a few times. In return Rachel had done free aura readings at a birthday party for one of Helen's friends. There had been a lot of white wine and canapés that night. Rachel had known full well that she was there as the entertainment for the evening, but she had hoped that it was the first step in building a circle of friends outside the Community, another step toward mainstreaming.

She knew now that she was never going to be accepted at the clinic. She had done her best to blend in, but pinning her hair into a tight bun and donning dark-framed, serious glasses and a white lab coat couldn't hide the truth. Everyone at Chapman was well aware that she was not a real para-psychologist. She wasn't even a licensed therapist. In addition, she qualified as a curiosity, especially among the men on the staff, because she had been raised in a Harmonic Enlightenment community.

She had discovered early on that there were a lot of myths and misunderstandings in the mainstream world concerning the harmonically enlightened lifestyle, and a number of them revolved around sex. The one aspect of her attempt at mainstreaming that had appeared promising at first was her social life. Men had lined up to invite her out on dates at the tearoom and later here, at the clinic. But the whirlwind of dating had dissipated rapidly after she had been forced to make it clear that women who lived by the Principles were not necessarily inclined to hop into bed whenever the opportunity arose.

Until a couple of weeks ago she had been making her living selling tea and giving aura readings every Wednesday and Saturday at the Crystal Rainbow Tearoom in the Old Quarter. She had been trying to recover her sense of inner balance following the disturbing events that had occurred on her last trip to Rainshadow Island.

Oakford had found her in the Crystal Rainbow. Why he had wandered into the tearoom that day, she had never discovered. It was not his kind of place. But a quick glance at his aura had warned her that he had some real talent. Her first thought was that he had found it amusing to watch her do the readings. A lot of people treated aura readings as a form of fortune-telling—a parlor trick that was not to be taken seriously.

But Oakford had been serious. He had ordered a cup of tea, sat down at a small table in the corner, and quietly observed her work for nearly an hour. In the end he had been convinced that she was a natural—a talent who could not only read auras but also diagnose disorders of the para-senses. He had concluded that she would be useful to him at the clinic and promptly dazzled her with the promise of a high salary and—more important—a respectable opportunity to practice her healing abilities.

He had said nothing about the monsters.

"Here's the problem, Dr. Oakford," she said. "Lancaster does not present with a simple instability of the aura." She was rather proud of the *does not present* line. It sounded clinical, she thought; very professional. "There's a whole chunk of the normal spectrum missing in his energy field. Think flatlined."

"That's not possible," Ian snapped. "If his aura was flatlined, he'd be dead."

"Not his entire aura. But there is a blank section on his spectrum. It's like someone shut down the lights in that region."

"I would remind you, Miss Blake, that it is your job—indeed, the mission of this clinic—to turn on those lights for our patients."

"Okay, maybe the light thing was a bad analogy. Let me try another approach. In the old days, people would have said Lancaster was soulless. That was always a big element in the traditional vampire myth, you know. Today most laypeople would tell you that Lancaster lacks anything resembling a conscience."

"This is a para-psychiatric clinic, Miss Blake," Ian said. It sounded as if he had his teeth clenched. "We do not deal in matters of religion or philosophy. We are focused on using modern science to diagnose and heal illnesses of the para-senses."

"And a worthy goal that is," she said quickly. "I'm all for it. In fact, I was thrilled when you asked me to come to work here. I've always felt I had a calling to do this kind of work. Oh, wait, that sounds sort of religious or philosophical, doesn't it? I mean, if my life had taken a different direction, I might have had your job."

Ian's eyes hardened. "Think so?"

Okay, that had been a tactical mistake.

"Well, no, probably not," she admitted. "I wasn't born for upper management."

Another poor choice of words, she realized.

Ian flushed a dark red. Alarmed, she rushed to calm the gathering storm.

"I'm more of an entrepreneur," she explained. "I could never do the kind of work that you do. What I'm trying to tell you is that I can't fix Marcus Lancaster or anyone else like him."

"In that case," Ian said evenly, "your services are no longer needed here at the Chapman Clinic. You've got fifteen minutes to clear out your desk. A member of the security staff will escort you to the door."

Although she knew an escort to the door was standard procedure when someone got fired, it hurt to know that Ian did not trust her.

"Afraid I'll steal some paper clips or a list of your drug company clients on my way out?" she asked.

Ian shook his head and exhaled heavily. "I'm sorry about this, Rachel. I really believed that you would be an asset to my team."

She rezzed her talent. The charms on her bracelet clashed lightly on her wrist, generating just enough ultra-light to allow her to view Ian's energy field. Ian was angry but he was also experiencing genuine disappointment and regret. He had taken a chance on her, hoping that she might give him an edge in the highly competitive world of para-psych drug research, and she had failed him.

She heard Carl and Marcus Lancaster in the hall

behind her. She did not turn around but she could feel the monster's energy.

"Isn't she lovely, Carl?" Lancaster asked. "Miss Blake is going to be my bride, you know. The voices tell me that she's my perfect match. We have so much in common."

"Congratulations," Carl said. "Be sure to send me an invitation to the wedding."

"I'll do that," Lancaster said, sounding pleased.

"Meanwhile, it's time for lunch."

"Yes, of course," Lancaster said. "Do you suppose there will be quiche and perhaps a nice white wine at lunch today? I haven't had a decent meal since I arrived here."

"This is Wednesday," Carl said. "That means meat loaf."

"I really don't like meat loaf," Lancaster said. "But I will tolerate anything so long as I can be near my beloved. Her radiance lightens my aura like a fine champagne."

"No wine at lunch, either," Carl said.

"I was afraid of that," Lancaster said.

Carl guided him along the hallway.

"Damn it, Rachel, whatever you did to Lancaster in that therapy session has worsened his condition," Ian said. He kept his voice low, but it was plain that he was not just angry; he was concerned for his patient.

Rachel shuddered but she did not turn around. She listened to the retreating footsteps, suddenly very glad to know that in fifteen minutes she would be out of the building and far away from the clinic.

"I know you don't want to hear this," she whispered

back, "but Lancaster is deliberately acting crazy. His aura is very stable—scary stable, in fact. He is in full control of himself and his talent. He's a full-on psi-path and he's dangerous, sir."

"You're wrong," Ian said. "There is definitely instability in Lancaster's aura. He is an ideal candidate for the drug trial that I am conducting."

"Right." She clutched her notebook to her breasts. She really needed to get out of the clinic. She fought the suddenly overwhelming urge to run. "If you'll excuse me, I'll go pack up my office." She started to move around him and paused. "I do have one piece of advice for you, although you probably won't take it."

Ian narrowed his eyes. "What?"

"Do not believe anything Marcus Lancaster says."

"If you have any proof that he's lying, now would be a real good time to provide it," Ian said, his expression fierce.

She tried to come up with something, anything that would impress Ian.

"His ear stud," she said.

Ian blinked. "What about it? The crystal isn't tuned amber. It can't be used to generate energy. That was checked out when he was admitted. The patients are not allowed to possess amber. And it's certainly not gem-quality. It's just a cold, decorative stone of some kind."

She took a deep breath. "Here's the thing, sir. I've seen stones like it before. Also, you should know that Lancaster doesn't need amber or charged crystal to use his para-senses. He's a natural. I think he has a mid-level talent for psychic hypnosis, but that's not my point."

"Ridiculous. There is no such talent."

"I didn't expect you to believe that, but think about this, sir: Why would a guy who wears designer suits and watches that probably cost more than the entire city-state budget wear a cheap ear stud?"

"Probably because it has sentimental value," Ian snapped, exasperated.

"Trust me, there isn't an ounce of sentiment in Marcus Lancaster."

"What makes you think that you are qualified to offer an opinion on Lancaster's para-psych profile?" Ian said. "You were selling tea and giving aura readings when I found you at the Crystal Rainbow."

"Yes, I was, and I think I'll go back to that career. I don't seem to be cut out for clinical work or for the mainstream world, come to that."

She tightened her grip on her notebook and stepped around Ian.

"Rachel—"

Surprised by the hesitation in his voice, she paused and turned back.

"Yes?" she said.

"Even though you were technically here on probation, I'll see to it that you receive two weeks' severance pay," Ian said quietly.

"Thanks. I appreciate that. I spent a fortune on new clothes for this job. I'll be paying off the credit card for a while."

"I suppose you'll be going back to the Crystal Rainbow Tearoom?"

"No," she said. "I think it's time for plan B."

"You're going to return to the Harmonic Enlightenment Academy?"

"No. The truth is, I don't belong there, either. Ever heard of Rainshadow Island?"

"No," Ian said.

"Not many people have. It's one of the islands in the Amber Sea. It's not even on most maps. My great-aunts ran a bookshop and café there for a couple of decades. Several months ago they retired and moved to the desert. They left Shadow Bay Books to me. I've just let the shop sit, closed up, until I could decide what to do with it. In the back of my mind the shop was my fallback plan in case things didn't work out for me here in Frequency City. Good thing I didn't sell it."

She started walking again, heading toward her office.

"One more thing," Ian said.

She paused and turned back to face him again. "What now?"

"You said you'd seen stones like the one in Lancaster's ear stud."

"Yes."

"Where?"

"On Rainshadow Island. As far as anyone knows, that's the only place they have ever been found. They're called rainstones."

She hurried away down the hall to the tiny office that had been allocated to her. Two months ago when she had accepted the position at the clinic she had been so excited at having her very own office that she had taken dozens of photos of the small, spare space and emailed them to everyone in the family. She shook her head at the naïve memory. As if an office was proof that she had found her place in the world.

"I should have known this wasn't going to work out," she said into the silence. "Not like I wasn't warned."

It took ten minutes, not fifteen, to gather up her personal possessions and dump them into a cardboard box. Carl was waiting at the door. He looked unhappy.

"I'm really sorry about this, Miss Blake," he said. "It's been nice having you here. The patients all like you. So do I. Things seem more cheerful and sunnier here when you're around."

She smiled. "Thank you, Carl, but Dr. Oakford is right. It's best that I leave. I don't belong here."

Carl cleared his throat. "I don't suppose you happen to have any more of that tea that you blended for me, do you?"

"Not here in the office but I'll mix up another batch and send it to you."

Carl brightened. "Thanks, I appreciate that."

Five minutes later she was alone on the street, the cardboard box containing her things tucked under one arm, her purse slung over her shoulder. The low, dark clouds opened up as she walked quickly toward the bus stop. Naturally she would get caught in the rain without an umbrella today, she thought. Some days were just flat-out unharmonic from start to finish.

The cold, sleeting rain plastered her tightly pinned hair to her head and soaked her new black low-heeled pumps. The shoes would be ruined. Not that it mattered, she told herself. No one wore black low-heeled pumps on Rainshadow. Boots, athletic shoes, and sandals were the norm there. And she just happened to own a new pair of boots.

She waited for the bus, chilled to the bone but aware that she felt a lot better now that she was away from the Chapman Clinic.

She would survive the rain and the loss of the job. What mattered was that she would never again find herself alone in a therapy room with Marcus Lancaster. Because she was quite certain it was no coincidence that he had manipulated the situation so that they had wound up together today. If she remained on the staff at the clinic, he would manipulate things to ensure that there were more such encounters. She knew that as surely as she knew the Principles.

Another shiver of apprehension swept through her. Rainshadow was Plan B, but the thought of returning to the island made her uneasy. Something had happened to her the last time she was there—something unnerving. Twelve hours of her life had vanished.

She had gone into a psychic fugue late one afternoon and wandered into the forbidden territory of the Preserve. Somehow she had not only survived the night in the dangerous woods, but she had also done what most people who knew the island considered almost impossible—she had managed to find her way out of the Preserve.

She had emerged at dawn the following morning but she had no memories of the night.

She had, however, collected some souvenirs along the way—dark dreams that now haunted her sleep, the faint memory of ethereal music being played somewhere in the night, and a handful of rainstones.

Chapter 2

HIS NAME WAS HARRY SEBASTIAN. HE MATERIALIZED ON her front porch in the middle of a raging thunderstorm. He was dressed in a long black raincoat that he wore over black trousers and black boots. Rain streamed off the coat. His near-black hair was plastered to his head. The flashes of lightning illuminated the hard, sharp planes and angles of his face and the sleek, powerful silhouette of his shoulders. The energy of his dark aura blazed with ultrasilver light and midnight shadows.

It would have been all too easy to believe that Harry was Lucifer, himself, come to collect her soul. But Rachel knew better. Harry was no angel, fallen or otherwise. Harry was the kind of guy who would walk into hell to rescue you from the devil—or send you to the inferno himself, if he thought that you deserved it.

She watched him through the screen door, instinctively slipping a little higher into her other senses. The gentle chiming of the silvery metal charms on her bracelet was drowned by the rolling thunder. The faint glow in the small stones went unnoticed in the white-hot crackle of lightning.

He looked at her with eyes that burned with smoky green fire, the same way that he had looked at her yesterday when they had been introduced by the new police chief, Slade Attridge. Her intuition had warned her then— as it did tonight—that the heat in Sebastian's eyes was a dangerous mix of sexual attraction and the aroused curiosity of a top-of-the-food-chain hunter. Yesterday she had been stunned by the thrill of awareness that had slammed through her senses. But that was nothing compared to the excitement effervescing in her blood tonight.

He was here—right here—at her door.

"Sorry about this," Harry said. "I was on my way into town to grab some dinner at a café. When the rain started, I decided to turn around and go back to the old gatekeeper's cabin, but there's a tree down across Gatehouse Road. Your place was closest, so I thought I'd see if you'd let me wait out the storm here."

On Rainshadow, neighbors looked after one another, Rachel thought. But Harry Sebastian wasn't exactly a neighbor. He had arrived two days ago, but she knew very little about him aside from the fact that Slade had summoned him to investigate some problems in the Preserve. The Sebastian family owned the Preserve and, therefore, most of the island, but none of them had ever spent much time on Rainshadow. Probably because they were all too busy making money, she thought. Sebastian, Inc. was a highly successful business empire. In some quarters the Sebastians were still considered to be pirates.

Before she could respond she heard an enthusiastic chortle at her feet. She looked down and saw Darwina. The dust bunny was fully fluffed and in full-cute mode. She resembled a large wad of dryer lint with two baby blue eyes. Yesterday she had made it clear that she liked Harry, flirting outrageously with him in the café at Shadow Bay Books. The attraction was of a somewhat superficial nature in Rachel's opinion. She was pretty sure that it was based almost entirely on the fact that Harry's big SUV with its powerful flash-rock engine promised a much more exciting ride than Rachel's bicycle or the little Vibe buggy that she borrowed from Brett at the service station when she needed something larger in the way of transport.

Darwina was new in Rachel's life, but it had already become apparent that she was something of an adrenaline junkie.

Fortunately for Harry, he had another, more solid character reference. Slade Attridge, a former Federal Bureau of Psi Investigation agent with excellent cop instincts, had made it clear that he approved of Harry as well.

Rachel pulled herself together, gave the situation about a half second's thought, and concluded that she had no alternative other than to play the gracious hostess. The little frissons of excitement feathering her senses warned her that she did not really want an alternative. It seemed as if fate had brought them together tonight. Not that a good Harmonic Enlightenment girl believed in fate, of course. But there was such a thing as the raw power that went with the energy of mutual attraction.

"Of course you're welcome to come in." She lowered her talent, unlocked the screen door, and stood back. "But I don't think you'll be going anywhere until morning. This storm looks like it will be hanging around for a while."

"Thanks."

Harry moved over the threshold and into the tiny front hall, filling the space with his intensely male presence. The cottage suddenly seemed a lot smaller and more intimate.

He stood dripping rainwater on the floor. For a heartbeat, she just stared at him, uncertain what to do next. Common sense and good manners came to her aid.

"Give me your coat," she said. "I'll get you a towel. You can dry off by the fire."

"I appreciate this."

Harry shrugged out of the long black coat and handed it to her. He wore a black crewneck pullover with black trousers. She looked at his wet boots.

"You had better take those off, too," she said. "I'll put them in the mudroom with your coat."

"Good idea." He sat down on the wooden bench and tugged off one leather boot. "I was only outside for the length of time it took me to get from the car to your front porch, but it's really coming down out there."

"People who have lived on the island for years are

saying this is the most severe storm season they've ever seen and the weather seems to be getting worse."

"I know." Harry went to work on the second boot. "Slade told me."

When he got the boot off she caught a glimpse of what looked like a leather sheath strapped to his leg just above his ankle. The sheath disappeared beneath his pant leg almost immediately.

"Backup," he said calmly. "I'm in the security business, remember?"

"Right." She cleared her throat. "Go on into the living room. I'll be right back."

Balance in all things. She chanted the mantra silently while she hung the coat on a peg in the little mudroom off the kitchen. She positioned the boots on a wooden rack and zipped back through the kitchen and into the living room, heading for the stairs.

When she went past the hearth she saw Harry warming his hands in front of the fire. Darwina was on the mantel, chortling to him. Little flirt, Rachel thought, amused. Darwina made it look so easy. But skilled flirtation was a talent that Rachel was afraid she did not possess. It was not one of the subjects taught in Harmonic Enlightenment schools, where the focus was on inner balance.

But it was hard to maintain her inner equilibrium around Harry. Something about his energy seemed to push her ever so slightly off balance. When he was in the vicinity she felt as if she was teetering precariously on some psychic high-wire—without a net.

She came back downstairs with a towel in time to see Darwina showing off her favorite toy, an old Amberella doll.

"She loves that thing," Rachel explained. She walked across the small living room and handed the towel to Harry.

"The doll, I assume, belongs to you?" Harry asked, smiling a little as he used the towel to blot water from his hair.

"Yes. I got it as a birthday present when I was a little girl. At the time I wanted it more than anything else in the world but my parents felt that the dolls were not suitable, harmonically enlightened toys for young girls. I had to do a lot of fast talking to convince them that Amberella was actually a fine role model."

"Slade mentioned that you were raised in an HE community and trained at the Academy of Harmony and Enlightenment," Harry said.

She listened carefully but there was nothing in his voice to tell her his opinion of the HE lifestyle. Her short experience in the mainstream world had taught her to expect either disapproval or prurient curiosity about the sexual practices in the Community—often a combination of both. But if Harry felt either disdain or a lurid interest, he hid it well.

"That's right," she said. "Amberella was one of the few things I took with me when I left the Community."

Harry glanced at her charm bracelet. She smiled.

"Well, the doll and my bracelet," she amended.

"When did the dust bunny show up?"

"Just a few days ago. I fed her a couple of times. She brought me some small stones. The next thing I knew she had more or less moved in. I keep Amberella on the mantel. Darwina saw her and went straight for her."

Harry studied Amberella with an amused expression. "That's a fancy dress for a doll."

"She's wearing her Restoration Ball gown. There were dozens of outfits you could buy for Amberella, but this one and the wedding gown were the dresses that every little girl wanted most. I knew I was probably only going to get one, so I chose the ball gown because of the little crystals sewn on it."

Darwina chortled happily and waved the doll. Harry took a closer look at the figure. His brows rose.

"The crystals aren't plastic. They're the real deal, aren't they?" he asked.

"My parents decided that if I was going to get an Amberella doll it should have some educational and enlightening aspects. Mom spent a whole day removing the original plastic crystals and replacing them with genuine stones."

"How did you talk your folks into giving you the doll?" Harry asked.

"Oh, I was subtle, believe me. In the end they managed to convince themselves that Amberella would be a good way to expose me to the ways of the Unenlightened."

Laughter gleamed in Harry's eyes. "The idea being to build up your immunity against the outside world?"

"Yep."

"I take it that didn't work out well for you?"

"Nope. It just made me all the more determined to go mainstream. I wanted to live the Amberella lifestyle."

Harry watched her with knowing eyes. "That didn't work out for you, either."

It wasn't a question.

"No," she said quietly. "I don't fit into either world now."

"Maybe that's why you wound up here on Rainshadow." Harry regarded her with a thoughtful expression. "A lot of folks who settle on the island don't seem to fit in anywhere else."

"So true." Time to shift the conversation, she thought. "I take it you never got dinner?"

"No. But I'll survive."

"Nonsense." She went briskly toward the kitchen. "I made some lasagna. Plenty of leftovers. I'll heat some up for you."

"I'm not going to turn down that offer." He followed her and stopped in the kitchen doorway, looking around with interest. "This is nice. Cozy or something."

"This cottage belonged to my aunts." She opened the refrigerator and took out the foil-covered pan of cold lasagna. "Most of the furniture and dishes belonged to them." She started to close the refrigerator and paused, noticing the partially empty bottle of white wine and two bottles of beer on the bottom shelf. "I've got some chardonnay and some beer."

"I could use a beer." He took the bottle she offered and glanced at the label. "This looks like Slade's brand."

"It is. He and his fiancée, Charlotte, came to dinner the other evening. Slade brought the beer. Charlotte and

I drank the chardonnay. Have you met Charlotte? She runs Looking Glass Antiques, which is just down the street from my shop."

"I met her yesterday. Slade introduced us." Harry propped one shoulder against the doorframe, swallowed some beer, and watched her go about the task of reheating the lasagna in the rez-wave oven. "They seem like a well-matched couple."

"They are but they didn't go through a matchmaking agency. They found each other here on Rainshadow. They're going straight for a full Covenant Marriage."

There was a sudden chill in the kitchen. Rachel glanced over her shoulder. Harry's expression had not changed. It was still all hard planes and angles, still politely unreadable. But a curious stillness seemed to have enveloped him. She knew that she had inadvertently stumbled into forbidden territory.

"No Marriage of Convenience to test the waters first?" he asked.

His tone of voice was a little too neutral. Rachel wondered at the undercurrents in the atmosphere, but it would be rude to inquire. She had discovered that when it came to the subject of Covenant Marriages versus Marriages of Convenience, people in the mainstream world often held strong opinions.

Dissolving a Covenant Marriage was a legal nightmare, not to mention prohibitively expensive for all but the very rich. The laws had changed somewhat recently, but divorce was still a devastating scandal that destroyed careers and ruined social status. Those who went through a divorce were considered unmatchable by legitimate matchmaking agencies.

Because it was so difficult to get out of a CM, many people favored a trial Marriage of Convenience. MCs had legal standing and some legal protections but they could be terminated by either party at any time—unless there were offspring. A baby automatically converted an MC into a full Covenant Marriage. Family was the most important social institution on Harmony and it was reinforced with all the power of law and custom.

"No," she said aloud. "No MC for Slade and Charlotte. They are very certain of their decision. They're also in a hurry."

"Yeah, I got that impression yesterday when Slade told me that he and Charlotte are leaving Rainshadow tomorrow for a week. They're going to Frequency City so that Slade can do the meet-the-relatives thing."

"I don't think Slade is looking forward to a weeklong round of family events but he'll do anything for Charlotte," Rachel said.

The oven pinged. She opened the door and reached inside with a pair of hot pads. She placed the pan on the counter and used a spatula to carve out a large square of the fragrant, steaming lasagna. She set the lasagna on a plate and carried it to the kitchen table.

Darwina scuttled in from the living room, Amberella clutched in one paw, bounced up onto the wide window ledge next to the glass jar filled with rainstones, and chortled hopefully.

Rachel gave her a stern look. "You already had dinner. If you don't watch out, we're going to have to buy you a dust-bunny-sized treadmill."

Darwina eyed the lasagna pan with an assessing gaze.

"Okay, okay," Rachel said. "But don't blame me if you don't end up with a figure like Amberella."

She cut another smaller square of the lasagna, positioned it on a saucer, and placed the saucer on the window ledge. Darwina set Amberella aside and settled in to devour the lasagna.

Harry pulled out a chair and sat down. "This looks great. Thanks. I didn't realize how hungry I was until it dawned on me that I might not get dinner tonight. Funny how a little thing like that concentrates the attention."

Rachel took the chair across from Harry and watched him dig into the meal. It was surprisingly satisfying to see him enjoy something she had prepared with her own hands.

"This is great," he said around a mouthful.

"I'm glad you like it." She smiled. "I consider lasagna to be an excellent example of a harmonically balanced dish."

"Yeah?" Harry raised his brows. "What constitutes a harmonically balanced dish?"

"Equal parts meditation and exercise."

"Meditation and exercise?" he repeated politely.

She winced. "Sorry. It's supposed to be a joke. I was taught that cooking is to be done in a spirit of active meditation. But after a high-calorie dish like lasagna it will be necessary to exercise. Hence the harmonic balance is maintained."

Harry forked up another bite. "Got it. An example of Harmonic Enlightenment humor."

She propped her elbow on the table and rested her chin on her palm. "Not exactly sparkling wit, is it? But, then, we're not really known for our sense of humor."

"Is that so?" Harry's eyes glinted a little. He put down the fork and drank a little more beer. "I hadn't heard that."

"During my short stay in the mainstream world I discovered that there are a lot of misconceptions and misunderstandings about the Community."

"Such as?"

She flushed. She was not about to bring up the misconceptions about HE attitudes toward sex, at least not while he was eating her lasagna.

"Never mind," she said. "You know, I've got a picture of the original Harry Sebastian in my shop. I sell a lot of prints as souvenirs. You look just like your ancestor. But I'll bet you get that a lot."

"Let's just say that when I walked down the main street of Shadow Bay yesterday a couple of kids wanted to know if I was the ghost of Harry the Pirate."

"Can't blame them. According to the legends, he never made it off the island after he buried his treasure. They say his ghost walks the Preserve at night."

The first Harry Sebastian was a legend in the islands of the Amber Sea and, as was usually the case with legends, very few hard facts had survived. Most historians were convinced that he was nothing more than a notorious buccaneer who had preyed on shipping and the tiny island towns during and immediately after the lawless Era of Discord.

But here in the islands, there were those who claimed that he had been a hero—if a mercenary one—who, for a price, had protected ships and the small communities from the real pirates. It all depended on your point of view, Rachel thought.

The only aspect of the story that everyone agreed upon was that the original Harry had vanished after burying his treasure. The most popular theory was that his partner in the pirate-hunting business, Nicholas North, who had accompanied him on the treasure-burying excursion, had murdered Harry inside what was now the Preserve. According to the tales, North had not made it out of the forbidden territory, either. He was presumed to have fallen victim to the strange forces at work in the dark part of the island.

"A few minutes ago you said there were a lot of misconceptions about the Harmonic Enlightenment community," Harry said.

"Yes," she said.

"Well, there are a few misconceptions—or maybe I should say historical inaccuracies—in my great-grandfather's legend."

"Of course," Rachel said. "It's the nature of legends to become inaccurate over time. That's what makes them interesting. What are some of the misconceptions about your ancestor?"

Harry took another bite of the lasagna. "Let's start

with the fact that he did not die here on Rainshadow. His partner, North, did not murder him. Both men made it off the island after they buried the so-called treasure."

"I sure hope you don't go spreading that word around town. It would be very bad for business. I sell gazillions of copies of the *Tales of Harry Sebastian* to the tourists. The books are a young adult series written by a local author named Jilly Finch. She works part-time in my shop. We could both be ruined if you squelch the legend."

"Don't worry; legends always survive the truth."

"Good point," Rachel said. "So what really did happen to Harry One and Nick North?"

"The Era of Discord was almost over by the time they came ashore with the treasure. They saw the writing on the wall. The days of pirate hunting for fun and profit were coming to an end, and they had both collected a sizeable circle of enemies."

"Not surprising. Pirating is probably the kind of business that attracts enemies."

"Got news for you, anyone who runs a successful, highly profitable business attracts enemies sooner or later," he said.

"Really? Do they teach that in business management school?"

"I don't know. I didn't go into finance or business management. I left that for others in my family. I got stuck with the same talent that Harry the Pirate had, so my options were fairly limited."

"You mean you could be either a pirate or a pirate-hunter?" she asked lightly.

For a second or two Harry appeared to be genuinely surprised by the question.

"How did you know?" he asked.

An effervescent sensation whispered across her senses. Her pulse kicked up a little. She cleared her throat and tried to calm her dancing energies.

"It just seemed obvious that whatever made Harry a successful pirate—and by all accounts he was *very* successful—would also have made him very good at catching other pirates. Same skill set, so to speak. It's a matter of harmonic balance."

"Yeah?" Harry looked intrigued.

"Well, sure. I mean, it's obvious, isn't it?"

He moved one hand in a dismissive gesture. "Not to everyone. Very few people outside my family understand—Never mind. To return to my tale, Harry and Nick North quit the business, promoted the story that they had both died on Rainshadow, and slipped quietly back into normal life, or maybe I should say what passed for normal in the first years after the Era of Discord."

"I suppose it wouldn't have been hard for two clever men to make themselves disappear," Rachel mused. "According to the history books, things were chaotic for a while after the battles in the catacombs ended. I suspect a lot of folks took advantage of the confusion and the lack of a paper trail to make major career changes."

"My great-grandfather got married, started a family and what proved to be a profitable corporation. He kept a low profile but he made sure that the family business claimed most of Rainshadow under the old Exploration

Laws and later he established the Rainshadow Preserve Foundation to manage things here."

"All that to protect what he and North had buried inside the Preserve?"

"Yes," Harry said.

"What happened to Nicholas North?"

"Unfortunately, he did not do as well as Harry One. Started a number of businesses but they all failed. Eventually he disappeared altogether. My great-grandfather died several years ago but he told me once that he thinks North may have come back to Rainshadow to try to recover the treasure and that he didn't make it off the island that second time."

"How do you know North didn't find the treasure and vanish with it?"

"Because as of eighteen months ago, it was still here, right where it was supposed to be," Harry said.

"Wow. You actually saw it?"

"I've checked up on it several times over the years."

"What is it?" she asked eagerly. "There has been speculation for decades. Rare amber or gems? Alien artifacts?"

"None of the above. It's not very exciting, just three chunks of murky gray crystal that my family brought with them from the Old World when they came through the Curtain."

"They brought three rocks all the way from Earth?" She was floored. "Good grief, those stones must have had some value to warrant space on one of the colonial ships."

"There's no record of the stones having any monetary

value, but according to what little we know about them, they may have had some paranormal properties. My great-grandfather considered them to be extremely dangerous but he did not want to get rid of them altogether by dropping them into a deep ocean trench. His theory was that someday they might prove to be very valuable. But he said that modern technology wasn't sufficiently advanced to control the energy in the stones, let alone find a profitable way to use them."

"So he hid them here on Rainshadow and left his descendants with instructions to protect them."

"That's pretty much the whole story," Harry said.

"You said you know where they're hidden."

"Harry One left an old psi-code map in the family archives. I was able to use it to locate the cave where Harry and Nick hid the stones. It's just a short distance inside the energy fence, not deep in the heart of the Preserve. My great-grandfather told me that he and North were afraid that if they went in too far they wouldn't be able to find their way back out."

Darwina finished her lasagna, picked up Amberella by the doll's long legs, and hopped down from the window ledge. She tumbled across the wooden floor and vanished into the living room.

Rachel looked at Harry. "I'm impressed. Most people can't even get through the energy fence that surrounds the Preserve. I knew Slade could track people who got lost inside and I assumed you could, too, or you wouldn't have come here to investigate whatever is going on in there. But here on the island everyone claims that there is no way to create a useable map of the terrain inside the fence because the energy is too disorienting."

"I've got a variation of my great-grandfather's talent, which is what it takes to read his psi-coded map. It's a matter of some complicated psychic genetics." Harry looked back at the counter with a hopeful expression. "Any chance of another slice of lasagna? It's the best I've had in a long time."

"It's my mother's recipe." Rachel got up and went to the counter to cut another piece. "You know, some of the really old maps of the island show the boundary of the psi-fence with everything inside marked 'Here There Be Monsters.'"

"The Foundation has an excellent collection of those old maps. There have always been plenty of myths and legends about the island because of the heavy paranormal radiation inside the fence. The energy in the Preserve can induce visions and hallucinations. But over the years we've sent several search-and-rescue teams in to pull out the occasional drunken yachtsman or doped-up thrill-seeker who managed to get through the barrier. There have been no reliable or confirmed sightings of monsters or ghosts. Believe me, the Foundation would be the first to know."

But monsters were showing up in her dreams lately, Rachel thought. And she was certain that the nightmares were linked to her missing twelve hours—the time she had been lost inside the Preserve. She was not about to mention that to Harry, though. He would think she was crazy. There were enough people on the island who believed she was psychically fragile due to her fugue experience. She did not want Harry to come to the same conclusion.

She carried the lasagna to the table. "But no one has ever ventured too deeply into the Preserve, right?"

"That's true," Harry said. "The working theory at the Foundation has always been that strong talents can go in for short distances but no one, not even the most powerful sensitives, can go into the heart of the island and make their way back out."

She sighed. "You know, don't you?"

"About your missing twelve hours inside the Preserve? Yes. Slade told me."

She made a face. "Well, it's not like it's a secret. Everyone on the island knows I slipped into some sort of fugue state one evening, went into the Preserve, and walked out at dawn the next morning. It's embarrassing, to tell you the truth. After all my Academy training and meditation exercises I should have had more control. Knowing that something like that can happen is . . . deeply unsettling."

"I understand. But the paranormal currents inside the Preserve have always been very strong, and lately the psi temperature has been rising. That's more than enough to explain your amnesia."

"That's what I keep telling myself. But getting back to those three stones that Harry One hid in the cave. What did you do with them?"

"I left them there." He shrugged. "I saw no reason to

move them at the time. I told you, according to my great-grandfather they're dangerous."

"In what way?"

"He didn't know exactly and neither do I. They've been in the family ever since the Late Nineteenth Century, Old World Date, but a lot of the Sebastian family records and archival materials relating to our ancestors back on Earth were lost in an explosion and fire that occurred during Colonial times here on Harmony. So, given that I didn't know what I was dealing with, it seemed best to leave them where they were."

"Sounds like a smart decision."

"Except it wasn't," Harry said. He finished the last of the lasagna and set the fork down very deliberately. "The first thing I did when I arrived on the island a couple of days ago was go into the Preserve to check on the stones."

"And?"

"And they're gone," Harry said quietly.

"You mean you couldn't find the cave this time?"

"I found the cave. But the crystals are gone."

"You think they were stolen?"

"I know they were stolen," Harry said. "What's more, I think they're at the core of the problem in the Preserve. Whatever is happening inside the fence involves some very high energy, and the one thing I do know about those rocks is that they are capable of channeling a lot of power. What we don't know is how to unleash or control the latent energy in the stones."

She took a breath and let it out cautiously. "I understand your logic."

"I have to find the rocks and I'm going to need your help to do it."

"*My* help?" She stared at him. "What in the world can I do to assist your investigation?"

"I want you to read some auras."

"Whose auras? And why should I read them?"

"I think one or more of the local residents is involved in this thing."

"What?" She flattened her palms on the table and pushed herself to her feet. "You want me to rat out my friends and neighbors? Forget it."

Harry looked at her very steadily. "Whoever took the stones is in way over his or her head. Something dangerous is happening out there in the Preserve, something that needs to be stopped."

"Even if you're right, what makes you think that one of the islanders is responsible? We've got regular, scheduled ferry service. That means day-trippers on the weekends. We've got B&Bs for tourists who want to spend more time. During the summer months we get the yacht crowd. And then there are those weeklong motivational seminars offered by the Reflections Institute out at the old lake lodge."

"You're saying that I need to widen my pool of suspects?" Harry asked politely.

"Absolutely. There are a lot of strangers coming and going on Rainshadow these days."

He appeared to give that some thought. "It's possible that a visitor is responsible for whatever is happening out there."

"It certainly is."

"The problem is that a tourist who drops in on the weekends doesn't fit my profile."

"What profile?" she asked. "You can't possibly have one yet. You've barely even started your investigation."

"No, but I'm actually pretty good at this kind of stuff."

"Okay, okay." She dropped back into her chair. "Tell me about this profile of yours."

"I think it's a good bet that whoever stirred up that energy in the Preserve has some long-standing connection to the island."

"A good bet? That doesn't sound like a real forensic profile."

Harry ignored the interruption. "It's a matter of opportunity. It would take time to find the stones, time to move them, time to do whatever the suspect did that is now causing problems. A day-tripper who was coming and going routinely into the Preserve would have been noticed by now."

She did not want to admit it, but he had a point.

"Maybe," she allowed.

"In addition, the suspect obviously has to be a powerful talent. Most people can't even get through the fence, let alone navigate the terrain once inside. That's where you come in, Rachel."

"You want me to identify all of the folks on Rainshadow who happen to possess a lot of talent?" she asked.

"That would be an invasion of privacy, not to mention a good way to lose business and maybe even get myself killed. In case you hadn't heard, folks on this island like their privacy. It's one of the reasons they come here in the first place."

"I'll try to make this as simple as I can. Whatever is going on out there in the Preserve must be stopped or I will have no choice but to order a full evacuation of the island."

She stared at him, shocked. "You can't do that."

"Yes," he said. "I can. And I will if I think it's necessary."

"But Rainshadow is home to the sort of people who don't do very well elsewhere. This is a special place."

"Trust me, I understand."

"Even if you do order an evacuation, I can tell you right now that a lot of the locals would ignore it," she said.

"In that case, I think there is a high probability that something very, very bad might happen to them."

"Do you have any idea what that something might be?"

"No," Harry said. "But this island is a powerful geothermal nexus, so I think a major paranormal explosion would be high on the list of probable outcomes."

She sat quietly, not speaking for a time.

"I see," she said finally.

"My goal is to save the island and the community of Shadow Bay. I'm not interested in old secrets and gossip. I'm just trying to identify a list of suspects."

"What will you do once you have your list?"

"I will ask questions," Harry said. "Slade will be working with me. You know him. He'll make sure that everyone's rights are protected."

That much was true, she thought. Slade was a dedicated lawman to the bone. He would keep an eye on Harry, assuming anyone could keep an eye on Harry Sebastian. There was a reason why those with Harry's brand of psychic ability were called shadow-auras. No one knew much about them.

"Look on the bright side," Harry said. "Working with me is the best way to keep tabs on my investigation and make sure I don't go down the wrong road with any of your neighbors."

She was trapped.

"Do you do this kind of thing a lot?" she asked.

"What kind of thing?"

"Piss people off?"

"Sadly, yes."

"I knew I shouldn't have answered the door tonight."

She got to her feet again, cleared the table, and carried the dishes to the sink. Behind her Harry's chair scraped a little on the floor. A sudden jolt of suspicion made her turn around.

He was on his feet, watching her warily. "What?"

"Some men have some serious misconceptions about women from the Community," she said.

"You mentioned that earlier."

"Just to clarify, you will be spending the night on the sofa or the living room floor, your choice."

He nodded once. "Believe it or not, I had figured that much out for myself."

She sighed and turned back to the sink. "Not that the facts will get in the way of the gossip."

"What gossip?"

"By seven o'clock tomorrow morning half the town will know that you spent the night here. The rest will find out at ten when they go to the post office to pick up their mail."

"So?"

She glared at him over her shoulder. "So everyone will assume the worst."

"Right. The worst. I don't suppose it will help if I say I'm sorry for putting you into this situation?"

"No," she said. "It won't help a bit."

Chapter 3

THE ETHEREAL CHIME AND CLASH OF HER CHARM BRACE-let brought him out of a light sleep. The fact that he could hear the gentle sound so clearly made him realize that somewhere in the past hour or so the storm had burned itself out.

He watched Rachel descend the stairs. All of his senses stirred, just as they had yesterday when he had walked into Shadow Bay Books with Slade. One look into those brilliant amber eyes and everything else that was important in his life dropped to second place on his list of priorities. In that first moment of meeting her he had known that even if he never saw her again he would not forget her.

His night vision was excellent. In the dim glow of the low-burning fire he could make her out quite clearly. She wore a pale, ankle-length robe over her nightgown and a pair of fluffy slippers. Her flame-red hair was loose and mussed from sleep and tumbled around her shoulders.

Even from across the room he was intensely aware of the strong energy that shivered in the atmosphere around her. It aroused him and heated his blood, made him want to reach for her and drag her down onto the sofa with him.

She moved with an elegant, feminine grace and confidence that spoke of dance or martial-arts training. He had heard that both were taught from childhood on within the HE community.

Darwina, Amberella clutched tightly in one paw, fluttered down the steps at Rachel's feet.

He lay unmoving on the sofa. Rachel was already more than a little pissed off at him. The last thing he wanted to do was startle or alarm her. When she reached the foot of the stairs, she turned toward the kitchen. The route took her past the sofa. She glanced his way but she did not pause.

"I know you're awake," she said in a normal tone of voice. "I'm just going to let Darwina out."

She kept going into the unlit kitchen. He pushed aside the blanket and sat up on the edge of the sofa. The back porch door opened.

"You and Amberella stay out of trouble, now," Rachel said softly. "I do not want to get a call from Officer Willis telling me to come bail you out of jail."

There was an answering chortle and then the door closed. A moment later Harry heard water run in the sink. A cupboard door opened.

He got up from the sofa and raked his fingers through

his hair, pushing it back behind his ears. He padded barefoot across the cold floor. He had removed his pullover but he still had on the black T-shirt and trousers so he figured he was reasonably decent. He stopped in the kitchen doorway. Another night-light illuminated the scene. Rachel was lounging against the sink sipping a glass of water. There were dark shadows in her eyes.

"Bad dreams?" he asked.

"Yes." She made a face. "Darwina sensed my agitation. She woke me. But once she knew I was awake, she decided to go check out the after-hours clubs with Amberella."

"After-hours clubs?"

"Or wherever dust bunnies go at this time of the night." Rachel glanced toward the windows. "Looks like the storm is over."

He followed her gaze and saw fog infused with cold moonlight pooling in the clearing around the cottage.

"For now," he said. "But there's more heavy weather on the way."

"You think it's another sign of trouble in the Preserve, don't you?"

"There's so much energy stirring inside the fence now that it's having a serious impact on the local microclimate."

"You're not the only one here who is saying that. There really is something big going on out there in the Preserve, isn't there?"

"Yes." He folded his arms across his chest and watched

her drink the last of the water. "Was there a storm the night you did your fugue-walk?"

"I don't think so. There was a lot of fog when I left the bookstore but I could see well enough to ride my bike back here to the cottage. My shoes and clothes were damp when I walked out of the Preserve the next morning but it seemed like the normal sort of dampness that you'd pick up walking through the woods and across rough terrain at night."

He studied her for a long time. "What do you remember?"

For a moment he thought she was not going to answer the question. But after a while she started to talk.

"Very little," she said. "I spent most of the day at the bookshop, conducting an inventory, dusting, just puttering around. I was still trying to decide whether or not I wanted to move to Rainshadow and take over the business as my aunts suggested or put the store and the cottage on the market. I locked up around five o'clock and started back here on my bicycle. Somewhere on the road everything went blank. Or maybe I should say mostly blank."

"Meaning?"

"Lately I've been getting more and more wispy little fragments of memories. At least I think they may be real memories. But it's like catching a glimpse of something out of the corner of your eye. When you turn to look, it vanishes. I've tried going back to the place where I later found my bicycle to see if the location stirs up any clear recollections."

"And?" he prompted.

"Sometimes I think I get an impression of a car. I feel as if I should know the driver, that if I just looked harder, I would recognize him."

"Him?"

She hesitated. "I think so but I can't be positive." She put the empty glass down very gently. "Could be recovered memories or false memories or simply hallucinations. But the dreams have definitely been getting worse."

"What do you see in your dreams?"

She looked at him, her eyes burning a little hotter in the shadows of the kitchen. "I see monsters."

The shudder of energy in the atmosphere told him all he needed to know. She was holding herself and her sanity together but deep down she was scared to death.

He walked to where she stood and wrapped his arms around her. She did not resist but neither did she return the embrace. Her tension was a palpable force.

"I don't know whether to hope that I'm recovering my memories or check myself into a para-psych hospital," she whispered.

"Tell me about the monsters," he said quietly.

"I can't get a clear picture. Tentacles. Eyes that glow. Too many eyes. Like creatures out of a prehistoric sea. Whatever they are, they see me as prey. In the dreams I'm running through the ocean but it's not dark. The water is infused with light."

"You're running *through* this sea?"

"Yes. But I'm breathing okay. I'm not drowning." She

shuddered. "The creatures are swimming all around me, above, below, to the sides."

"But they don't attack?"

"No. It's as if they can't get at me."

"What's the source of the light in the water? Sunlight?"

"No." She hesitated. "Energy, I think. The water is infused with ultralight." She pulled back a little and looked up at him. "Yes, ultralight. That's the first time I've understood that the water is hot with psi."

"What's your first clear memory the next morning?"

"I emerged from the Preserve just before dawn. There was fog again—I recall that much. And there was music."

"What kind of music?"

"Clear, beautiful, bell-like notes." She smiled. "I followed them out of the Preserve and came through the fence near Calvin Dillard's place. He's got a cabin out on Mills Road. His property is close to the boundary of the psi-fence."

"Tell me about Calvin Dillard."

"Calvin is a very talented musician and a composer. He can play almost any instrument. He told me I gave him quite a scare because he never gets visitors, and certainly not at that hour. When he realized I was dazed and disoriented and that I couldn't remember what had happened to me, he figured I'd been in an accident and banged my head. It's as good a theory as any."

"Is he a professional musician?"

"No, I don't think so, at least not any longer. His music

is a personal passion. He's lived here on Rainshadow for nearly a decade. Retired. He's one of the loners here on the island but he's not totally reclusive. He comes into town to collect his mail and buy groceries. He's bought some books from my shop. I've always liked him."

Harry made a mental note to take a closer look at Calvin Dillard. The first witness on the scene was often the most closely linked to the situation.

"You said you found your bike on the road?" he said.

"What?" Rachel blinked a couple of times and then her expression cleared. "Oh, the bike. Yes, it was lying in a ditch on the side of the road. Which does lend credence to the theory that I took a fall and banged my head, doesn't it?"

"You're not buying that theory, I take it?"

"There was no sign of an injury. No blood or bruises on my head."

"So, somewhere in between the bike ride in the fog and walking out of the Preserve near Calvin Dillard's cabin you remember seeing monsters under the sea. Is that all?"

"Isn't that enough to get me labeled a bit wacky?"

He smiled. "Not nearly enough, at least not here on Rainshadow."

"Which is probably why I wound up back here." She paused, looking past his shoulder to the window ledge. "I do have one souvenir of that night."

He glanced at the window ledge and saw the glass jar filled with little crystals. "The rainstones?"

"I found them in the pocket of my jacket that morning

when I walked out of the Preserve. But I have no memory of picking them up."

"Or why you picked them up?"

"No. My intuition tells me that they're important but I don't know why. It's not as if you can't find rainstones all over the island. There doesn't seem to be anything special about those particular stones."

He released her and moved across the kitchen to the window ledge. He picked up the glass jar and turned it slowly, examining the stones. In the dim glow of the night-light they were dull and colorless.

"Why would a strong crystal talent like you think that a handful of cold stones were important?" he wondered aloud.

"I don't know why I thought they were important, but they aren't entirely cold." She walked to where he stood and took the glass jar from him. "There is a little latent energy in them but I doubt that many people could sense it, or work it unless they were strong crystal-talents."

"Are you saying you can work rainstones?"

"Sure. I've done it for some of the kids who come into the shop. Whenever they find a rainstone they bring it to me and ask me to do my magic trick."

"What is this trick?" he asked.

"I'll show you."

She rezzed the overhead light and unscrewed the lid of the jar. He watched her pour some of the crystals into her palm. Energy pulsed in the atmosphere. Her bracelet chimed gently and he thought he saw some of the tiny stones set in the charm brighten.

The crystals in her hand started to heat with a little colorless ultralight. And suddenly Rachel was holding a palm full of water. But unlike real water the liquid did not drip through her fingers. It was transparent but it had a viscous quality. There was another shiver of energy and the quicksilver-like material transformed swiftly back into crystalline form. She was once again holding a handful of rainstones.

He whistled softly. "I'll be damned."

"The kids love it when I do that." She dropped the stones back into the jar. "But aside from being a clever piece of magic, there's not much point to it. As far as I can tell that's all the stones do, go from crystal to liquid and back again."

"But only someone with your kind of talent can make them shift back and forth?"

"I think so, yes."

"You walked out of the Preserve at dawn with a pocketful of magic crystals," he said. "That tells me one thing for sure."

"What?" she asked.

"Those stones are important to this investigation." He reached out and cradled her delicate jaw in his hand. "And so are you. But, then, I've known that all along."

"Because you think I can be useful when it comes to identifying possible suspects. I know. You've already made that clear."

"Not just because of that. There are other ways to come up with a list of suspects. Less efficient, maybe, but doable. No, Rachel Blake, you're important to me for a lot of other reasons."

She watched him intently, her spectacular amber eyes heating a little with equal parts feminine awareness and caution. Energy swirled in the atmosphere, the kind of intimate energy that stirred the senses. He was taut and hard and on edge.

He leaned forward and kissed her ever so slightly. Just enough to get a taste of her. It was a mistake, because the small caress acted like a match to kindling. Desire roared through him.

She did not pull back but she did not throw herself into his arms, either. When he raised his head and looked at her, he saw the deep shadows in her eyes. He could read the signs. She wanted him but she did not trust him, at least not in the way she needed to trust a man before she went to bed with him.

He lowered his hand. She was right to be cautious around him—more right than she could possibly know.

She stepped back, folded her arms, and slipped her hands into the sleeves of her robe.

"I'm going upstairs now," she said, exquisitely polite. "Please de-rez the light when you go back to bed."

She swept out of the kitchen, the hem of her robe whipping around her ankles. He listened to her light footsteps on the stairs. She was practically running from him.

He de-rezzed the kitchen light and went back to the sofa. He did not lie down. Instead he sat there for a time, watching the glowing embers in the fireplace and wondering why a woman who could access the latent energy of almost any kind of stone would flee the Preserve with a handful of crystals that had no obvious value.

When that line of thought did not lead anywhere helpful, he abandoned the effort and concentrated on the mystery of Rachel Blake, instead. He didn't make any progress in that direction but he discovered that he could sit there, gazing into the fire and thinking about Rachel for the rest of the night.

Which was pretty much what he did.

Chapter 4

THEY CALLED HIM THE MERCHANT ON THE STREETS OF Frequency City. He specialized in the high-end black market. It was said that, for a price, he could get you anything you wanted.

At that moment, however, he could not get what he wanted most for himself. Time was running out. Everything had gone wrong. The frustration and rage were building.

He picked up the sledgehammer and slammed it against the frozen waterfall. Aside from the jarring jolt to his shoulder, nothing happened. The blow did not take so much as a chip out of the door of the big crystal vault.

"Shit."

Frustration and fury roared through him. He dropped the hammer and stared into the transparent chamber. He was so damn close.

The crystal vault extended from one side of the cavern wall to the opposite side and from the floor to the ceiling. It blocked the entire passage. Cascades of solid rainstone sealed both ends.

He could see the treasures inside—the artifacts of ancient Alien technology were worth a fortune on the black market. But nothing he had tried could smash through the doors of the chamber. The crystal walls had proved equally impenetrable. The transparent stone was as hard as the green quartz that the Aliens had used to build their cities and the catacombs. Nothing made by humans could put a dent in it.

He made a fist and pounded it against the rainstone. He only did it once.

"Shit."

Grimacing from the pain, he turned and went back through the psi-lit cavern and into the crystal tunnel through the artificial sea.

The sea monsters that swam and crawled through the depths watched him with their cold, unblinking eyes. Their tentacles writhed and their fins rippled in the currents. The Merchant ignored them.

There was only one person who had the talent to open the vault doors. Things had gone wrong the last time, but Rachel Blake was once again back within reach. Unfortunately, there was a new twist. Harry Sebastian, the man in charge of security inside the Preserve, was now on the island. It was no secret in town that he was conducting a full-scale investigation.

But that was not the worst of it. The real problem was

that Sebastian had obviously sensed that Rachel was the key. He had closed in on her with a hunter's intuition almost immediately after he had arrived.

The Merchant's frustration threatened to swamp his logic. He forced himself to step back emotionally and think like the smart guy he was. One thing was clear: To get to Rachel, he would first have to get rid of Harry Sebastian.

Chapter 5

THE BELL OVER THE DOOR OF SHADOW BAY BOOKS jangled brightly. Charlotte Enright, the proprietor of Looking Glass Antiques, entered. Rex, Slade's dust bunny companion, was on her shoulder. Rex had his favorite object, a small, elegant, and very expensive antique clutch purse in one of his six paws. He chortled excitedly at the sight of Darwina and bounded down to the floor.

He scooted across the bookshop and into the café at the rear. Darwina waited for him on the windowsill, and he hopped up to join her. She graciously gave him part of the day-old cookie that she had been munching. They murmured to each other.

Although Rachel had unlocked the front door of the shop, the Closed sign still hung in the window. The official opening time was nine. It was only eight thirty. Jilly Finch, Rachel's part-time assistant, had not yet arrived.

Rachel and Charlotte and the dust bunnies had the premises to themselves.

"Young love in bloom, do you think?" Charlotte asked. She nodded toward Rex and Darwina.

"Or a hot fling," Rachel said. She went behind the counter to pour some tea. "Hard to say with dust bunnies."

"Or humans, at least at the beginning," Charlotte said. "Takes a while to figure out what's really driving a relationship at first, doesn't it?"

Amusement and friendly commiseration gleamed in her hazel eyes. Rachel gave her a rueful smile. They had met and become "summer friends" in their teens. Their families had vacationed on the island and they each had aunts who had been local residents.

After graduating high school, however, life had taken them in different directions. Charlotte had gone to college and eventually pursued a career as a dealer in paranormal antiques. Rachel had studied crystal healing at the Harmonic Enlightenment Academy and moved on to practice at the Enlightenment Institute until she had decided to try to find a place for herself in the mainstream world.

Now they were both back on Rainshadow and it was as if their friendship had been in hibernation during the time they were apart. It had blossomed immediately when their winding paths had brought them back to the island.

"No need to be subtle." Rachel put two cups of tea on the counter. "I'm well aware that the news that Harry spent the night at my place is the chief topic of conversation in town this morning. I fed him breakfast and kicked him out of the house as soon as I could, but Hank Levenson, the fish guy, drove past just as Harry was pulling out of my driveway in that big SUV of his."

"Hard to disguise that vehicle. Everyone in town knows it belongs to Harry."

"So true."

"How did he end up at your place?" Charlotte asked.

"He went into town for dinner. When the storm hit, he decided to turn around but there was a tree down on the road. At least that's the story I was given."

"Do you doubt it?"

"Let's just say that I'm sure there probably is a tree down on the road to the old gatekeeper's cabin. Whether or not the road was impassable is an open question."

Charlotte smiled. "Meaning?"

"Meaning that if Harry did give me a story, he would have made certain that it would hold up under scrutiny."

"Well, for what it's worth, Slade says there are several trees down on various roads."

"Okay."

"And to be fair, if he couldn't get back to the cabin, it's not like Harry would have had a lot of options," Charlotte said. "Your place was the closest."

"Uh-huh."

"I can tell that you are not entirely convinced."

"Huh-uh."

Charlotte smiled. "That was a really bad storm."

Rachel folded her arms on the counter. "I thought about posting a banner outside the shop window today that reads NOTHING HAPPENED LAST NIGHT but I decided it would be a total waste of time and energy. Also, not entirely honest."

"Oh, wow." Charlotte's eyes widened behind the lenses of her stylish glasses. "Something *did* happen?"

"Yes, but don't get too excited. I fed him leftover lasagna and then he more or less blackmailed me into helping him investigate what is going on inside the Preserve."

"Blackmail?" Charlotte straightened, incensed.

"I know what you mean." Rachel made a tut-tutting sound with her teeth and tongue. "What is the modern dating scene coming to?"

"Wait until I talk to Slade."

"Thanks, but don't bother. I exaggerated somewhat. It would be more accurate to say I was pressured into agreeing to assist with the investigation. And it's too late to back out now. I've already committed myself."

"But why? How?" Charlotte frowned. "And what in the world could Sebastian possibly use to pressure you?"

"The entire town of Shadow Bay, for starters."

"Excuse me?"

"Here's the problem," Rachel said. "Harry thinks someone in town is responsible for what is going on in the Preserve. If I don't use my talent to help him narrow the field of suspects, he'll handle the investigation his way and most likely order an evacuation."

"Oh, crap. Slade said something about a possible evacuation but I didn't think it would come to that." Charlotte paused, frowning. "I doubt if it would work. You know folks on this island. A lot of them would simply ignore or defy an order to leave. They would conclude that it was some sort of conspiracy to seize their property or expose their secrets or something. There are a bunch of people on Rainshadow who have reasons to keep their pasts buried."

"I did warn Harry but he thinks that whatever is going on in the Preserve is potentially quite dangerous."

"So you've agreed to help him."

"Yes, but mostly because I think he's flat-out wrong."

"About the situation in the Preserve becoming dangerous?" Charlotte shook her head. "Slade agrees with him. I've been inside the fence and I can tell you that there is a lot of ambient psi in the Preserve."

"I didn't mean that I think Harry is wrong about the trouble in the Preserve. I meant that I think he's wrong about one of the locals being responsible. Most of the residents have been here for years. Why would the trouble start now if one of them was involved? Why not a long time ago?"

Charlotte cleared her throat discreetly. "Not all of us have been living on the island for a long time. Take me, for instance. And Slade. We both moved here recently."

Rachel winced. "Same with me. But we're the exceptions. Regardless, I think it's best that I keep an eye on Harry Sebastian. I know most of the locals and I understand them. I'll try to keep Harry from leaping to the wrong conclusions."

"I agree. And you won't be on your own for long. Slade and I will be back in a week—sooner if necessary.

You know Slade. He'll stay in close contact while we're doing the meet-the-relatives routine in Frequency City. He takes his responsibility as police chief here very, very seriously."

Rachel smiled. "I know."

"If there's any trouble, he can be back here within a few hours."

"Reassuring," Rachel said.

"So that's what didn't happen last night, hmm?" Charlotte gave her an assessing look. "A little lasagna and some delicate blackmail."

"That's about it, I'm afraid." Rachel picked up her teacup. She decided not to mention the kiss in the kitchen. *Not like it amounted to much,* she thought.

"Well, as it happens," Charlotte said, "I've got a little gossip to give you."

"Sounds good," Rachel said. "Let's have it."

Charlotte shook her head. "You were never meant to be a member of the HE community, were you?"

"Hey, according to the Principles, all knowledge is enlightening. As far as I'm concerned, that includes gossip."

"In this case, what I have to tell you may balance the harmonic scales a little because it concerns Harry." Charlotte lowered her voice even though there was no one else in the shop. "Slade did a background check on him as soon as he learned that Harry was the security expert the Foundation was sending to the island."

A flicker of unease ruffled Rachel's senses. "What did he find out?"

"Harry Sebastian was married in a Full Covenant Marriage wedding ceremony two years ago."

The floor fell away beneath Rachel's feet. The shock took her breath and left her dazed. *How could she have been so wrong about Harry Sebastian?* She struggled to come to grips with the reality of what Charlotte had just said.

"Are you sure there isn't some mistake?" she whispered. "I got the impression that he wasn't married, not even a Marriage of Convenience."

"He's not married," Charlotte said. "At least, not any longer."

Rachel managed to breathe. "Widowed?"

"No. Three weeks after the wedding, Harry's wife filed for divorce."

Rachel felt as if she had fallen into a very deep hole, yet again.

"Oh my," she managed. "Leaving aside the issue of the scandal involved, divorce is a legal and financial nightmare."

"Yes, it is."

"It must have cost a fortune."

"I'm sure it did. But the Sebastians happen to have a fortune. Harry is very wealthy in his own right."

Rachel drank more tea and lowered the cup slowly. "There aren't many grounds for divorce. The ones that do exist are narrow and quite strict."

"In this case we can rule out most of them. Both parties were well above the age of consent. There was no mental illness and it was not a case of bigamy. Neither individual was already married to someone else."

Rachel shook her head, more bewildered than shocked now. "Then what in the world were the grounds?"

"Get this," Charlotte said. "Evidently the divorce was granted under the new laws providing for the dissolution of a marriage in cases of *intolerable psychical incompatibility*. Harry's wife asked the court to grant the divorce on the grounds that the nature of Harry's talent caused her to fear for her safety and her sanity."

Rachel sniffed. "Well, that's pure ghost-shit."

Charlotte cleared her throat. "I beg your pardon? Did I just hear you use the term *ghost-shit*?"

"Being raised HE doesn't mean I don't know the language."

"Obviously."

"The bride must have come down with a very bad case of bridal jitters *after* the ceremony," Rachel said. "Terrible timing on her part. I would have thought that she would have figured out that she didn't want to marry Harry at some point during the engagement."

"The engagement was quite short. It lasted only a couple of months. Harry and his bride did not meet through a matchmaking agency."

"Probably because no agency would take Harry on as a client," Rachel said. "His talent is a little unusual."

"Tell me about it," Charlotte said. "You're talking to a woman who was declared unmatchable by every agency in Frequency City, remember?"

"I remember."

"Whatever the case, the marriage ended three weeks after the wedding. The whole thing was handled as discreetly as possible, but divorce always leaves a social stigma."

"In this case it was Harry who took the hit, though," Rachel said.

"Yes. The ex-wife came through it all unscathed. She was the innocent, injured party. In fact, she is now engaged to another man. This time she found someone through an agency."

"Poor Harry."

"Excuse me? Poor Harry?"

"For the rest of his life he'll be the guy whose wife divorced him because he scared the living daylights out of her," Rachel said.

"Hard accusation for a man to live down, that's for sure. If he was unmatchable before the divorce, he's got no chance of finding an agency who will take him on as a client now."

Rachel drummed her fingers on the counter and thought about the heat that had swirled in the kitchen last night when Harry had kissed her.

"Something tells me there's more to the story," she said.

The bell over the door tinkled again. Harry walked into the shop with Slade Attridge. The energy of the men's powerful auras charged the atmosphere of the small space. *A pair of hunters,* Rachel thought.

Rex chortled a greeting from the windowsill and flapped his clutch a few times.

Charlotte spun around on the stool to face Slade.

"Hey there, handsome," she said in a mockingly sultry voice. "Come here often?"

"Mostly when I know you're here," Slade said. He crossed the bookshop into the café and kissed Charlotte. It was a quick, proprietary kiss that left no doubt as to the powerful bond and the sense of commitment between the two of them.

Rachel was intensely aware of the energy in the atmosphere around the pair. Out of the corner of her eye she noticed that Harry was suddenly very absorbed in a painting of the tiny town of Shadow Bay that was hanging on the wall. She knew that he, too, sensed the currents that swirled in the room. The psychic bond between Slade and Charlotte was so strong that even those with a minimal amount of awareness could sense it. Certainly everyone on the island was convinced that the two were meant for each other.

According to the Principles, love was the most powerful of all energies. It ran the gamut of the spectrum from the normal zone all the way into the furthest reaches of the paranormal. Rachel could believe that when she watched Slade and Charlotte together.

True, the process of falling in love had been rocky for them. They had met as teens one summer here on Rainshadow, but life had taken them in different directions for several years. When they had returned to the island as adults, however, they had rediscovered each other. There had been one or two other small glitches—someone had tried to kill them, and Slade had discovered that all was not going well somewhere deep in the heart of the Preserve.

Still, there was a wedding in the offing, and Rachel was thrilled for both of them. They deserved their happiness. Charlotte and Slade had found something very precious and very rare—a love that would endure and grow ever stronger as the years passed.

A tingle of awareness flittered through Rachel. Intuition made her glance at Harry. He was no longer studying the painting. He was watching her with a thoughtful— one could even say *suspicious*—expression.

Darwina and Rex were watching her, too. They blinked their baby blues and did their best to look adorable. They didn't have to try hard, she thought. Dust bunnies, in general, tended to look cute in a scruffy sort of way—at least until they went into hunting mode. As the old saying went, by the time you saw the teeth it was too late.

"You're in luck," she told them. She went to the end of the counter and removed the glass dome lid off the tray that she used to display cookies and treats. "I've got exactly two of yesterday's batch of chocolate-coffee zingers left."

Nearly delirious with excitement, Rex left his precious clutch on the windowsill and launched himself across the floor. He catapulted up onto the counter. Rachel handed him the cookies. He seized them in his front paws and rushed back to the windowsill. He gallantly offered one of the treats to Darwina.

"Great," Slade said. "Just what a dust bunny needs, chocolate laced with caffeine. They'll both be bouncing off the walls."

Harry watched Rex and Darwina devour the cookies. "Probably a good thing I'm from Rainshadow Foundation security and not from the Board of Health. I'm not sure the health inspectors would approve of dust bunnies dining in a public restaurant."

"The public health authorities aren't a big problem for us here on the island," Slade said. "The nearest inspector is stationed over on the mainland in Frequency City. We don't see much of him. In fact, we don't see a lot of officials of any kind around here. When it comes to enforcing local laws and ordinances, the Rainshadow Police Department is all there is."

Harry gave him an amused, knowing look. "That would be you and your two-person department."

Slade smiled, coolly satisfied. "Yes, it would." He turned back to Charlotte. "All set over at Looking Glass?"

"Yes," she said. "Jasper is going to watch my shop while we're off the island. I just gave him the keys."

"In that case, it's time you and I went home and grabbed our bags." Slade glanced at his watch. "Next ferry leaves in an hour." He looked at Harry. "We're scheduled to be out of town for a week. After I meet Charlotte's relatives, we're going to attend the wedding of some friends of mine, Marlowe Jones and Adam Winters. You've probably heard of them."

"I'd have to have been living in a cave not to have heard of them," Harry said. "According to the media, they saved the Underworld and, possibly, all four city-states, as well. That makes for a lot of press."

Rachel whistled softly and propped her elbows on the

counter. "I'm impressed with your social connections, Slade. Adam Winters is the boss of the Frequency City Guild, and Marlowe Jones is from an old Arcane family. That is going to be a huge wedding. Full-on traditional Guild ceremony combined with all the trappings of a high-ranking Arcane Society affair. I can't wait to see pictures of Marlowe Jones's dress."

"Trust me, I don't usually move in those circles," Slade said. He looked grim. "And I can think of a lot of other ways that I would rather spend that particular afternoon, but Winters and I go way back."

Charlotte patted his arm and looked at Rachel and Harry. "Slade is grousing because it means he has to buy a tux."

"Think of the bright side, Slade," Rachel said, "you'll have the tux available for your own wedding."

Slade visibly cheered. "Good point." He turned back to Harry. "Officer Willis is covering for me while I'm off-island. If you need anything, just ask. He's solid. Learns fast but he's young and hasn't had a lot of experience. If you think you're going to require more backup than he can handle, call me. I can get here within a few hours either by ferry or float plane."

"Sure," Harry said. "But this is just an initial security assessment. I won't take any action until I get a handle on what's happening inside the Preserve. That will probably take a few days."

"You've got the files I pulled for you and my notes," Slade said. "If you need anything else, Myrna Reed at the station will get it for you."

"Thanks," Harry said. "I appreciate that."

Rachel was amused. "Don't worry, Slade. Rainshadow will survive without you for a few days."

"The question is, will I survive the meeting-the-relatives marathon," Slade said. He scooped Rex off the windowsill. "See you all next week."

"Bye," Rachel said. "Have fun meeting the parents and all the rest of the in-laws."

Slade narrowed his eyes. "Can't wait."

Charlotte laughed. "You're an ex–FBPI agent. You can handle anything, including my family."

"Not unless we get moving," Slade said. "We now have forty-five minutes to grab the bags and make the ferry."

He ushered Charlotte out the door and then all three of them were gone. Rachel found herself alone with Harry.

"Coffee?" she asked.

He glanced at the elegantly lettered menu of tea and coffee drinks that hung on the wall. "It says that something called Harmony Tea is your specialty. 'Specially blended to enhance the unique harmonic resonance of the aura.' "

She went still, her intuition flaring. "Harmony Tea is very popular with the tourists. I sell a lot to the locals as well. But this morning at breakfast you told me that you prefer coffee."

"I drank that green tea you served."

"Because it was all I had on hand."

"Slade gave me coffee when we met at the station. I've had my fix. I'm ready to try a cup of Harmony Tea."

She tapped one finger on the counter. "This is a test,

isn't it? You want to find out if I really can use crystals to read auras or if I'm a fraud."

"A lot of people can see auras or at least sense the energy of them," Harry said gently. "But reading them and interpreting them is a very different level of talent."

"Is that so?" she said very politely.

"Can you really do it?" he asked. "Read and interpret auras?"

"Mmm-hmm."

"How about mine?"

"What about it?" She was all innocence now.

"Can you read it?"

"Nope. I can see it but not very clearly."

He frowned. "So the whole aura-reading thing is just a sales gimmick to sell tea?"

"The reason I can't read your aura at the moment is because it's still daylight outside. You're a true shadow-aura. That means it's a lot easier to read you at night."

Harry looked amused. She had to hand it to him—he didn't miss a beat.

"Nice try," he said. "But we both know that there is no such thing."

"I admit that you're the first one I've ever encountered, but we studied the phenomenon at the Academy. The para-bio-physics involved is fairly simple. The ultralight in your aura simply comes from the far end of the spectrum, which makes it very hard to detect. Only a very strong aura reader can perceive it."

Harry did not stir but there was a sudden chill in the atmosphere. "What makes you think I'm a shadow?"

"Well, among other things, I did see your aura quite clearly last night," she said, exasperated.

"Shadow-auras are supposed to be invisible."

"To most people, maybe, but not me." She realized she was getting irritated. "Look, I'm not in the mood to be tested. I don't have to prove anything, certainly not to you. If you aren't convinced that I've got the kind of ability you need to assist you in your investigation, just say so. No hard feelings on my part, believe me."

"I'll take some of your special blended tea," he said quietly.

She narrowed her eyes. "I'm not giving it away for free, you know."

She winced as soon as the words were out of her mouth.

But Harry merely inclined his head politely. "I understand."

"I'm running a business here," she added somewhat gruffly.

"I know."

"There's an extra charge for one of my special blends." She gestured toward the fine print on the menu board.

"I think I can afford it," he said.

It was a challenge. She knew she could not resist.

"Okay," she said. "All right."

She turned, rezzed a little talent, and began selecting jars from the array on the back counter. There was no recipe for what she was about to do because shadow-auras were so rare that no one at the Academy had been able to run any experiments. But her intuition and train-

ing guided her toward some of the more exotic psi-
infused ingredients in her extensive collection.

She went to work, putting pinches of dried herbs from
several different jars into a glass pot. She was aware that
Harry was watching her every move.

"I'm not planning to poison you," she said, not both-
ering to turn around.

"But you could if you wanted to?" He didn't sound
worried. He sounded interested.

"Sure." She took the kettle off the stove just before
the water boiled. The herbs she had chosen were delicate
and subtle. Boiling water would shock them and lessen
their restorative effects. "But I'd have to deal with the
psychic fallout afterward and that would be a real pain.
No telling how many hours of crystal meditation it
would take to rebalance my harmonic energies."

"Good to know you're not real enthusiastic about
slipping me a little poison."

"I've got better things to do. At least at this moment."
She poured the hot water carefully into the glass pot.
"You do realize that when the word gets out that you're
looking for suspects among the locals you're going to
run into a few issues. There are some very odd and reclusive residents here on Rainshadow. They consider their
secrets and their privacy sacrosanct. If you try to question them, they're as likely as not to meet you at the front
door with a mag-rez pistol or a really big knife."

"I'm aware of that problem. Slade briefed me on the
local customs and attitudes toward authorities. That's
another reason why I'd prefer to work through you when

I interview the locals. Everyone around here seems to trust you."

She glanced at the row of glass tea and herb canisters that lined one wall. "It's probably the tea. Word has gotten around the island that my blends are special. People like them."

"In other words, you're the local dealer."

She raised her brows. "You could say that. But in case you're wondering, nothing I sell in this shop is on any government agency's list of banned or regulated drugs."

"This isn't tea-growing country. Where do you get your supplies?"

"The traditional teas come from the usual commercial vendors on the mainland. But I pick a lot of the herbs that I use in my special blends here on the island."

"Where, as Slade pointed out, the various government agencies don't have a presence."

"I know my herbs," she said.

"Mushroom hunters say something similar just before they get fast-tracked to the ER after eating one of the poisonous variety."

She glanced at him over her shoulder. "You're a real suspicious sort of guy, aren't you?"

"Goes with the job. But you seem to be the suspicious type, too. Is there a reason for that?"

"Look, there's something we need to get straight here," she said. "I trust Slade and I know he's genuinely concerned about whatever is going on inside the Preserve. I realize he would not have called in Foundation security if he didn't think the situation was serious. For his sake and the sake of the other people here on the island, I'm willing to help if I can. But as I told you last night, I will not help you dig up old secrets and buried pasts just to satisfy your suspicions."

"You've made it clear that your first loyalty is to your friends and neighbors. I'm good with that."

"Just so we're clear."

She rezzed her senses and inhaled cautiously. The strong, bright energy felt right—a harmonious counterpoint for Harry's midnight-dark aura. She poured the brew into a cup and put it on the counter in front of him.

"There you go," she said. "A specially blended harmony tea for a shadow-aura."

He picked up the cup, examined the golden-hued brew for a few seconds and then inhaled cautiously. "Smells good, like the woods after a rain. Or maybe the ocean."

She smiled coolly. "That's an indication that I got the blend right for you."

He took a cautious sip. His eyes heated a little. He lowered himself onto one of the stools and took another sip.

"I like it," he said. "I've never enjoyed tea in my life but this is good."

"Technically speaking it's not tea. It's an herbal tisane. But that's just semantics."

Neither of them spoke for a while. Harry drank his tea in silence as though it were a fine wine or rare scotch, clearly savoring it.

The back door opened, shattering the stillness that had settled over the bookshop. A wall of bookshelves blocked the view of the rear door from the café, but

Rachel heard Jilly Finch's familiar footsteps. Darwina heard her, too. She chortled enthusiastically and bounced down from the windowsill to greet Jilly.

"Good morning, Rachel," Jilly sang out from the other side of the book wall. "And good morning to you, too, Darwina. Looks like you both got here ahead of me today. Saw the bicycle out back."

"Hi, Jilly," Rachel called. "Everything okay out at your place?"

"Yes. Didn't lose the power, thank goodness, because I was right in the middle of a terrific scene involving Harry Sebastian and a ghost."

"The ghost of what?"

"Never mind, it's complicated. Let's get to more important stuff. Alice Wilkins called first thing to tell me that the bridge over the creek is out. That's not all she told me. I hear you had an interesting overnight guest. You are the talk of the town today, boss. Is it true? Did Harry Sebastian actually spend the night at your place? Because if so, I've got a gazillion questions for you. All in the name of research for my books, of course."

Jilly came around the corner of the book wall, Darwina tucked under one arm, and saw Harry at the counter.

"Oh, shit," she said.

Horrified chagrin widened her eyes. A handsome woman in her mid-forties, Jilly had platinum blond hair cut in a short, spiky style. An array of small studs adorned her ears. Metallic rings decorated with designs taken from Old World mythology graced most of her fingers. Wide metal cuffs with additional ancient motifs circled each wrist. She was dressed in a flowing, ankle-length caftan.

"Jilly, this is Harry Sebastian," Rachel said calmly. "Harry, meet Jilly Finch."

Unruffled, Harry got to his feet and inclined his head politely. "Nice to meet you, Jilly. You must be the author, the one who writes that series about my great-grandfather."

"That would be me," Jilly said. "And now that I've gotten past my initial mortification, I've got to tell you that I would really, really like to interview you about your great-grandfather."

"Some other time, maybe," Harry said. "I'm a little busy at the moment."

"Sure," Jilly said quickly. "Anytime that's convenient with you is good for me. Your perspective as Harry's great-grandson would be incredibly helpful. It would allow me to add more insight and historical accuracy to my books. I write for the YA crowd, and kids love details."

"I'll get back to you." Harry finished the tisane and put the cup on the counter. "Now if you both will excuse me, I've got some research of my own to do. Slade gave me the old police files dealing with incidents connected to the Preserve. I'm going to go through them today and see what turns up."

"Don't run off," Rachel said coolly.

"Got a lot of work ahead," Harry said. He started toward the door. "But I'll stop by your place this evening and let you know what I found in the police records, if anything."

Panic sparkled through her. She was not going to let him invite himself to her house a second time, she thought. That would mean that she would have to offer him coffee or tea at the very least and that, in turn, could lead to a glass of wine, which could slide all too easily into letting him stay for dinner. *That way lies madness,* she thought. It would be easier to control the situation if she could escape whenever she felt it was necessary.

Jilly must have seen the deer-in-the-headlights expression on her face.

"Don't forget we've got that special tea-tasting event with the Reflections seminar crowd at five today, boss," Jilly said.

"Oh, right," Rachel said quickly. "Thanks for reminding me." She gave Harry a bright smile. "I don't know when it will conclude. Could run late. But at this time of year there is daylight until after nine in the evenings. When I finish with the Reflections event, I'll drop by the old gatekeeper's cabin. You can update me then."

"That works," Harry said.

Well, that was a little too easy, Rachel thought. *What's wrong with this picture?* Maybe he thought he could control things better if he got her on his turf.

"Excuse me," she said.

Harry was halfway to the door. He paused.

"Yes?" he said.

"You didn't pay for your tisane. That'll be ten dollars."

Jilly blinked, clearly stunned. She started to say something but she took one look at Rachel and closed her mouth.

"Ten dollars for a cup of tea?" Harry said very neutrally.

Rachel rezzed up another brilliant smile. "Next time ask the price before you give the order."

He nodded and reached for his wallet. "I'll remember that advice."

He put ten dollars on the counter. Said another round of polite good-byes and went out the door.

Jilly looked at Rachel. "Most guys would have been pissed off at having to pay ten bucks for a cup of tea."

"Something tells me it would take more than being overcharged for a cup of tea to make Harry Sebastian mad."

"Like what?" Jilly asked, her writer's curiosity instantly aroused.

"I have no idea," Rachel said. She contemplated the front door of the shop. "And I don't think I want to find out."

Chapter 6

"THIS EVENT HAS BEEN VERY SUCCESSFUL." EMERSON Eubanks smiled at Rachel across the counter. "I wasn't entirely convinced a tea-tasting would fit into my message but I'm glad Nathan talked me into giving it a try. Rest assured I'm a believer now."

Emerson Eubanks could have been called up by central casting for the role of motivational speaker in a film. He was in his early forties, brown-eyed, attractive, dynamic, and endowed with a disarming, quite brilliant smile. He was pleasant enough, in Rachel's opinion, but he was one of those high-energy people who made you tired just looking at them. People like Emerson never had problems. They had *challenges*. His message was printed on the Reflections Institute brochures: *Creating Positive Awareness*.

The tea-tasting program had lasted nearly two hours. Rachel could tell that not only was Eubanks pleased, but so were the attendees. Almost all of them had bought some tea and several had picked up copies of Jilly's *Tales of Harry Sebastian* books. Jilly was still busy checking out the last in a long line of customers.

"I'm glad it worked out so well," Rachel said. "I know a new group arrives every week to attend your retreats. Would you like to set up a schedule?"

"Let's do that," Emerson said. "But since this was Nathan's idea, I'll let the two of you coordinate future tastings."

Emerson clapped Nathan Grant on the shoulder and went off to join the seminar attendees who were making their way outside onto the street.

Nathan smiled and winked at Rachel. "Thanks for making me look good in front of Eubanks. This job is important to me."

"Anytime," Rachel said. She ignored the wink. "I'm glad the event turned out so well."

"You and me both. Eubanks is all about his message. He insists that every seminar event enhance Positive Awareness. He wasn't sure a tea-tasting would be a good fit but between the two of us, it looks like we changed his mind."

Nathan was one of the instructors at the Reflections Institute. She had talked to him on the phone when he had called to discuss the possibility of a tasting, but she had not met him in person until today. Like everyone else on the Reflections staff, he was attractive, well dressed, and upbeat, but Rachel found him to be more laid-back and not nearly so exhausting as Emerson.

It was too bad about the winking thing. His murky aura was off-putting, as well.

"The seminars run from Saturday through Friday," Nathan said. "What do you say we settle on Wednesday afternoons for the tastings?"

"That will work out very well," Rachel said.

"Great. See you on Wednesday."

Nathan gave her another wink and followed Eubanks and the seminar attendees outside. When the door closed behind him, Jilly turned the Closed sign in the window and flung herself across the counter with great drama.

"Whew, what an afternoon," she said. Then she straightened, grinning. "But it was worth it. We both made some money today. You sold several pounds of tea and I sold twelve copies of my book."

"Hooray for us." Rachel picked up a tray and headed toward the cluttered tables in the café. "Now all we have to do is clean up."

"Yep, there's always a dark side to success," Jilly said. "I'll wash. You dry. By the way, did I see Nathan Grant wink at you?"

"Twice."

"He probably thinks it's charming."

"Probably."

FIFTEEN MINUTES LATER RACHEL PICKED UP THE LAST OF the twelve freshly washed cups. The misty dreamscape image flashed out of the darkness of her lost memories, disappearing as quickly as it had appeared.

The cup slipped from her fingers and shattered on the floor.

"Are you okay, boss?" Jilly asked.

"Yes." Rachel stared at the pieces of the broken cup, mentally trying to recover the fleeting scene that had flickered across her awareness when she'd picked up the cup. But it was gone.

"You sure?" Jilly asked. "You look like you just saw a ghost."

"I think I did see one," Rachel said.

Chapter 7

HARRY STOOD ON THE FRONT PORCH OF THE OLD GATE-
keeper's cabin, his hands wrapped around the railing, and
watched Rachel ride out of the fog on her bicycle. She
wore the snug-fitting black jeans she'd had on earlier,
boots, and a leather jacket. Her hair was clipped back in a
frothy little twist.

He wondered about the black jeans and leather. The
edgy outfit did not quite fit the profile that he was putting
together. He was no expert on the HE lifestyle, but what
he had learned suggested that the members of the Community dressed in loose-fitting robes that were the colors of various kinds of amber and crystals. The robes
were often adorned with tiny bells sewn into the hems.
He had read somewhere that the bells were supposed to
encourage good energy.

It was hard to imagine Rachel in a white lab coat at

the Chapman Clinic, and the thought of her doing aura readings to amuse the customers in the Crystal Rainbow tearoom seriously annoyed him. She was a powerful talent who cared about others. She deserved respect. He did not like the idea that she had been treated as a low-rent fortune-teller during her time in Frequency City.

But he also understood intuitively that she did not belong in the cloistered environment of an HE community with its emphasis on maintaining a cerebral detachment from the world and an inner psychic balance in all things. She was too curious, too adventurous, and far too passionate to live apart from the world. She needed the rough-and-tumble of real life. She needed to be free to lose her temper at times, free to become giddy, free to cry or laugh out loud.

Most of all she needed a lover who appreciated her strengths, her talent, and her spirit. *A lover like me,* he thought. His hands tightened a little on the railing.

No. He needed a lover like her.

She brought the bicycle to a halt at the bottom of the porch steps and dismounted with the fluid grace of a dancer. Or one skilled in martial arts, he reminded himself. He smiled.

"The fog seems worse out here," she said.

"Probably because this place is so close to the fence boundary." He went down the steps, picked up the bike, and carried it back up the steps. "Where's your pal?"

"Darwina disappeared with Amberella just before the tea-tasting event started. Haven't seen her since. Maybe she went off to meet a guy or maybe she wants to impress her friends with the doll. Who knows? Slade says Rex vanishes frequently into the woods. Dust bunnies don't seem to have any problem with the psi-fence or the Preserve."

He propped the bike against the wall of the cottage. "You don't have a car?"

"Can't afford one yet. Things didn't go well for me financially in Frequency City. My boss at the Chapman Clinic was decent enough to give me two-weeks' severance pay, but I had to hand over most of that to my landlord when I broke the lease on my apartment. I get a lift from a friend or borrow a Vibe from Brett at the service station when the weather is bad."

"Come on inside," he said. He held the door for her.

Just before she crossed the threshold she glanced toward the dark woods that crowded around the cottage. "I didn't realize how close this place was to the psi-fence. You can really feel the energy of the Preserve from here."

"And it's getting stronger."

"So you and Slade keep saying." She moved into the front room of the cabin. "I'm not arguing that point."

He took another look at the fog-shrouded woods before he followed her inside. There was a lot of energy in the atmosphere this evening and not all of it was coming from the Preserve.

"There's another storm on the way," he said, closing the door.

The territory of the Preserve covered nearly 75 percent of Rainshadow. There was no physical fence. Instead, the boundary was secured with an invisible barrier of paranormal energy that had been in place as long as anyone could remember. Most people assumed that it was some sort of natural phenomenon generated by the unusual currents on the island. Harry wasn't so sure. He and the others in his family had another theory.

Regardless of the origin of the fence, the Foundation had recently reinforced the barrier with some very high-end security technology that had come out of one of the company labs. But the enhancement wasn't working. Slade Attridge and others, including a couple of the local kids and Rachel, had all managed to get inside lately.

Rachel stopped a few steps away and turned to face him. "I just had a thought. Maybe it's the heavy storm pattern we've had lately that is responsible for agitating the energy in the Preserve."

"No," he said. "I'm sure it's the reverse. The Preserve is stirring up the storms. But there is bound to be a synergistic effect, which makes things worse over time. This island is a major geothermal para-nexus. There's a lot of natural energy in the vicinity—unusually powerful ocean tides and currents, deep-sea volcanoes offshore, hot springs, tectonic movement—and Rainshadow sits right in the center of the convergence zone. It wouldn't take much to destabilize things here even without the added problem of a new source of paranormal radiation firing up unpredictable oscillation patterns."

"Those three stones that your ancestor hid in that cave?"

"Yes."

She nodded somberly. "I understand. 'All things in

nature survive on the razor's edge that separates harmony and chaos.' "

"One of the Principles?" he asked, amused.

"I'm afraid so. 'You can take the girl out of the Community but you can't take the Principles out of the girl.' That's another quote, by the way. One of my dad's."

"According to my research, your father is one of the highest-ranking scholars in the Community. He probably knows what he's talking about. If you'll give me your jacket, I'll hang it up."

For a couple of beats he was afraid that she was going to refuse. But she finally unfastened the jacket, slipped it off, and handed it to him. His fingers brushed hers when he took the garment from her. The fleeting contact aroused his senses again. He had to exert some real effort to suppress the reaction. That should have worried him but it didn't. It made him feel reckless.

"Mind if I ask a personal question?" he said.

She narrowed her eyes. "How personal?"

"Just wondered about the leather." He indicated the jacket and boots. "Somehow you don't look like the leather type."

She was surprised, as if she had been braced for a different question. Then she relaxed.

"It goes back to those missing twelve hours of my life," she said. "I went into the Preserve dressed in a pair of sandals, slacks, and a short-sleeved shirt. When I came out the next morning after the trek through the woods, I was a real mess. My arms and my feet were in especially bad shape, all scratched up and bruised because I'd been brushing up against branches and thorns and stumbling over rocks. If I go into another fugue state, I want to be prepared."

She spoke casually enough, but the shadows in her eyes made it devastatingly clear that the fear of a second fugue haunted her days as well as her dreams.

When he hung the jacket on the ancient coatrack, he caught a fleeting trace of her scent laced with a residue of her energy. He felt a little intoxicated.

He turned back to her and discovered that she was watching him with a cautious expression. There was some heat in her eyes. He knew that she was well aware of the attraction between them and that she was wary of it. He smiled.

"What?" she demanded.

"It struck me that the principle you just quoted, the one about all things in nature being balanced on the line between harmony and chaos applies to what is going on between you and me," he said. "I'm on edge when I'm around you. I don't think it would take much to push me off balance."

"Don't even think about it, Sebastian." She beetled her brows and held up one hand, palm out. "I am not in the mood to be seduced."

"But your mood could change, right?"

She grimaced. "Now you're making fun of me."

"No. But I might be laughing at myself."

"Why?"

"Forget it. Sit down." He moved a hand slightly to

usher her toward the old chairs near the fireplace. "Let's get to work."

She hesitated and then turned to walk briskly toward one of the chairs. He watched her, allowing himself a few seconds to contemplate the lush shape of her rear framed in denim.

Just too damn much energy in the atmosphere tonight, he thought. And a lot of it was circulating right here inside the cottage. He reined in his overheated senses.

"You do realize that you are the first person who has made a connection between the unusual weather pattern and the Preserve?" Rachel asked.

"That's what I do," he said. "Look for connections and logical explanations."

"Do you ever come up with the wrong conclusion?"

"Yes. But not often."

She settled gracefully on one of the oversized leather chairs and held her hands out to the fire. "Because you're that good?"

"Not at everything but when it comes to this kind of stuff, yeah. I'm good. You could say I have a talent for the work."

A knowing look came and went in her eyes. "Just as your great-grandfather had a talent for hunting pirates?"

"Something like that, yes."

"I can't stay long this evening," she warned. "Regardless of how this new storm is being generated, I don't want to get stuck out here after dark. It's tough to ride a bike at night here on the island because there are no streetlights."

"I promise you that you won't be riding your bike home alone in the dark," he said. "I'll drive you back to your place if the storm hits before you leave. How did the tea-tasting event go?"

To his surprise she seemed to hesitate.

"It went fine," she said. But she didn't look at him; she gazed into the fire. "Made some money. Emerson Eubanks, the man who runs the seminars, seemed pleased. So did the instructor who organized it, Nathan Grant. They both said something about making it a regular event at each seminar."

"That would be a good thing, right?"

She nodded. "Definitely."

"So what went wrong?"

Her mouth curved in a wry smile. "Do you always assume a negative?"

"I don't have to be psychic to know there was a problem."

She wrinkled her nose. "That's the thing. I don't know if there was a problem or not. Ever hear the Old World expression, 'it felt like someone just walked over my grave'?"

A chill went through him. "Something happened at the tasting that made you think of that saying?"

"Uh-huh. When Jilly and I washed the dishes, I picked up a cup. For some reason my intuition stirred, and I sensed a little psychic residue on the cup. I got a small psychic shock and dropped the cup."

"You can sense that kind of energy?" he asked.

"I can't read it but like a lot of strong talents, I can catch traces of it, especially if it was laid down by another powerful talent. At any rate, for a few seconds I could have sworn that I half remembered a ghostly aura, one I could not quite see. The harder I tried, the more it faded."

"Another dream fragment?"

"I think so," she said. "Now I'm starting to worry that my dream images are messing up my real memories. False memories are worse than no memories."

"This could be important, Rachel. Do you think that one of the people who attended the tea-tasting is connected to what happened to you?"

A small tremor went through her. She clasped her hands tightly together. "I thought about that possibility, believe me, but I don't see how that would be possible. The seminar attendees are all new on the island as of last Saturday. I know I've never seen any of them before."

"What about Eubanks and the instructor, Grant?"

She shot him a sidelong look. "I haven't forgotten your theory about a local resident being responsible for whatever is happening inside the Preserve. Eubanks has been on the island for several months. I heard that Nathan Grant joined the staff a few weeks ago. I took a quick look at their auras this afternoon. I've never seen either one before."

"Unless you've forgotten one of them?" he suggested gently.

She sighed. "Unless I've forgotten one of them."

"I don't understand, you must have met Eubanks previously."

"Yes, briefly." Her eyes widened. "I see what you mean. I've met him in person, but today was the first day I've had a reason to examine his aura. As for Nathan Grant, I've talked to him on the phone, but today was the first time I'd met him in person and, therefore, the first time I've had a chance to view his aura."

"You don't automatically view an individual's aura whenever you see him or her?"

"If I'm in my senses, I can perceive some paranormal energy around everyone but I can't read that energy with any degree of accuracy unless I focus through crystal. Frankly, most of the time I prefer not to look at people's auras."

"Why not?"

"Well, it's a terribly intimate experience, for one thing," Rachel said. "Much worse than reading someone's diary or learning an individual's most closely held secrets."

"It feels intrusive."

"It *is* intrusive," Rachel said. "What's more, it's often depressing because I can see weaknesses and flaws that I know people could overcome if they just exerted the willpower to do it."

"But you know they probably won't make the effort to change."

"And I also know that they will go through the rest of their lives blaming their problems on others," she concluded. "But that's not the worst of it. The most unpleasant thing about doing in-depth aura readings is discovering how many people are actually low-level, garden-variety psi-paths—people who will lie, cheat, or steal without a qualm just to get what they want. Then there are the real monsters."

"I get the picture."

"Take my word for it, if I read the aura of every person I encountered on the street, I'd probably end up in a para-psych ward."

"But you did read Eubanks's aura today," he said. "What did you see?"

"Just what you'd expect in someone who is in the motivational seminar line. He's a con man who has managed to con himself into believing that he really does have a message that others need to hear."

"What about Nathan Grant, the instructor?"

Rachel frowned. "His aura was murky. I couldn't get a good fix on it. That happens sometimes. To do a reading on him I'd probably need physical contact."

"How many murky auras do you run into?"

She raised one shoulder in a small, graceful shrug. "It's not all that uncommon."

"But you didn't see anything in his aura that would lead you to believe that he's involved in whatever is going down out in the Preserve?"

She sat back in her chair. "It doesn't work like that, Harry. I'm not a human lie detector. Everyone has a dark side and most people are capable of doing dangerous or illegal things if the goal is worth it."

"I'll add Eubanks and Grant to my list of persons of

interest." He indicated the files spread out on the low table. "Meanwhile, I went through the records that Slade pulled for me. These are the ones I thought might have some significance. I'd like to go over them with you."

"Okay, but I'm telling you again, you're wasting your time. I have no idea what's going on in the Preserve, let alone who in town might be responsible."

"You've made that clear."

He sat down across from her and opened his senses a little to luxuriate in the exotic, mysterious energy that she had brought with her into the small cabin.

She surveyed the room. "No one has lived here in a very long time."

"This place is the property of the Foundation. In the old days there was a gatekeeper stationed here on the island, but we rarely use it now."

Rachel looked amused. "For goodness' sake, why did the Foundation need a gatekeeper? There aren't any actual gates in the fence, are there?"

"Okay, in reality the gatekeeper functioned as a guard."

"To protect the treasure?"

"Back in the day, no one at the Foundation was worried that someone might find the damn rocks. The problem was that people kept searching for a legendary treasure that never existed."

She smiled. "The lure of pirate amber."

"During the first few years after my great-grandfather's legend started to circulate around the islands of the Amber Sea, a fair number of treasure hunters disappeared inside the Preserve, never to be seen again. To discourage the treasure hunting, the Foundation experimented with keeping an armed guard stationed on the island for a time. It didn't work well."

"Treasure hunters tend to be the obsessive type."

"Yes," he said. "But eventually the Foundation techs came up with ways to enhance the effectiveness of the fence. It was decided that a guard was no longer necessary."

"Rainshadow has always been forbidden territory. The tales of ghosts and monsters existed long before your ancestor came ashore to bury those crystals. They go back to the days of the First Generation explorers who mapped the Amber Sea islands and the Colonial-era fishermen who worked these waters."

"That's why my great-grandfather and North chose this place to bury the three stones," he said. "They figured that even if someone did get past the energy fence, he or she probably wouldn't be able to locate the treasure, let alone get out alive. Entire expeditions have disappeared into what is now the Preserve. The interior has never been mapped because the energy inside is so disorienting that compasses and other instruments don't work. Can't even get a visual fix on landmarks from the air because of the distortion created by the paranormal currents."

Rachel watched him very steadily. "I've always wondered what made the first Harry Sebastian think that he could go through the psi barrier, bury his treasure, and find his way back to his ship."

"He was a very powerful talent."

"Strong talents have started appearing recently in the

population, but, statistically speaking, they're still rare. They would have been a lot more scarce when your ancestor was working these waters. I'm guessing that the members of your family didn't start developing psychic abilities after settling here on Harmony. Your First Generation ancestors were talents before they arrived, weren't they?"

"Yes," he said.

"Arcane?"

"No. The Sebastians have never been what you would call 'joiners.' What about your family?"

"My ancestors were members of the Arcane Society for generations back on Earth, but after they arrived on Harmony they lost contact with the organization. I think they just assumed that they wouldn't need its protection and social connections any longer. They thought things would be different here for those with psychic talents."

Harry smiled grimly. "They weren't the only ones who believed that. Some things have definitely changed in the past two hundred years here on Harmony, but most strong talents still try to keep a low profile."

"Power is power, and a person who possesses a lot of psychic talent tends to make other people nervous and with good reason. Some talents can do as much damage with their paranormal abilities as other folks can do with a knife or a mag-rez."

"Are you quoting from the Principles or are you speaking from experience?"

"Both." Shadows came and went in her eyes. "As far as I'm concerned, a powerful talent with a criminal mind is far more dangerous than a thug with a mag-rez. A strong psychic can do a lot more harm before he's caught. *If* he's ever caught."

"When was the last time you encountered a strong criminal psychic?"

"I met one during my short career at the Chapman Clinic." She shuddered. "I still get cold chills when I think about Marcus Lancaster. But the worst part was that I couldn't convince my superiors to listen to me. Lancaster has Dr. Oakford and the rest of the staff completely fooled."

A flicker of intuition crackled through Harry. "Is that why you were let go? You disagreed with the staff's professional diagnosis of Lancaster?"

"You knew I was fired?" She made a face. "Yes, of course you did. You're in the security business. You would have done your research. To be honest, I don't think I would have lasted long at Chapman, even if Lancaster had not been an issue. I didn't fit into the clinical setting."

"They didn't appreciate your talent," he said. He had never met Dr. Ian Oakford and probably never would, but he had an explicable urge to rip Oakford's head off his shoulders.

But Rachel was suddenly laughing, a warm, bright, from-the-heart laugh that sent good energy swirling around the room.

"Nope," she said. "Oakford did not appreciate or respect my talent. And really, how often does that happen in life?"

He smiled. "You're right."

"Let's get back to your little problem."

"My little problem?"

"I'm aware of the history of the island before it was claimed by your family's corporation," Rachel said coolly. "But the details are very murky after that. The Rainshadow Foundation has never been what anyone would call transparent about the way it manages the Preserve."

"Mostly because there's nothing to manage except the damn fence. You're going to have to trust me when I tell you that we don't know anything more about what is going on inside the Preserve than anyone else does. We've never had any control over the forces in the interior. All we can do is try to protect folks from themselves by keeping treasure hunters, adventurous kids, drunken boaters, and thrill-seekers out. We didn't put up the first psi-fence, by the way."

For the first time, Rachel looked startled. "Really?"

"According to the records, there has always been a strong force field around most of the island."

"It's no secret that the island has always had a serious woo-woo factor, but I've never heard that there was an actual psi-fence around it before the Foundation took over."

"That's because the early one was only partially effective when it came to keeping humans out. My theory—and the experts at the Foundation agree with me—is that the Aliens installed the original psi barrier to keep their own kind out."

"So it was set to the frequencies of Alien psi?" she asked.

"Sure. Why would they have been concerned about a bunch of stranded colonists from some no-name planet who landed a couple of thousand years after they left? They never saw us coming."

"Okay, your logic makes sense. The fence wasn't originally tuned to human frequencies. Your point?"

"My point," Harry said deliberately, "is that the Aliens must have erected the original energy fence for a reason, probably a very good reason."

Rachel stilled. Her amber eyes heated with sudden comprehension. She pursed her lips and shook her head in wonderment.

"Now that," she said carefully, "is a rather scary thought. What was inside the Preserve that was so important or so dangerous that the Aliens would have put up a high-tech psi-fence?"

"We don't know and it didn't seem to matter because until now, the Preserve has been quiet ever since my ancestor claimed the island. The assumption was that whatever had once been locked up on the other side of the boundary had died or disintegrated centuries ago."

"Died or disintegrated?"

"We have no way of knowing what was locked up inside. Could have been animal, vegetable, or mechanical in nature."

"I see," she said.

"Remember, at this point it's all wild speculation based on the existence of what we think was intended to be an energy fence. We could be wrong about our basic assumption. Whatever the case, now that the currents are getting hot inside we need some answers and we need them fast."

She frowned in thought. "But why would the Aliens have kept something that was vitally important to them here on an island in the middle of nowhere?"

"Good question. The para-archaeologists and other experts concluded years ago that something about the surface environment of Harmony was poisonous to the Aliens. That's why they went underground and bioengineered an entire rain forest, and that's why ninety percent of the ruins are down below in the catacombs."

"Exactly. Everything that seems to have been crucial to their well-being is belowground, not up here on the surface."

"Yet they paid special attention to this one lone island located in the middle of an unimportant chain of islands in a remote sea," Harry said.

"Are you absolutely sure of that? There aren't even any ruins on the island."

"None that have been discovered yet," Harry said. "But like the Underworld, most of Rainshadow has never been explored."

"If the Foundation researchers believe that there was something very important happening inside, why haven't they conducted some major expeditions into the Preserve?"

"Because very few of our people can get more than a hundred yards beyond the fence," he said, "let alone conduct serious research. As I explained, once inside, most instruments and high-tech equipment is useless."

"Just like in the catacombs and the rain forest," she said. "But you can come and go the way Slade can."

"The deeper you go into the Preserve, the more powerful the currents become. Talents like Slade and me can go farther than most, but there are limits, even for us. None of the navigational instruments that have been developed for the catacombs and the rain forest can handle the heavy psi in the center of Rainshadow."

She looked at the old files on the table. "So your plan to get answers starts with drawing up a list of people who might have the ability to go through the fence, is that it?"

"It's a start."

She raised her eyes to meet his. "Well, then, I guess you'll have to put me at the top of your list. We know for a fact that I was not only able to go through the fence, I managed to find my way back out all by myself."

He exhaled slowly, with perfect control. "Yes."

Understanding lit her amber eyes.

"Oh," she said. She gave him a cool smile. "I see. You already had me in the number-one spot on your list. That explains why you've asked for my help, isn't it? This is a twist on the old advice to keep your friends close and your enemies closer."

"Rachel, let me explain—"

The blast of rain struck with enough force to rattle the windows. Sheets of water cascaded down the glass. The flames flared on the hearth in response to sharp updrafts.

The wind howled beneath the eaves. The darkness outside was suddenly absolute. Thunder rumbled.

The lights flickered and went out.

"Oh, damn," Rachel said. "I thought I had a couple of hours, at least, before the storm struck."

Lightning flashed in the inky night, briefly illuminating the room. Harry got to his feet.

"Looks like you're going to be here for a while," he said. "The power's out, so there goes a hot meal. Lucky I picked up enough cheese and crackers for two."

MARCUS LANCASTER HATED EVERY MINUTE THAT HE WAS forced to spend at the Chapman Clinic, but the nights were the worst.

During the day he was occupied, playing the model patient and able to take some pleasure in manipulating Oakford and the other members of the staff. But after dark he was alone in his locked room on a locked ward and he was consumed with thoughts of Rachel. She was his but she did not yet understand that essential fact. She needed to comprehend that she belonged to him, that although she was strong, he was more powerful. Her talent was his to control.

It had been weeks since she had been fired. The first few days after she had left had been hell. He had immediately begun planning his escape. The knowledge that Rachel was out in the world and out of his immediate control made him seethe with frustration. He had been ready to walk out the door of the clinic when his associate had contacted him and informed him that Rachel was back on Rainshadow. The long-delayed project to retrieve the artifacts was going forward.

It was only the knowledge of the considerable risk involved in the Rainshadow operation that kept him here at the clinic. It made sense to let his associate take the fall in the event that the FBPI got involved, Marcus reminded himself. Being locked up here at the clinic would provide the perfect alibi if things went wrong. And given that so much had already gone wrong—a representative from the Foundation was now on the island—there was a strong possibility that the project would end in disaster.

His own personal survival was his first priority, and the best way to survive the failure of the Rainshadow operation was to remain right where he was.

But knowing that Rachel was beyond his control for now was almost too much to bear.

He stood at the small barred window of his room and looked out into the night. The ruins of the ancient Alien city glowed green in the heart of Frequency.

Not much longer now. One way or another the operation would soon be over and he would be free to claim Rachel.

Chapter 8

"I HOPE DARWINA IS OKAY." RACHEL SELECTED A SLICE OF cheese and positioned it on a cracker. "This is a serious storm and she's out there in it all by herself."

She was reluctant to admit it but it was rather pleasant to be sitting here in front of a cozy fire with Harry, drinking the wine he had poured and snacking on cheese and crackers, while the tempest raged. *Even if I am Suspect Number One,* she thought. Clearly she needed to get out more.

"I'm sure Darwina is doing fine." Harry paused his wineglass halfway to his mouth and fixed her with his riveting gem green eyes. "Don't forget she's got that great little girl's role model with her, Amberella."

"The doll is made of rez-plastic. Her hair and clothes are all synthetic. Amberella will definitely survive."

"And so will Darwina. She's a creature of the wild. She's been through other storms on her own."

"I know." Rachel flinched as lightning crackled in the darkness, briefly illuminating the windows in a white-hot glare that reminded her of the silver shadows in Harry's aura. "But this is a bad one. The worst yet, I think."

"Why did you name the bunny Darwina?"

"I'm not sure." Rachel took another bite of the cheese-and-cracker combo and munched while she considered the question. "Probably because dust bunnies are such an interesting example of evolution here on Harmony."

"What does the name *Darwina* have to do with evolution?"

She blinked and then smiled. "Sometimes I forget that not everyone outside the Community got stuck with the same reading list in school that I got stuck with. Darwin was an Old World figure who had a lot to do with developing the concept of evolution."

"Yeah? Did he write about para-bio evolution?"

"Well, no, I don't think he got that far but I'm sure he would have if he had lived long enough. His theories were so elegant that they apply to paranormal biology as well as normal biology."

"Can you see Darwina's aura?"

"Nope, of course not, at least not in the same way I view human auras. But all living things produce energy fields, and I can pick up some of Darwina's vibes if she's in the vicinity. *Just as I will always know when you're close,* she thought, *even if I can't see your aura.*

Thunder rolled through the night. The next flash of lightning was so powerful it lit up the entire front room of the cottage. Rachel looked out the window. In the hot, glaring light she caught a glimpse of Harry's big black SUV parked in the drive and the dense trees that surrounded the cottage.

In the next instant the scene went dark again, but for a few seconds black-and-white afterimages sparked disconcertingly in front of her eyes. She could have sworn she saw ghostly figures moving in the trees. The hair stirred on the back of her neck. She blinked several times to clear her eyes. When she looked out the window again, there was nothing but darkness. She heaved a small sigh of relief.

"Are you okay?" Harry asked.

"Yes. The storm is making me a little jumpy."

"I know the feeling. A lot of energy out there tonight."

She decided not to mention that it didn't take much to put her nerves and her senses on edge these days. Most of Shadow Bay already considered her psychically fragile because of her lost night. She did not want Harry to come to the same conclusion. She made a note to do some deep meditation when she got back to her cottage.

"Looks like Darwina has adopted you the way Rex did Slade," Harry said. "Or maybe bonding with you would be a better way to describe it."

"I hope so. I like my cottage but it feels a little empty at times."

"I'm sure she'll be okay," Harry said. "Darwina is

probably kicking back in some comfy little cave at this very moment."

"Probably."

Thunder rolled and the rain beat furiously at the windows, an intruder demanding entrance. An unfamiliar excitement feathered Rachel's senses. *It's the energy of the storm,* she thought. But that wasn't the full explanation. It was being here alone with Harry that was sending sparks of awareness and anticipation through her. The intimacy swirling in the atmosphere between them was distracting, intense, and incredibly arousing.

Would he try to kiss her again tonight? If the edgy, sexy heat in his eyes was anything to go by, the answer was probably yes. But he would not force himself on her, so the more important question was, would she let him kiss her? And would she respond?

You're at the top of his suspect list; of course it would not be a good idea, she thought. *Talk about sleeping with the enemy.*

But it was hard to think of Harry as the enemy. An adversary, yes, an opponent, perhaps, a challenge, definitely. But not the enemy, never the enemy.

She picked up her wineglass and took a fortifying swallow. She needed the drink. Her imagination was running wild.

"What was it like growing up in an HE community?" Harry asked.

Startled, she looked at him over the rim of the wineglass. "What?"

"Sorry. That was a very personal question."

"No, no, it's okay." She pulled her scattered thoughts together. "It was good. Life is what it is when you're a kid. You take what you get and deal with it, especially if you don't know that there is another way of doing things. I had a happy childhood. I love my parents and I know they love me. I was taught to use my talent in a positive, fulfilling way."

"But you chose to leave the Community."

"Yes." She took another sip of wine and looked into the fire. "The members of the Community are challenged to live in a very self-disciplined way according to the Principles of Harmonic Enlightenment. Balance and focus in all things is the goal."

"You had trouble with that?"

"Unfortunately, yes. Luckily, my parents understood. They knew, even before I did, that I would never find true inner harmony if I forced myself to try to live my whole life within the regimen of the Community. As my father said, I needed to run the experiment—give the outside world a shot and see if it was for me."

"But it wasn't."

"No." She smiled. "But I also knew I couldn't go back to the Community, at least not to live full-time. Rainshadow feels right, though, at least for now. What about you? What was it like growing up in the Sebastian family?"

"Like you, I can't complain. Good parents. My brother and sister and I are close. But I wasn't cut out for the corporate world."

"So they put you in charge of security?"

He smiled. "After I screwed up in every other department of the family business. Between you and me, sooner or later I'm going to screw up running security, too."

"Why?"

"Because I wasn't cut out for upper management. I don't like sitting behind a desk. I don't like meetings. Don't like dealing with personnel issues. Don't like looking at charts and graphs. I need to be outside the office."

The charms on her bracelet shivered lightly.

"Of course you do," she said. "You need to hunt."

He went very still. His eyes burned. "Do you see that in my aura?"

She was surprised by the question. "Yes."

"You really can see it, can't you?"

"Uh-huh." She sipped more wine.

"Technically speaking, I'm not supposed to exist. I'm one of the monsters, a psychic vampire."

Rachel waved that aside with a small movement of her hand. "Nope, not even close."

"You're sure of that?"

"Oh, yeah, positive."

She sipped some wine and tried to think of a polite way to ask about his divorce. But some things you just don't ask, not even on a second date.

Date?

Time to change the subject, she thought.

But it was Harry who changed it.

"You do realize that after tonight no one is going to buy the excuse that we accidentally got caught in a storm together again," he said.

"Between you and me, no one in Shadow Bay bought it the first time."

A muffled *thump* at the window interrupted her. Rachel sucked in a sharp breath and turned quickly. There was a dark shadow perched on the ledge. It was approximately the size and shape of a rain-drenched rat. The shadow scratched at the glass.

"Take it easy," Harry said. He set down his glass, got to his feet, and started across the small space. "Probably a broken branch or some debris kicked up by the wind."

"No, there's something out there," Rachel said. She jumped to her feet. "It's Darwina."

Another ragged bolt of lightning cracked in the darkness, illuminating the wet blob on the window ledge. Darwina stared into the fire-lit room, all four eyes wide open. She batted at the window again.

"I wonder how she found you way out here," Harry said. "That psychic bond between the two of you must be damn strong."

"She's probably looking for refuge from the storm. The poor thing must be soaked through."

Rachel flew across the room and reached the window ahead of Harry. She struggled futilely with the old window latch. "This thing is stuck."

Darwina was huddled on the narrow ledge, her wet fur plastered around her small body. She blinked her second set of eyes, the amber pair that dust bunnies opened only for hunting or when they were threatened. She clutched a bedraggled-looking Amberella in one paw.

Rachel jerked harder on the latch. It didn't move. Darwina bounced up and down and scratched at the glass, clearly agitated.

"I've never seen her like this," Rachel said. "She's very anxious, probably terrified by the lightning."

"I'm not so sure about that," Harry said. "But it's obvious she wants inside. If you'll step out of the way, I'll deal with the window."

"Thanks." Rachel moved aside.

Harry gripped the old latch in one powerful hand and forced it to move. There was a grinding sound from the rusty metal, but the latch gave. There was another protesting groan when Harry forced the window open.

The storm roared into the room, bringing a blast of rain. Darwina bounded through the opening, Amberella in her paw, and vaulted up onto Rachel's shoulder.

Harry got the window closed. Darwina growled and shook the rain out of her fur, showering Rachel in the process.

"Okay, now we're both wet," Rachel said. Smiling, she reached up to pat Darwina. Her hand froze when the dust bunny rumbled in warning.

Harry watched Darwina with narrowed eyes. "She may look cute and cuddly but she's a wild animal, Rachel."

"I'm sure she won't hurt me," Rachel said. "But she is very agitated."

Darwina gave another low, ominous growl. She was half-sleeked, and her gaze was fixed on the window.

"She may have been fleeing a predator," Harry said. "I wonder what hunts dust bunnies here on the island."

"No animal with any common sense would be out hunting in this weather."

They both looked at Darwina, who was still growling. Her attention was fixed on the dark night outside the window.

"Shit," Harry said. But he said it very quietly.

He wrapped one hand around Rachel's arm and hauled her to one side.

"What are you doing?" she gasped, stumbling a little to keep her balance.

"Stay away from the windows." He used his free hand to yank down the shade and then released her to glide swiftly around the small room, closing the other blinds.

Rachel chilled. "Are you thinking what I think you're thinking?"

"Whatever is out there has Darwina seriously alarmed," Harry said. "It occurs to me that there is only one kind of animal that might be dumb enough or desperate enough to come out in a storm like this. No sense making targets of ourselves."

She thought about the flickering afterimages she had seen earlier in the wake of a lightning strike. Maybe the ghostly figures in the trees had not been a product of her imagination.

"Oh, crap," she said. "Do you really think there is someone out there?"

"We're not taking any chances." He clamped one hand on her shoulder and pushed her to a crouching position against one wall. "Stay in this room and stay down." He opened the hall closet and took out the long black storm coat. "The lights are out but the fire is going strong. I don't want you silhouetted against the shades."

"What are you going to do?" she asked.

"Take a look around." He fastened the jacket.

"You're going to go outside? Are you crazy? If there is someone out there, he might have a gun."

"Believe it or not, that possibility did cross my mind. I'll use the kitchen door. Remember, stay away from the windows."

"Harry, I don't think this is a good idea. You won't be able to see a thing in this storm and if you use a flashlight you'll make a perfect target of yourself."

He went toward the kitchen. "I won't need a flashlight."

"Are you saying you can see in the dark?"

He paused in the doorway and looked back at her over his shoulder. In the shadows his eyes were already hot with his rising talent. "You said you saw my aura, but I never got around to telling you about the nature of my talent."

"No," she said. "You didn't."

"I told you, I'm one of the monsters. You should have believed me."

He disappeared into the darkness of the small, unlit kitchen. Darwina rumbled anxiously in Rachel's ear. She reached up to pat Darwina reassuringly.

"It's okay. Harry is a professional," Rachel said. "Not sure exactly what he's going to do out there, but whatever it is, he'll do it very, very well."

Glass exploded in the bedroom. The sound of the

shattered window stunned Rachel for an instant. Before she could recover from the shock, there was another explosion and then firelight flashed violently in the room at the end of the short hall.

Darwina hissed. She was fully sleeked out now, her fur flattened against her small body. Her tufted ears were exposed. She vibrated with urgency. It didn't require a psychic link to know that she was all in favor of heading for the door.

Rachel scrambled to her feet, grabbed her leather jacket off the coat rack and ran toward the kitchen. Darwina's claws dug into her shoulder.

The inferno gathered energy with a speed that indicated a powerful accelerant had been used in the firebomb. The roar of the flames leaping down the hallway was louder than the thunder of the storm, a great, insatiable beast that would not be satisfied until it had consumed everything in its path.

Darwina chittered wildly.

Rachel flew into the kitchen.

And collided with a solid dark shadow.

"Harry?"

"Change of plans," he said.

There was something wrong, she thought. She knew he was there. She could hear him and feel the heavy currents of his energy swirling in the kitchen. But she could not see him. The small space was swathed in shadows, but the fire was racing down the hall now, throwing off enough light to reveal a portion of the stove, the counter, and the refrigerator. *But she could not see Harry, who was right there in front of her.*

But that was not the worst part of the disorienting experience. It was the terrifying chill that rattled her nerves, the icy sensation coalescing rapidly into a blood-curdling terror. Mindless panic threatened to overwhelm her. This was what it felt like when the monsters came out from under the bed. This was what it felt like when you were cornered by the creature from the depths of the Obsidian Lagoon. This was the sensation that over-whelmed you when you woke up inside the coffin, the sensation that destroyed sanity, the sensation that made you welcome death. . . .

"Rachel," Harry said. "Trust me."

It was an order.

This was no monster. This was Harry.

She pulled herself together with an act of will and focused a little talent through her bracelet. Harry's fierce silver-and-midnight aura blazed reassuringly in the dark-ness. Her heart was still pounding, but the panic receded quickly. She took a deep breath.

"Okay," she said. "I'm okay."

His fingers clamped around her wrist and suddenly she could make him out more clearly.

"What did you do?" she whispered, stunned. "You were invisible except for your aura. And the cold sensa-tion—"

"I'm still invisible and so are you as long as we stay in physical contact. The bastards outside will be watching both doors but they won't be able to see us. Do exactly what I tell you."

"Right." She wanted to ask him who *they* were and how he even knew that there was more than one person waiting out there in the night, but it didn't seem like a good time.

He opened the kitchen door. Rain and wind blasted into the space. Rachel glanced back and saw that the fire was already devouring the living room. There was something not quite normal about the flames. In the next instant she understood. The colors that burned in the heart of the inferno were from the paranormal end of the spectrum. The fierce oranges and white-hot yellows were streaked with a palette of violent shades of ultralight—magenta, blue, and crimson.

Before she could do more than wonder about the odd nature of the flames, Harry was pulling her through the kitchen door and out onto the porch.

"Whatever you do, don't let go," he said.

"I won't," she vowed.

At that moment, Harry's steel-clad grip on her wrist and the feel of Darwina's small claws digging into her shoulder seemed like the only real things in a night that was spiraling out of control.

Chapter 9

THE FLAMES FROM THE BURNING CABIN LIT UP THE immediate vicinity in a hellish glare, the lightning and thunder adding to the nightmarish scene. Rachel could feel her own energy field sparking wildly. The wind lashed at her, clutching at her clothing and hair. The force of the driving rain soaked her to the skin within seconds. Darwina huddled close, no longer growling.

A figure dressed in a gray squall jacket, the hood pulled down low, stood watching the small house burn. Heedless of the pounding rain, he appeared entranced by the spectacle. He had an object clutched in both hands—a gun, Rachel realized. It was pointed at the kitchen door. She could not breathe. She and Harry had to be starkly silhouetted against the flames. But the figure in the slicker gave no indication that he saw them.

We really are invisible, Rachel thought. *This is sort of cool. Very high-rez, as the kids would say.*

"Vince, the kitchen door's open," the man in the squall shouted to his companion. "Looks like he's trying to come out on this side of the house."

The voice—shrill and edgy—told Rachel that he was a young male, maybe no more than eighteen or nineteen.

Vince charged around the corner of the house. "Whatever you do, don't let him get into the woods or we'll never find him."

Like his companion, Vince, too, was clearly flying on a wave of adrenaline and nerves but he sounded a little older and maybe a tad more under control.

Harry drew Rachel swiftly down the back steps. The roar of the fire was as loud as the thunder now.

The two men with the guns kept the weapons aimed at the open door. Harry kept the great cloak of his talent swirling around Rachel, Darwina, and himself, wrapping the three of them in deep shadows.

At the bottom of the steps, he pulled Rachel to one side, out of the direct line of fire. But the attention of the two young gunmen did not shift. They kept their weapons aimed at the kitchen door.

"Where is he?" Vince stopped a few feet away from Gray Jacket. "I don't see him."

"The door opened a few seconds ago but he never came out." Gray Jacket sounded suddenly uncertain. "Maybe the fire got him. Shit. What a way to go. Burned alive."

"Okay. All right." The taller youth used one hand to

wipe rain away from his face. He sounded unnerved but determined. "That was the plan, remember? It worked the way it was supposed to work."

"Shit," Gray Jacket said again. "We've got to get out of here before the fire department comes."

"Are you crazy? Nobody is going to report this fire tonight. No one lives close enough to see it. The fire won't spread beyond the house anyway, not in this rain."

"Freakin' weird, isn't it?" Gray Jacket stared at the blaze. "Never saw a fire burn like that."

"Yeah, real high-rez, huh?"

Rachel looked at the faces of the two gunmen as Harry drew her past them. The pair stood only a few yards away, oblivious to anything except the fire. In the glare of the flames it was plain to see that both appeared astonished by what they had done.

Gray Jacket jerked and spun around in a tight circle, as if searching for an enemy.

"Did you feel that?" he asked.

"What?" Vince turned quickly, searching the shadows. "What happened?"

"Forget it," Gray jacket said. "Come on, let's get out of here."

Harry came to an abrupt halt. Rachel, her attention on the firebombers, stumbled into him. Darwina scrambled to keep her balance.

"Don't move," he said. "You're very close to the psi-fence. With all the hot energy bouncing around tonight, you could accidently stumble into the Preserve. If that happens, it might take me hours to find you."

"I'm not going anywhere," she promised. "But what about you?"

"I'll be right back."

He released her and promptly vanished. The frightening cold sensation returned, but now that she knew what was causing it, she could suppress it. Darwina muttered darkly in her ear.

The gatekeeper's cabin was fully engulfed now. The roof had fallen in and the walls were crumbling. The stone fireplace was the only thing still standing. The fire beast was consuming its prey, flesh and bone.

Rachel reached up to touch Darwina, seeking comfort. "It's okay, I told you, he's a professional. This is what he does."

But she knew that it was herself she was trying to reassure. Harry was a powerful talent but he was going up against two mag-rez guns.

Chapter 10

HARRY KICKED UP HIS SENSES AND WENT SWIFTLY BACK across the clearing. His talent cloaked him in shadows at any distance because it enveloped him. But he knew from hard experience that others did not feel the shock waves of black ice that he projected when he went into the shadows until he was within a radius of about five to fifteen feet, depending on the sensitivity of the target.

Gray Jacket reacted first. A visible spasm of alarm arced through him. He jerked like a puppet on a string and staggered around in a small circle, searching the darkness.

"There it is again," he shouted above the roar of the fire and thunder.

"What?" Vince shouted back.

"There's something out there. You heard the talk in town, all that stuff about monsters in that place they call the Preserve."

"Just stories for kids," Vince said. "Come on, we're finished here. I want to get out of this rain. Got a long walk ahead of us back to the buggy."

"I'm telling you, there's something out there." Terror shivered in Gray Jacket's voice. "Can't you feel it?"

"Stop talking like that. Are you going crazy on me?"

"The cold. Don't you feel it?"

"It's not cold tonight," Vince said. "You're losin' it, man. Come on, we need to leave now."

Harry was close enough to Vince to catch the frequencies that linked directly to his darkest dreams, the place where his nightmares originated.

Gray Jacket screamed, a high-pitched keening cry of fear. He stumbled backward, flailing wildly, whirled, and started to run blindly toward the fire.

That was the problem with hitting an individual's nightmare button, Harry thought. The results were unpredictable. Some people simply fainted. Others, like Gray Jacket, lost all touch with reality and did something stupid like run into a burning building.

Harry went after him. The kid ran like a demon was on his heels but he couldn't outrun the surge of dark energy that Harry slammed into him. This time the icy tide overwhelmed him. The kid fell to his knees and then sprawled, unconscious, in the wet grass.

Vince lurched toward his comrade and then stopped a short distance away.

"What's wrong, man? Get up. We gotta get out of here."

"Your turn," Harry said quietly.

Vince screamed and tried to flee the unseen wave of

darkness that swept over him. He got two shaky steps before he fell to his knees.

Harry dissolved the cloak of shadows he had used to conceal himself. Vince stared up at him in stupefied horror.

"No, you're dead. *You're dead*. You just burned up in that house."

Evidently watching his intended victim materialize out of the night was the last straw. Vince's eyes rolled back in his head. He crumpled, unconscious, to the ground.

Nothing like having a talent for becoming someone else's worst nightmare, Harry thought. Hell of a career path. But that was nothing compared to what it did to a guy's love life.

He sensed the first stirring of the fever when he leaned down to collect the guns. The rush of unnatural awareness and the rising heat in his aura caught him unaware, blindsiding him. It shouldn't be happening. He hadn't used that much energy to take down the two firebombers.

The flames, he thought. There had been some kind of paranormal energy in the damn fire. It had stirred up his talent, making it harder to control. He had used more energy than was necessary and now he was going to pay the price.

It promised to be a very bad night.

"Just what I needed."

He focused on the two things he had to do before the psi-fever took him.

Chapter 11

"WHAT DO YOU MEAN, YOU'RE GOING TO LEAVE ME HERE and come back for me in the morning?" Rachel demanded. "Are you crazy?"

They were standing in the clearing at the back of what was left of the house. The fierce fire was rapidly burning itself out. The rain was still coming down in heavy sheets, drowning what was left of the blaze. Harry was grim-faced and his eyes were psi-hot.

He had secured the two gunmen, hand and foot, and stashed them in the old woodshed. The small window-less outbuilding at the edge of the clearing had not been touched by the fire.

"It's better this way," he said. "Trust me."

"I am not going to spend the rest of the night alone in your car," she said.

"I don't have time to explain, Rachel. Hell, I don't

even know how to explain. All I can tell you is that what's happening to me is a side effect of my talent. It will wear off in a few hours. Now get into the damn car and stop arguing. I don't have much time left."

"You're experiencing some major after-burn, that's all. It happens sometimes when a dark-end talent goes too far out on the spectrum. This can't be the first time you've been through this."

"No, but it shouldn't have happened this time. The fact that it's kicking in so hard makes me think it's going to be worse than usual. You do not want to be anywhere in the vicinity when the burn peaks, believe me."

"If you think I'm going to let you wander around in the woods in this condition and in this weather, with the Preserve only a few yards away, you really are out of your mind. We will both spend the night in the SUV."

"No." There was a flat finality in his voice. "I need to find a place to wait out the fever. You'll be safe inside the car. I won't be far away. I'll keep an eye on you."

Rachel jacked up her senses and took another look at the heat in his aura. The silver lightning and the shadows were hot and getting hotter, but there was no instability.

"What are you so worried about?" she asked. "Psi-fever isn't contagious."

"My kind of post-burn fever is different. I'm not worried that you'll catch anything from me. That's not the problem."

"The problem is that we're standing out here in the rain, arguing. We can finish this conversation inside the SUV."

"There's nothing to discuss."

"Oh, yes, there is." She raised one arm and aimed a finger at the SUV. "You're going to get into the damn car."

"No."

"Yes. Harry, listen to me. I can deal with your fever. Balancing auras is what I do, remember?"

"My aura is different," he growled. "That's why my fever is different."

"Powerful, yes, and there are some unusual currents coming from the far end of the spectrum, but nothing I can't handle."

"How?"

"I'd really rather do this somewhere out of the rain, but since you're going to be stubborn—"

She heightened her talent so that she could view the whole spectrum of his aura. The currents were hot and blazing, but she was quite certain she could deal with the over-rezzed frequencies.

Bracing herself for the jolt she knew was coming, she pushed a little energy through her charms, reached out, and took Harry's hand. He flinched, as if the shock of physical contact had jarred him more than it did her. She didn't know what he was experiencing but she found herself warding off waves of glacial-cold energy. For a few heartbeats she was completely disoriented. The horrible, mindless panic she had experienced earlier threatened to return, but she steadied her senses quickly and went to work.

She was vaguely aware of Darwina chortling a cheerful farewell. The dust bunny bounded down to the ground with Amberella and disappeared into the trees.

Rachel pulled hard on her talent and her Academy training and pulsed the necessary counterpoint waves into the flood tide of Harry's graveyard-cold energy. The charms on her bracelet brightened like molten silver. The crystals glowed, creating a sparkling rainbow of ultralight.

The flood tide of coffin ice receded quickly and resumed its normal pattern.

Harry's fingers tightened convulsively around hers. He stared at her with eyes that were still a little hot.

"What the hell did you just do to me?" he asked. His voice was rough and a little hoarse.

"What I was trained to do," she said. "I rebalanced your aura. You should start feeling more in control now."

He looked down at their clasped fingers, uncomprehending.

"Yes," he said.

"Now can we get into the car?"

He took a deep breath and scrubbed rain off his face. "Will the effects last?"

"Yes." She hesitated. "All I did was push a psychic reset button to return your frequencies to normal. You would have gotten there on your own in time but I speeded up the cooling process. Does this kind of thing happen to you a lot?"

"No, not unless I go a lot deeper into the zone and stay there for a while."

"As you said, it was probably the result of all the wild energy blowing around out here tonight. We can discuss the para-biophysics of recent events if you like but I'd rather not do that while we're standing out here in the rain waiting to get struck by lightning."

"Lightning. Good point." Harry wrapped one hand around her wrist and started toward the SUV. "Can't risk trying to drive you home until this storm is over. There will be trees and branches down everywhere. We'll wait it out in the car."

They went quickly through the downpour toward the big vehicle parked in the drive. Harry opened the front passenger door. Clutching her jacket in one hand, Rachel grasped one of the handholds and started to hop up into the cab. She paused, one foot inside the SUV, the other dangling in midair, looked toward the dark woods.

"Darwina," she called.

"She'll be all right," Harry said.

Rachel hesitated until Harry gave her an assist that was more of a gentle shove. Whatever the intent behind the push, it propelled her up into the front seat with enough force to make her bounce a little.

Harry closed the door. Rachel watched through the windshield as he loped around the front of the vehicle. He was right, she thought. Darwina could take care of herself.

Harry opened the driver's side door and got in behind the wheel.

"Where will she go on a night like this?" Rachel asked.

"Last I saw of her, she was headed for the Preserve fence."

Rachel thought about that. "I guess she concluded that her work here was done."

"Looks like it. You were in danger. Now you're safe."

"But how did she know that I was in danger tonight?"

"Beats me." Harry shrugged out of the wet storm coat, wadded it up, and tossed it over the backseat into the cargo bay. "Like I said, the psychic bond between the two of you must be damned strong."

"Yes, but it's not magic. Somehow she sensed that I was in trouble before I realized—" She broke off, smiling a little. "No. She sensed that there was danger nearby at exactly the same time I did. The difference is that she took my inner alarm bell seriously. I didn't. You'd think a good psychic would know better."

"What are you talking about?"

"I remember looking out the window several times when the lightning flashed. On one occasion I saw what I thought were the kind of afterimages that you get when a bright light goes off in front of your eyes. At least, I told myself they were afterimages, but my intuition kicked up. I should have paid more attention. I realize now that a couple of those flashing images were actually glimpses of the firebombers in the trees."

"You think Darwina picked up on your intuitive vibe?"

"That's the only thing that makes sense in terms of para-physics. A flash of intuition jacks up a lot of hot energy, at least for a short period of time. That energy goes out into a person's aura. Darwina is obviously sensitive to my aura, even over some distance."

"Huh."

He unfastened his shirt, stripped it off, and used the garment to dry his hair and face. Rachel was intensely aware of the fact that he was now nude to his waist. The fading firelight revealed the powerful contours of his shoulders.

They sat quietly for a time, studying the smoldering remains of the cabin through the rain-washed windshield. Rachel knew they were both decompressing, but Harry needed to come down a lot further than she did. The bio-cocktail that had been kicked up by adrenaline and the use of his high-rez talent combined with the strange energy of the fire had unleashed a lot of very hot psi. She had extinguished the after-burn, but that still left a lot of heat brewing. Nature and time would take care of it.

"What was that about?" Rachel said after a while.

"I think it's obvious." Harry leaned his head against the back of the seat. "Someone does not want me investigating whatever is going on in the Preserve."

"That fire—"

"Was partially paranormal in nature," Harry concluded. "I know."

"I would not have thought that sort of technology would be widely available."

"It's not. It's cutting-edge para-technology. The more important question is who would send a couple of kids out on a night like this with that kind of exotic explosive device?"

"One thing's for sure, those two young men are not locals," she said. "I didn't recognize either of them."

"Doesn't mean they aren't working with someone here on the island."

"You do not give up on a theory easily, do you?"

"Not until a better one comes along," Harry said.

"Well, one way or another, it appears that I'm now in the market for another bicycle," she said.

"The Foundation will buy you a new bike. Hell, it will buy you a new car."

"A bike is fine. Good exercise."

"You need a car for rainy days and other bad weather."

"I can always get a lift or borrow a Vibe when I need something larger."

"I'll see to it that you get a car," Harry said grimly.

"I can't take a car from you."

"Why not?"

"It's too much of a gift." She waved one hand. The charms jangled in a discordant fashion. "It will upset the balance."

"We're talking about a business expense for the Foundation; it's not a matter of harmonic balance."

"I can't believe that after we both nearly got barbequed in a paranormal fire we are sitting here in our wet clothes arguing about whether your stupid Foundation will buy me a bike or a car."

Harry turned his head to look at her. "Stupid Foundation?"

"Sorry." She took a steadying breath. "I got carried away. Of course your Foundation isn't stupid. How can a Foundation be stupid? It's the people who run it who are— Oh, never mind."

"You're right. We should not be arguing about the car."

"No, we should not."

There was a short silence.

"Thanks," Harry said after a while. He did not take his eyes off the smoldering ruins. "For the aura fix, I mean."

"You're welcome." She pushed her wet hair back behind her ears. The outside temperature was still balmy, in spite of the storm, but she was getting chilled sitting in her damp clothes. "I don't suppose you have anything I could use to dry off?"

Harry shook off his preoccupied air and switched on the interior lights. "I can't believe you took the time to grab your jacket."

"I went right past the coatrack on my way to the kitchen." She paused. "The jacket cost a lot of money. I'm still paying off the credit card."

For a moment she thought he was going to lecture her on the proper priorities to keep in mind when fleeing from a raging inferno. But in the end he evidently thought better of it.

"I keep some emergency supplies in the back. I'll get them." He started to open the door to go around to the back of the vehicle.

"No need for you to get drenched again," she said quickly. "I'm smaller than you, I can crawl back to the cargo bay."

She scrambled into the rear seat and then into the cargo area. She smiled a little at the sight of the neatly stowed emergency kit.

"You guys in the security business are prepared for anything," she said.

"Goes with the job. There should be a couple of blankets back there."

"Found 'em."

"You're soaked. Take off those wet clothes and wrap yourself up in one of the blankets."

She stilled. The thought of undressing in such close quarters was more than a little unsettling. But the notion of spending what remained of the night in her wet clothes was not particularly appealing, either.

"What about you?" she asked.

"I'm okay. Boots are wet and so are the bottom edges of my pants but the rest of me is mostly dry."

He leaned down and went to work removing his boots.

Rachel held one of the blankets to her throat. "Would you mind turning out the light?"

"Huh?" Harry glanced back at her, frowning. Then understanding struck. "Oh, yeah, sure. Sorry."

He hit the switch, plunging the interior of the SUV into deep night. Outside, the fire continued to smolder, but it no longer gave off enough light to illuminate the inside of the vehicle. Satisfied that she was not going to be doing a silhouette striptease, she peeled off her wet clothes. There was a fair amount of fumbling around involved. It wasn't easy tugging off the wet jeans while simultaneously trying to hold the blanket around herself. By the time she managed to get out of the denim she was breathing heavily and the windows were fogged up.

When she got to her underwear, she stopped, intensely conscious of the heavy silence from the front seat. She finally concluded that since the panties amounted to nothing more than a gossamer scrap of synthetic lace she might as well keep them on. They would dry faster from the heat of her body. The bra, however, had to come off. It was sticky and uncomfortable.

She draped the jacket carefully over one rear seat and then arranged the bra, shirt, and jeans alongside it. Clutching the blanket around her, she made her way forward into the other rear seat. She settled in, knees pulled up to her chin beneath the blanket.

Harry stirred in the front seat. She could see the outline of his head and shoulders when he turned to look at her.

"Are you going to stay back there?" he asked, his voice very neutral.

"More room for both of us this way," she said quickly.

"Right."

The rain thundered on the roof of the big vehicle. Another bolt of lightning lit up the atmosphere.

After a time Harry spoke again.

"There are some experts who claim that people with my kind of talent are the original source of a lot of the old horror stories," he said.

"Your talent is so rare that no one has ever been able to study it. If you can't study something, you can't explain it. The unexplained is frequently the source of myths and legends."

"More HE philosophy?"

"Yes."

"I scared the daylights out of you, didn't I?"

"Only for a couple of seconds. Don't take it personally. After all, you didn't give me any advance warning."

"Would that have made a difference?"

"Sure." She smiled. "You got away with the scare factor once but you won't be able to pull off that stunt again."

"Why not?"

"Because I know your frequencies now. Try it and I'll dampen your energy field until it feels like a wet blanket."

Harry gave an unexpected bark of laughter. "Can you really do that?"

"Yep, provided I can get physical contact. My ability is one of the reasons the matchmakers—both the agency that handles members of the HE community and the one I registered with in Frequency City—labeled me unmatchable."

"You, too?"

"Turns out no one wants to sleep with a wife who can suppress a man's aura if she gets seriously ticked off. You may be the source of the monster-under-the-bed myth, but women with my kind of talent are the source of the legends of the black widow—the bride who murders husbands in a serial fashion in order to inherit their fortunes."

"Some guys don't like a challenge."

For a heartbeat she didn't think she had heard correctly. Then she started to giggle. The giggle turned into laughter. *Over-the-top laughter,* she realized. Very unharmonic. But she couldn't seem to stop. There were tears in her eyes before she regained her control.

"Guess not," she finally managed. She used the corner of the blanket to blot her eyes.

"So, why aren't you afraid of me?" Harry asked.

"I told you, you've got a powerful talent but you're not a monster."

"When you look at me now, what do you see?"

"I see you," she said. She frowned. "Or at least I would see you if there were more light. What kind of question is that?"

"People who have been exposed to my talent never look at me the same way again. They see the monster."

"What do you care if the bad guys find you very scary? You're in the security business. I would think being considered scary by criminals would be an asset."

There was another tense silence from the front seat.

"It's not just the bad guys who think I'm scary," Harry said eventually. "Other people who get too close to me when I'm in the zone find me terrifying."

The hard, flat edge in his voice told her that he was thinking of one other person in particular.

She was not at all sure she wanted to pursue the conversation down this particular road but she could not stop herself.

"Girlfriend?" she ventured.

"Wife."

She cleared her throat. "I believe I did hear something about a divorce."

"Figured you had. Slade would have done a background check."

Rachel wasn't sure where to go next. "Must have been expensive."

"You have no idea."

She knew that he was not referring to the financial

aspects of the divorce. Harry had paid a high price in other ways as well.

She abandoned the attempt to be subtle. "Why did she marry you in the first place if she thought you were a scary guy?"

"She was an aura talent. She thought she could handle it."

"She was probably not as strong as me."

"No. What happened was my fault. I had allowed her to experience some of my talent while we were dating but I never went all the way into the zone before the marriage."

"So she never knew the real you?"

"Something like that," Harry said. "In any event, I do some regular psychic exercises to make sure that I'm always in control of my senses. At home I have a special room paneled in glass. I lock the door when I work out to make sure that no one walks in on me unexpectedly."

"But something went wrong?"

"Laura got the code for the door," Harry said. "I had warned her never to interrupt me during a session. I told her that I wanted to protect her from the full force of my talent when I was running hot. She respected that line before the wedding but afterward—"

"Eventually she had to know your secret."

"I think that's what it came down to, yes."

"Any woman would want to know the truth," Rachel explained gently.

"The truth was that the man she thought she loved was suddenly her worst nightmare. I was running hot— very, very hot—that day."

"She got hit with the full blast of your talent."

"I shut down as fast as I could, but Laura started screaming and then she was running away from me. I went after her, tried to calm her down, but she kept on screaming."

"When it was all over, you knew the marriage was doomed."

"A few years ago we would have been trapped. There would have been no option but to live separate lives. But we were able to take advantage of the new legislation that allows for grounds of intolerable psychical incompatibility."

"But that meant that you had to declare yourself psychically deranged and dangerous," she said.

"Figured it was the least I could do for Laura. And it's not like it wasn't the truth."

"It isn't the truth. You're not deranged."

"I hear a but," Harry said.

"Okay, you may be dangerous. But only to the bad guys, not to everyone else."

"You may be the exception," he said dryly.

"You tried to protect Laura. When that didn't work, you behaved like a true gentleman. You took the hit."

"Like I said, it was my fault."

There was a short silence.

"Big wedding, I'll bet," Rachel said after a while. "Covenant weddings are always very big affairs, especially for a wealthy family like yours."

"It was big enough."

"Must have been a lot of very expensive gifts to return."

There was another short silence from the front seat. And then it was Harry who was roaring with laughter. It was a deep, hearty, healing laughter, she thought. She raised her talent a little. Her charms clashed musically as she observed Harry's aura. The powerful energy looked strong and well balanced. She smiled and lowered her senses.

When Harry's laughter had subsided, he looked back at her.

"It's been a tough night," he said. "You've got to be exhausted. Why don't you get some sleep?"

"Are you kidding?" She gave a tiny sniff. "After what happened? I won't be able to sleep a wink."

"You might as well try. Not like there's anything better to do."

There was something better to do, she thought. She wanted to go on talking to him. It was so easy being with him here in the darkness. The danger they had been through together had created a bond, at least from her end. She was quite sure she could go on chatting with him until dawn.

But she was getting the distinct impression that he wanted to shut down for a while, go into his own head to do some serious thinking. She had to respect that. Besides, the sense of intimacy generated by the brush with death and reinforced by the close confines of the SUV was potentially misleading. This kind of situation could make a woman say and do things she might seriously regret come dawn. When you got right down to it, Harry Sebastian was still very much a stranger.

"Okay," she said, "I'll try to sleep."

She turned on her side in the seat, tucked her legs under her, and pulled the blanket more securely around herself. She couldn't be certain, but it seemed to her that the rain wasn't falling quite as hard now. The thunder was fainter and the lightning strikes were not as powerful. The storm was starting to dissipate. She hoped Darwina was somewhere safe and warm and dry.

THE HUMAN MONSTER WAS WAITING DEEP IN THE SHAD-
ows, his ice-blue eyes glittering with anticipation and lust. The rainstone in his ear stud glowed darkly.

"You are mine," he whispered.

"No," she said.

He came toward her. "My bride. My destiny."

She whirled and ran through the sea. Sensing prey, the creatures swarmed around her. Their tentacles writhed in their desperation to get to her.

She saw the frozen waterfall of energy that sealed both ends of the crystal chamber, and somehow she knew it was her only hope. The human monster could not follow her through the solid cascade of stone.

"Why do you run from me?" the human monster said. "You were meant for me."

"No." She tried to scream the word but she could barely manage a whisper.

She forced herself to keep moving through the strangely illuminated sea. She had to get through the frozen waterfall. . . .

"Rachel, wake up. You're dreaming."

She recognized the voice. Harry was calling her out of the glowing sea. She struggled up through the depths, riding a wave of shivering panic. For a couple of heartbeats the real world and the dreamscape merged. She sensed the human monster closing in on her but now she could see Harry in the shadows. He was in danger.

"Run," she gasped. She was breathing as hard as if she had been fleeing for her life. Her pulse pounded. "He's here. *Run.*"

"It's all right," Harry said. His arms closed around her, crushing her against his chest. "I've got you. He can't touch you."

Harry's heat and energy enveloped her. She was safe. She opened her eyes, trying to catch her breath. It was still dark, but the storm had dissipated into a gentle, steady rain.

"Sorry," she whispered, mortified. A woman who had grown up in the Harmonic Enlightenment community and trained at the Academy was supposed to have better control of her dreamscapes.

"It's okay." Harry held her close. "It's okay."

For a moment or two she allowed herself the luxury of being cradled against his chest, her head resting on his shoulder. Gradually the remnants of the dreamscape faded and the real world closed around her. She listened to the light drumming of the rain on the roof of the SUV.

After a while she forced herself to stir in Harry's grasp even though she would have preferred to remain right where she was for whatever was left of the night.

"Well, that was embarrassing," she said.

"You're embarrassed by a bad dream?" Harry asked.

"Of course. I've studied dream theory, lucid dreaming, and focused dreaming techniques since I was a kid. I control my dreams; they don't control me."

"Sounds like a slogan or a bumper sticker."

"It is for a member of the Community. When I was five, my mother embroidered those words on a pillow for me. I've also got them engraved on the inside of my bracelet."

Automatically she raised her hand to show him the band of silvery metal that she wore around one wrist. The charms tinkled lightly, but the action caused the edge of the blanket to fall away. Belatedly she remembered that the blanket was all she was wearing unless you counted the panties, which, she concluded, were hardly worth mentioning. At least the darkness inside the vehicle offered a semblance of modesty. Then she remembered Harry's excellent night vision.

"Oh, geez." Hastily she grabbed the edge of the blanket and clutched it to her throat. "This is getting more and more awkward by the second."

"Take it easy." He released her, allowing her to sit up. "I'm not going to assault your virtue."

"I know." Now she had offended him. Chagrined, she tried to wriggle off his thighs and into the other seat. In the process her hand came in contact with his bare shoulder. She froze, fascinated by the compelling heat and the sleek, masculine power of muscle beneath skin. "You're all wet."

"I couldn't squeeze over the front seat to get to you. It was easier to get out on my side and climb in beside you. That meant a couple of seconds in the rain. I'll live."

"Yes, I know." She did not take her hand off his shoulder. She was keenly aware of his scent, an exciting blend of the rain, the wild woods, and the essence of all that was male and Harry. She was enthralled. "But, still, it's my fault. I'm sorry you had to get out in the rain again because of me."

In the shadows his eyes heated a little. Mostly with irritation she thought. But there was something else, there, as well, a hard, edgy flicker of arousal. It did not take a psychic's intuition to recognize sexual desire in a man. She was suddenly very conscious of the hard muscles of his thighs beneath her hips.

"You can stop apologizing anytime," Harry said.

"Okay. Right. No more apologies."

She should move. Now. But she did not want to move. Her hand was still on Harry's rain-dampened shoulder. She tightened her fingers ever so gently and opened her senses to savor the full spectrum of sensation.

Energy danced and shivered in the atmosphere. *Her own,* she thought. *And his, too.* She was well aware that her sexual experience was quite limited by the standards of most people her age. Nevertheless, her intuition assured her that whatever was happening tonight was not the norm. True, physical contact between two people of talent sometimes had unpredictable effects on the auras of both parties, but this flashing, sparkling excitement effervescing through her senses was unlike anything she had ever known. She did not need to see the paranormal heat in Harry's eyes to know that he was aroused. She could feel it the old-fashioned way—through the fabric of the blanket and Harry's jeans. His erection was pressing against her bottom.

"It would probably be a really good idea to get off my lap," he said. He sounded as if he was speaking through tightly clamped teeth.

She raised her hand from his shoulder and touched the side of his hard jaw. "You saved my life tonight."

"You doused my after-burn fever. That makes us even."

"No." She thrust her fingers through his hair. "It doesn't."

"Damn it, Rachel—"

"Would you mind very much if I kissed you?"

For the first time he seemed to be caught off-guard.

"A gratitude kiss?" he asked, sounding wary. "Because you think I saved your life?"

"No."

"Because I woke you out of that nightmare?"

"No. I just want to kiss you."

He stilled. "Why am I getting the feeling that you're trying to run some kind of experiment?"

"I suppose you could call it that. Do you mind? Don't worry. I'll make it quick and painless. It will be like it never happened."

He breathed in deeply. The heat in his eyes went up a

notch, but she sensed that he was pulling hard on the fierce control that he used to handle his talent. She wondered briefly why he needed that kind of mag-steel power to deal with a simple kiss. *Probably the result of the fever-burn earlier,* she decided.

Clutching his shoulder, she raised herself up a little and touched her mouth tentatively against his. It was meant to be a light, fleeting kiss; a butterfly kiss. But without any warning the intimate energy smoldering in the atmosphere flashed across the spectrum, igniting her senses. She was suddenly intoxicated with the dazzling excitement that swept through her.

"Harry?" she whispered against his mouth.

He did not answer—not with words, at any rate. She felt a shudder go through him, heard the groan deep in his throat, and then his arms clamped around her, crushing her against his chest.

Chapter 12

HE COULD NOT REMEMBER THE LAST TIME HE HAD MADE out in the backseat of a car. Not since his teens, he thought. Things were definitely different this time.

The fierceness of his arousal should have been all the warning he needed to know that the situation was getting out of control. But at that moment he just did not give a damn about maintaining control. He no longer cared if she was running some weird aura experiment.

The hot currents of passion burned in the close confines of the backseat of the SUV. In its own way the energy flaring in the atmosphere was hotter than the paranormal fire that had consumed the gatekeeper's cabin. He could not remember ever wanting or needing a woman as much as he wanted and needed Rachel tonight.

He cradled the back of her head in one hand and deepened the kiss until her mouth opened beneath his.

He heard a soft little moan and then she released her grip on the edge of the blanket and wrapped her arm around his neck. He could feel her soft breasts pressed against him. Her scent was an exotic drug, intoxicating all of his senses. Her feminine energy, teasing and tantalizing, flowed around him.

She knew him for what he was and she did not fear him.

He moved his free hand down to the sweet curve of her shoulder.

"You're so delicate," he said against her mouth. "And warm. And soft."

She flattened her palm on his chest and spread her fingers. "You're so hard. And so very, very hot."

Dread sliced through him. "The psi-fever?"

"Not that kind of hot." She laughed lightly. "The good kind of hot."

The touch of her hand on his bare skin was incredibly exciting. It took everything he had to keep from coming then and there.

"Harry," she said in an aching whisper. "I think something weird is happening here. Something about our auras."

"Define weird."

"Amazing."

"Amazing works for me."

He didn't try to say anything else because he was pretty sure he was hovering on the brink of incoherence. Besides, he had better things to do with his tongue than talk.

He pulled free of her mouth and kissed the warm, fragrant place just behind her ear. She twisted in his arms, curling into him. He slid his hand down to her breast and covered the tight bud of her nipple with his palm. She tensed and her nails sank into his chest but she did not pull away. Instead, she shivered and started to sip air in quick, shallow breaths.

He shifted his hand down her side, savoring the feel of her sleek, smooth, resilient skin and the delicate bones beneath the surface. The curve of her hip was lush and firm and elegantly rounded.

When he moved his hand between her thighs, she tensed, murmured something he could not quite catch, and then parted her legs. She kissed his chest. Her mouth was wet and warm.

When he explored further, he discovered that she was as hot as liquid amber. He eased aside the thin scrap of fabric that barred his path. The panties were damp and not from the rain. When he eased a finger inside her, he found her tight and full. She shivered again and clutched at him. He sucked in a ragged breath.

"If we're going to stop, this is the time to do it," he said.

"Okay," she gasped. "Okay."

She sounded distracted, as if her attention was focused on something far more important than the answer to his question. He realized that her fingers were on his belt buckle. He held his breath, everything in him taut and hard. The need for release was almost overwhelming.

"I need clarification here," he managed. "Was that okay, as in we should stop, or okay, as in let's keep going?"

"Okay, as in we should find out what this is all about." She rested her forehead against his shoulder. "I need clarification, too."

"Clarification." What the hell did that mean?

She tugged on his belt. "Absolutely."

He caught her face in his hands and raised her head. His senses were sparking wildly because of his aroused state. He did not have to focus his talent to see that her eyes were glowing like molten amber.

"Rachel," he said.

"Yes?" She was a little breathless, shivering in his arms.

"You're sure you won't regret this in the morning?"

"Positive." In the shadows her smile was a tantalizing mix of feminine invitation and challenge. "Are you always this hard to talk into bed?"

A sound that was half laugh and half groan rumbled at the back of his throat. He pulled her head down on his shoulder and held her there while he ripped off the panties. Then he finished the job that she had started on his belt buckle and went to work on his zipper. At last his straining erection was free.

He settled her so that she rode him astride, clamped his hands around her thighs, and urged her downward. He stopped when he discovered that she was clenched tightly against him.

"Relax," he whispered.

"I can't relax," she said. Her nails dug into his shoulders. "I feel like I'm about to come apart."

"So do I. We'll do it together."

He stroked her until she was hot and melting and shivering with need. Then he pushed slowly into her, gently forging a passage through the tense little muscles.

"Harry."

At last he was inside where he needed to be, and she closed snugly around him. She rose once, twice, three times, and then her release struck. He could not have resisted the compelling heat and energy even if he had wanted to do so—and that was the very last thing he wanted.

He thrust into her one last time and then his climax powered through him, taking him out of himself. Energy flashed in the heated atmosphere. And suddenly the wavelengths of his aura were no longer clashing and challenging Rachel's—just the opposite. He could have sworn that their currents were resonating in a harmonious pattern that increased the power of both energy fields.

The breathtaking intimacy of the experience was beyond anything he had ever known. He longed to hold on to the sensation forever. Somewhere in the darkness he heard the sweet, seductive music created by the gently clashing charms on Rachel's bracelet.

Chapter 13

A LOUD THUMP ON THE HOOD OF THE SUV AND A MUFFLED chortle woke Rachel. She opened her eyes to the gray light of dawn. The rain had stopped and she could no longer hear any wind.

She lay quietly for a few seconds, orienting herself. She was a little stiff and cramped and she was wrapped in the blanket. She realized she was looking at the roof of the cargo bay.

Another muffled chortle sounded from the front of the vehicle. She sat up cautiously, wincing a little when she felt the slightly bruised sensation between her legs.

She looked out the window and saw Darwina, Amberella in one paw, bouncing up and down on the hood. There was no sign of Harry. Beyond the charred remains of the cabin she could see the woodshed. The door was open.

The hot memories flooded back. After the heated

lovemaking—no, after the hot sex, she mentally corrected herself—Harry had lowered the rear seats to make room for both of them to stretch out for the rest of the night. She had a vague recollection of him pulling her into the curve of his body and locking her there with one strong arm. After that, she had slid into a deep, dreamless sleep.

She found her clothes draped over the front passenger seat where Harry had moved them. Getting dressed proved to be a serious struggle. Her panties and bra were dry but the pullover top and jeans were still damp. So were her socks and the new boots. Her lovely leather jacket would never be the same, but she told herself that the coolest leather jackets always looked somewhat battle-scarred. Her hair was a disaster.

All in all, she could not wait to get home and into a hot shower.

She took two energy bars from the emergency kit, opened a door, and got out. Although the storm had cleared, the atmosphere still shivered with the currents of psi leaking out of the Preserve. The smell of charred wood drifted on the air. The temperature was warming up rapidly, but in her damp clothes she felt chilled.

She unwrapped one of the bars as she walked toward the front of the SUV. Darwina cackled cheerfully, waved Amberella, and vaulted onto her shoulder. Rachel gave her the other energy bar.

"And where did you spend the night, missy?" Rachel asked.

Darwina, munching enthusiastically on the energy bar, ignored the question.

Rachel took a bite out of her own bar and started around the blackened ruins, heading toward the woodshed.

The two firebombers stumbled out into the clearing, their hands secured behind them. In the dreary light of the cloudy dawn they looked as young as they had sounded last night. She doubted that they were even out of their teens. When she raised her talent a little, she could see that they were dazed and scared. *A couple of kids who were in way over their heads,* she thought. She could have dredged up some sympathy for them if they hadn't torched the cabin and tried to kill Harry and her.

Harry emerged from the darkness of the shed. He did not look like a man who had survived a raging inferno, taken down a couple of young thugs, engaged in torrid sex, and then spent the rest of the night sleeping in the cramped confines of an SUV. On second thought, maybe he looked *exactly* like that kind of man—one who did that sort of stuff on a routine basis and took it all in stride. Whatever the case, he definitely looked good in the early light.

He was back in black. Her jeans might be damp and uncomfortable but evidently *his* clothes had dried just fine. She might be moving somewhat stiffly this morning, but he glided across the clearing with a virile, masculine grace. Her hair was straggling around her face, but it was obvious that he had raked his fingers through his own dark hair, pushing it back behind his ears where it had obediently stayed.

Awareness fluttered through her, and more memories of the night heated her senses. *My lover,* she thought. *At least for one night.*

Harry glanced at her. There was no psi-heat in his
eyes this morning, just the familiar everything's-under-
control-here look.

"Good timing," he said. "I was about to wake you.
We're going to put this pair in the back of the SUV and
drive them into town, assuming the road is passable after
that storm. Officer Willis can lock them up. I want to talk
to each of them separately."

"Sounds like a plan," Rachel said. "Want me to call
Kirk Willis and give him a heads-up?"

"I just tried to do that," Harry said. "No luck. The
phones are out."

"Not surprising after that storm."

Darwina stopped munching the energy bar long
enough to growl at the two young toughs.

"It's okay," Rachel said. She gave Darwina a small,
reassuring pat. "Thanks to you, they won't be torching
any more houses for a while." She looked at Harry. "What
will you do if these two start yelling for a lawyer?"

The one named Vince brightened. "Yeah, I have a
right to a lawyer."

Harry looked at Rachel. "Are there any lawyers on
Rainshadow?"

"Good question," she said. "If they're here, they are
keeping a very low profile."

Harry nodded once, satisfied. "In that case, we won't
worry about that problem."

"You can't put us in jail," the other kid said. But he
sounded uncertain.

"Watch me," Harry said. He gave Rachel a brief, assessing glance. "I don't suppose there's any chance you can handle a mag-rez?"

"Are you kidding?" she said. "I'm HE, remember? We don't do things that involve weapons. Guns are associated with violence, and violence creates all sorts of disharmony in the aura. Very Unenlightened. Takes hours of meditation to get the currents resonating properly again."

"In that case I'll keep an eye on these two while you drive us all back into town."

"Sure," Rachel said. "I can do that."

She stopped and watched Harry march the firebombers past her toward the SUV. It was the first time she had gotten a close-up look at them. Each man had a tattoo on the back of his hand. The image was that of a griffin.

"Harry," Rachel said. She spoke very quietly.

He registered the urgency in her voice immediately.

"What?" he asked.

"I don't think that what happened last night had anything to do with your investigation here on Rainshadow."

"What are you talking about?"

"I'm the reason this pair torched your house last night," she said. "You almost got killed because of me."

Chapter 14

"YOU NEVER TOLD ME THAT SOME PSYCHO CRIMINAL PSI-path was obsessed with you," Harry said. It took more effort than he would ever have imagined just to keep his voice locked down a notch or two below a roar. "And what were you doing working with a bunch of criminal psi-paths, anyway? Were you out of your not-so-enlightened mind?"

"We were supposed to call them patients, and as a matter of fact it seemed like a golden career opportunity at the time," Rachel said. "I thought it would give me a chance to prove that my Academy training had some real-world value—that it wasn't all Harmonic Enlightenment woo-woo stuff. And as for Lancaster, I did tell you that he was the reason I got fired."

"You said you were let go because you disagreed with the staff's diagnosis but you never told me that you were alone with Lancaster in a therapy room. You never mentioned that he was dangerously obsessed with you."

"I didn't see the point. He's in a locked ward at the Chapman Clinic and he'll be there for another few months. Dr. Oakford doesn't think that Lancaster is a psipath but he is convinced that Lancaster is suffering from a severe breakdown of the para-senses."

"When were you planning to tell me about Lancaster?" he said.

"Harry, calm down. In my own defense, I would like to point out that until this morning I didn't realize that Lancaster was still obsessed with me. He hasn't made any effort to communicate with me. Stalkers always want their victims to know they're being stalked. And there's something else."

"What?"

"You and I have only known each other for about three days. A girl doesn't usually mention that she might have a stalker until at least the third date."

"Do not try to make a joke about this," he warned. "I am not in the mood."

"Right. I can see that."

They were in her kitchen. She was at the counter, a row of glass jars, lids open, lined up in front of her. She was using small tongs to select an assortment of dried leaves, flowers, and herbs from the jars. Each judiciously chosen specimen was carefully placed in the white tisane bag. An empty pot and a small round cup stood ready.

The power was out, so Rachel had set the kettle to heat on the small wood stove.

He could tell that the jars Rachel used to store the tea and tisane ingredients here in her kitchen were not standard-issue canning jars. Each was elegantly shaped and delicately etched with botanical designs. The lids were set with amber stones. The tongs were fashioned of some intricately engraved silver metal. The pot and the cup were obviously handmade.

Rachel had explained that she was going to brew another cup of the exorbitantly priced restorative tisane that she had concocted for him yesterday in her shop. When he had declared he wasn't going to pay ten bucks for another cup of tea, she had said there would be no charge. It wasn't like he could stop her, he thought. They were in her kitchen, after all. But he sure as hell didn't have to drink the stuff.

As far as he was concerned, his energy field had been just fine until she had started talking about Marcus Lancaster. Nothing like a night of World Class Extreme High-Rez Sex to restore a man's aura, he thought. It was the news that Rachel had been doing one-on-one therapy sessions with dangerously disturbed crazies that had messed up his harmonic resonance.

He studied her as she went about the task of brewing the tea. In spite of the fact that a couple of thugs had tried to murder her last night, the energy around her was as bright and positive and resilient as ever. How did she do it? he wondered. He was ready to kill a few folks at the Chapman Clinic, starting with Lancaster and Dr. Ian Oakford, but Rachel was serenely focused on making tea.

"After last night I've got nothing but respect for your

abilities," he said, "but you're not exactly a trained para-shrink. How did you end up working at the Chapman Clinic?"

"Dr. Oakford observed my readings at the tea shop where I was working. He has enough talent of his own to recognize that I really can read and diagnose auras. He thought having me on the staff would give him an edge in his research."

"What went wrong?"

"I told him that Lancaster's aura could not be balanced either by me or by the new drugs that were being used in the trial. I explained that Lancaster was missing a vital band of energy on the aura spectrum and that I could not fix what was never there in the first place."

"Oakford didn't believe you?"

"No." Rachel picked up the kettle and filled the pot with hot water. "He concluded that he had been wrong about the range of my talent."

"And he fired you."

She set the kettle aside. "Oakford did give me two weeks' severance pay. I think he did feel bad about the whole thing."

Harry stopped in front of the windows and looked out at the gray horizon. It felt like another storm was brewing. The sense of impending disaster that had been riding him ever since he had landed on the island was still building. His hunter's intuition flared.

"Tell me about Lancaster."

"He's a true psi-path, a genuine psychic vampire, in my opinion. He's smart and he's got a high-rez talent for manipulation. He made a fortune running scams and defrauding people. I strongly suspect that he arranged the murder of his wife in order to get his hands on her money but he made it look like an accident. I'm sure that her death will never be investigated."

"Yet, instead of lying low and spending his dead wife's fortune, he checks himself into the Chapman Clinic claiming he's had a breakdown due to the trauma of her death?"

"I knew that was an act, but no one would believe me," Rachel said.

"The question is why would he get himself locked up like that?"

"I don't like to sound egotistical but I've got a nasty suspicion that he did it because of me."

"All right, he's obsessed with you. But how did he learn about you? When did you meet him?"

"As far as I know, we never met until that day at the clinic. I would have remembered, believe me." Rachel went very still. "At least I think I would have remembered."

"I know where you're going here," he said. "But if you had experienced another fugue state, you would know it the same way you know about the one that took you into the Preserve. There would be a blank spot in your memories."

She cheered up a little at that. "Right. Well, I can tell you that Lancaster never came into the tearoom for a reading."

"But you think his obsession with you is genuine? He wasn't faking that?"

"Yes, I'm sure. I'm also quite certain that he wore that rainstone ear stud to our initial therapy session to send me a message."

Harry gripped the edge of the window. "The 'I know where you live' kind of message."

"Yes." Rachel paused, her fingers elegantly still in midair over the teapot. "But there is something here that doesn't fit properly."

"Got news for you." He turned away from the view of the gathering storm. "There's a lot of stuff here that doesn't fit right. Why do you think this bastard fixated on you?"

"Hmm?" Rachel shook off her distracted air and went to the stove to pick up the kettle. "Oh, that part is quite straightforward. He realizes that I know him for exactly what he is. What's more, I can resist his psychic seduction talent, therefore I fascinate him."

"Because you're the one woman he can't have?"

"And because I see him for the monster that he is. In some ways that makes me a challenge."

"I would think the fact that you know his true nature would make you a threat, not the bride of his dreams."

Rachel smiled and carried the pot across the kitchen to the table. "Shows how much you know about psychic vampires."

"And here I thought I was one."

"The fact that you don't understand Lancaster is proof positive that you aren't one of the monsters. Come, sit down and have some of your special blend."

He watched her for a moment. Last night she had

come close to being incinerated alive by a paranormal-enhanced fire. Afterward she had matter-of-factly dealt with the side of his nature that others considered monstrous. And then she had made passionate love with him in the backseat of his car. This morning she was calmly pouring tea and talking about the psychic vampire who was stalking her from afar.

He smiled and crossed the room to sit down at the table.

Rachel raised her brows. "Something amusing?"

"Not amusing. Amazing."

"What?"

"You. Are all the women in the Harmonic Enlightenment community as strong as you?"

She blinked, startled. "What an odd question. I'm one of the weaker members of the Community. I had to leave to try to find a place where I belonged."

"Just because you have a foot in both worlds doesn't make you weak, Rachel. The opposite is true."

Her brows crinkled. "I don't see how."

"Never mind. Tell me more about Lancaster."

"The long and the short of it is that he wants to seduce and control me. He isn't particularly interested in me physically. Possessing me sexually would be more symbolic than anything—evidence of his power over me. What he really wants to do is enslave me psychically. As long as I am unobtainable I am both a threat and an object of desire."

"In other words, he looked at you and he knew that he had two options. Control you or kill you."

She blinked a couple of times. "That does sum up his thinking processes quite succinctly. But I would remind you that there has been no follow-up on his part."

"Until last night."

She sighed. "Until last night."

"So he sends two young street kids to burn you alive?"

Rachel frowned. "That's what doesn't quite add up. I doubt that he's reached the stage where he's concluded that he has to kill me. I'm sure he's still at the point where he wants to prove to himself that he can seduce and control me. The only thing that makes sense is that he somehow found out about you. He wants me to know that no other man can have me."

"But you were in the cabin with me last night."

"I've got a hunch that was where things went wrong. I have a feeling those two firebombers were after you, not me. They probably didn't know that I was in the cabin. How could they? There was no second car in the drive. My bike was on the porch. The violence of the storm would have made it impossible for them to get a clear view through the windows."

"I've only been on the island a few days. How could Lancaster know about me—about us?"

"I have no idea," Rachel said. "But I think he somehow found out about that first night we spent together. We were the talk of the town yesterday morning, if you will recall."

Harry contemplated that while he picked up the cup and inhaled the invigorating fragrance of the tisane. "If Lancaster found out about the night I spent at your place so quickly, it can only mean that he's got a spy here on the island—someone who is keeping an eye on you for him."

"That would appear to be a distinct possibility," Rachel said. She shook her head with a wistful air. "But I just cannot imagine that any of my friends and neighbors would do something like that. And as I keep reminding you, those two young men he sent to blow up the cabin are not locals."

"You say he's got a talent for seducing and manipulating his victims. Whoever informed on you may not realize that he or she was putting you in harm's way."

"I suppose that's possible." Rachel cheered a little at that. "Whoever told him about me may have believed that I needed Lancaster's protection. He may have convinced the person that you were a threat."

"All right, we've got motive. But it wasn't Lancaster who torched the place last night, it was a couple of young toughs."

"Those two kids have griffin tattoos," Rachel said. "The image is the same as the figure on the ring that Lancaster wore the day I met with him. That can't be a coincidence."

"No. There's a link between the three of them. Now I need to find it. It shouldn't be too hard to break them."

Rachel frowned. "Break them?"

"Make them talk."

"No, probably not." Rachel watched him uneasily. "What, exactly, do you plan to do to make them talk?"

"Relax, I'm not going to torture the kids any more than I already have, if that's what's worrying you."

She perked up immediately and gave him an approving smile. "Good."

He wrapped one hand around the cup. "It won't be necessary."

She stopped radiating approval. "I see. That's the only reason you don't intend to subject them to any more of your talent? Because you think you can get the information you want without scaring them half to death?"

"Something tells me that's a trick question," he said.

"Not really."

But it was and damned if he was going to answer it. He did not like it that her faint air of disappointment bothered him. He reminded himself that even though she had been out in what she called the mainstream world for a while, she'd lived a very sheltered life.

When he inhaled the aroma of the gently steaming tisane, however, he immediately felt better about himself and more optimistic about everything else, including his odds of finding the answers he sought. He could not identify the herbs but he liked the spicy fragrance they produced. He liked it a lot. There was something clean, centering, and invigorating about their scent. He could feel the pleasant effects across all his senses. He took a deeper breath.

"Smells good," he said.

"I'm glad you like it." Rachel rewarded him by looking pleased. "Those herbs resonate nicely with your aura."

He glanced at the jars on the counter. "You sure they're all legal?"

She gave him a serene smile. "Do you care?"

"Not right now. Is this cup of tea going to cost as much as the last one?"

"Anything that is worthwhile comes with a price," Rachel said demurely.

"Sounds like another quote from the Principles."

"I'm afraid that bit of wisdom is much older than the philosophical tenets of the Principles."

He took a swallow. It tasted as good as it had the first time he had tried it in the bookshop café. It was as if Rachel had distilled the essence of sunshine and rain. The stuff rezzed all his senses in a subtle way.

"You know, this tea is actually worth ten bucks a cup," he said.

Rachel laughed. "I'm glad you agree with my pricing strategy."

He studied the amber-hued brew. "Could you create a tea like this for one of the guys you call the real monsters? Lancaster, for example?"

"No. I could create a tisane that would have a sedating effect or one that would act like caffeine on someone with Lancaster's aura. But I couldn't brew a drink that would balance his energy field for even a short period of time because there's an entire chunk of his spectrum that is simply dead. There is nothing that will harmonize a psi-path's aura."

"But you could poison a monster."

"Yes." She watched him drink. "I could poison him. But as I told you, killing, no matter how justified, exacts a heavy psychic toll."

"Except for the monsters," Harry said. "They can kill or damage without remorse and without taking any psychic damage."

"Because they are already damaged." Rachel moved one hand. Her bracelet jangled lightly. "That's what makes them monsters."

He lounged back in his chair and stuck his legs out under the table. "You know, you could make a fortune selling your teas and tisanes on the mainland."

"Sadly, it's not that easy. Each batch has to be individually blended to suit the customer's aura. There's no way to go into mass production. What's more, an individual's aura is never static. The oscillation of the currents is affected by any number of factors like age, health problems, and emotional issues. Even the weather has an effect. The blend that is beneficial one day may not be so effective the next day or next week."

"Okay, I can see the problems involved," he said. "Sounds like the best way to make real money off your products would be to charge a lot more than you do for each individually blended batch. Make everyone pay ten bucks a cup or more."

She shook her head. "No. That approach would mean turning away too many people who need my brews but can't afford them."

"Didn't think you'd go for that business plan."

She made a face. "Making a lot of money is not a big priority for those of us who were raised in the Community."

"Strange. For those of us in the Sebastian family, making a lot of money has always been a major priority."

"Maybe because your family has a talent for it. Mine doesn't, trust me."

"I'll take your word for it."

It was good to sit here with her like this, he thought. He drank some more of the brew and enjoyed the gentle stirring of his senses.

"I wonder where Lancaster got the hired muscle," he said after a while. "That pair sitting in the Shadow Bay jail this morning look like they came from the streets, but they don't have the vibe of hardened criminals. And what's with the griffin tats?"

"Some kind of gang symbol?" Rachel suggested.

Harry pondered that. "Maybe. But why would a slick con man like Lancaster get involved in a low-rent street gang? Doesn't feel like his style."

Rachel's eyes widened. "It's not. But there is another kind of organization that fits with Lancaster's para-psych profile perfectly. A cult."

"Yes." Harry sat forward abruptly, automatically reaching for his phone. He stopped, irritated, when he remembered that the phone service was still out. "No way to research that angle until we can get online or make a call to the mainland, but it makes sense. A cult that pulls in young street toughs would provide an excellent source of muscle for a guy like Lancaster, especially if he used the operation to recruit kids like those two, who both have a little hunter talent." He finished the tisane and got to his feet. "I'm going to talk to that pair we've got locked up."

"Okay, but I've got to warn you, I don't think you're going to get any useful answers from them, regardless of whether or not you use your talent."

"Why not?"

"You saw them this morning. They were dazed and bewildered. They didn't seem to remember anything of what happened."

"They were faking it."

"I don't think so," Rachel said. "I got a brief look at their auras last night and again today. There was something odd about some of the currents in both spectrums. I think you should let me observe the boys when you question them."

"Now they're just boys? What happened to young toughs and thugs?"

Rachel flushed. "I don't know. They just seemed awfully young and very scared this morning."

She was right, but that didn't mean they weren't young, scared thugs.

"What good will it do to read their auras?" he asked.

"I might be able to provide you with additional information."

He thought about it. Maybe it was the effects of the tisane but it sounded like a reasonable suggestion.

"More information is always good," he said. "But I can't put you behind a one-way observation window. The facilities at the local police station don't run to those sorts of amenities. You'll have to sit in on the questioning."

"That's fine. I don't like to work through glass, anyway. You know how it is with glass when it comes to the paranormal."

He nodded. "Unpredictable."

Everyone with an ounce or more of talent knew that in the field of para-physics, glass was one of the least understood materials because it possessed properties of both crystals and liquids, to say nothing of its reflective and refraction qualities. In addition, there were an almost unlimited number of variations of glass and glasslike substances ranging from the naturally fused versions such as obsidian to precision optics.

"Glass tends to distort aura readings because it masks some portions of the spectrum and it often alters the colors of certain bands of energy," Rachel said.

"All right, you can sit in when I do the questioning," he said. "But let's get one thing clear. No matter what happens or what is said, you are not allowed to interrupt. Understood?"

"Absolutely," she said a little too quickly. "I understand that you're the expert when it comes to that sort of questioning."

"Uh-huh." Keeping her quiet while he was grilling the pair was going to be a problem. He pushed that issue aside and began to pace the kitchen. He needed a strategy before he confronted the two firebombers. "At this point, all we've got linking Vince and his pal to Marcus Lancaster are those tats."

"And the fact that you were their target."

He thought about that. "Maybe it's all connected."

"How?"

"I don't know yet, but it feels like there must be some link."

"I'll take your word for it," Rachel said. "Meanwhile, there's something you should keep in mind about guys who go into the cult business."

"What?"

"At the start, they view their organizations as profitable power trips. But sooner or later they start to believe their own press."

Chapter 15

THERE HAD BEEN NO WORD FROM RAINSHADOW FOR nearly twenty-four hours. All Marcus Lancaster had been able to discover was that a storm in the Amber Sea had knocked out communications on the island. It had been difficult getting even that minimal amount of information because the clinic severely restricted access to outside news. Under normal circumstances, he relied on reports from his associate on the island, but now those had been cut off.

His intuition told him that something had gone terribly wrong. He could not let her escape.

"Tell me about your recurring nightmare," Dr. Oakford said. "The one you say you've had ever since childhood."

Marcus forced himself to pay attention. It was unsettling to discover that he needed to concentrate in order to employ his talent today. He should have been able to deal with Oakford without even having to think twice about it.

He must have done a halfway decent job of concealing his inner agitation, though, because Oakford was clearly oblivious. He conducted the therapy session in the same superficially calm, emotionless tone that he always employed. Marcus was not fooled. He could read voices and faces the way others read GPS maps. Beneath the surface of Oakford's well-modulated, blandly professional speech patterns, currents of anticipation were infused with the need for positive feedback.

Marcus reminded himself not to smile. Smiling was not an appropriate response in this particular situation. What was the matter with him today? He had been handling Ian Oakford and the other members of the staff with exquisite ease ever since Rachel had left the clinic. He had been biding his time, performing the role of the model patient brilliantly and always, *always* keeping in mind that it was in his own best interests to remain at Chapman until the project on Rainshadow was completed.

It was getting increasingly difficult to fake his diagnosis, though. Today he had to rez a little talent just to get himself into the part. It was critical that he remain in character because Oakford wanted to talk about the recurring dream. That was dangerous territory because the dream was linked to his childhood.

He had gone to great lengths to bury his past—quite literally. Now here was Oakford trying to pry open the places where he kept his secrets.

Truth be told, the memories were very good. What a rush it had been coming into his talent as a teen, Marcus thought. What kid wouldn't have reveled in the realization that he could make almost anyone believe almost anything, at least for a while? And what young male wouldn't have savored the delights of being able to manipulate any girl into bed?

Later, in his early twenties when he discovered that he could pull off the perfect scam—that he could persuade seemingly intelligent, well-educated, sophisticated investors to trust him with their money—he thought he had found his true path in life. For a while he had convinced himself that the exhilarating sense of power that he experienced every time he added another financial trophy to his growing empire was enough.

But it wasn't enough. He had begun to wonder if anything would ever be enough.

It was not until fate had led him to Rachel Blake that he had comprehended the shattering truth. She was what he required to fulfill his destiny.

"I've had the nightmares for years," Marcus said. "They started when I was sent to the orphanage. I was twelve years old."

Dr. Oakford consulted his notes. "That happened after the fire that destroyed your family's home and took the lives of your parents."

"Yes."

Oakford occupied the chair on the opposite side of the table, the same chair that Rachel had sat in a few weeks ago.

When this was all over, Marcus thought, Oakford was going to suffer an unfortunate accident.

"Walk me through your recurring dream," Oakford suggested.

Marcus jacked up his talent a little, just enough to get a fix on the vulnerable wavelengths in Oakford's aura. It wasn't hard. The doctor was desperately anxious for feedback that would tell him that the experimental psi-drugs were working.

"I'm in my bed in my parents' house," Marcus began. "It's night. I know that something terrible is about to happen. I want to warn my folks but I can't speak. I can't move. Can't get out of bed to go down the hall to warn them."

"Go on," Dr. Oakford said.

"I lie there, frozen. I sense someone or maybe something coming down the hall. I know that whoever or whatever it is, it's coming for me."

"You're not sure if the creature in the hall is human?"

"It's the monster-under-the-bed thing, Doctor. You know what it's like when you're a kid."

Oakford made a note. "Please continue."

"I finally manage to get out of bed. I can't go out into the hall because the monster is there. My only hope is to crawl out the window. But I'm moving in slow motion. I know I won't be able to escape. I hear the door open behind me. I turn around."

"What do you see, Marcus?"

"Nothing," Marcus said. "I always wake up at that point."

"When was the last time you had this dream?" Dr. Oakford asked.

Marcus made himself frown a little, as though he could not recall the exact date. The truth was, although he had dreamed the dream frequently over the years, it never went quite the way he had described it to Oakford. The real version had a slightly different twist and a very different ending.

"It's been a while now," he said. He blinked a couple of times and allowed his expression to clear, showing just the faintest hint of surprise. "Not for a couple of weeks, in fact."

Dr. Oakford nodded. "What do you think that means, Marcus?"

"I'm not sure," Marcus said. He risked a sliver of a smile that was tinged with relief. "But I will say I'm sleeping better these days, even if I am locked up in a parapsych ward."

"Better sleep is a sign of progress." Dr. Oakford's smile held more than a hint of satisfaction. "We'll continue work on the meaning of your dream tomorrow."

"Do you think that it's important that I've stopped having the old nightmare?"

"It's very, very important, Marcus. It means that you are moving toward recovery."

"I do feel calmer."

"I'm glad to hear that." Dr. Oakford closed his notebook. "We have a lot of work ahead of us, but the medications are working."

Marcus allowed himself another hopeful smile. He

made sure it looked like the kind of smile a grateful patient would give the doctor who was saving his sanity.

Oakford got to his feet and went to the door to summon the orderly. Marcus stood, wondering with some amusement what Oakford would say if knew the truth about the dream.

In the real version of the dream—the version Marcus had dreamed off and on for years—he was not the terrified little boy lying helplessly in bed. Oh, no. He was on his way down the hall to set a fire.

Chapter 16

"I'M JUST A SMALL-TOWN COP," KIRK WILLIS SAID. "I'M not ex-FBPI like the chief, but for what it's worth, I've got a feeling that those two perps are telling the truth. I don't think they remember much about what happened last night. Probably high at the time. That would explain the memory loss."

"I agree they were flying last night," Harry said. "Drugs would account for the inability to recall the actual torch-lighting ceremony at the gatekeeper's cabin, but they don't explain forgetting how and where they came into possession of a high-tech accelerant and the device that was used to start the fire. That required planning, and you don't do that under the influence of dope that is strong enough to cause a blackout."

They were sitting in Willis's small office at the Shadow Bay Police Station. Kirk was in his early twenties and still figuring out what kind of man and what kind of cop he wanted to be. It was obvious, though, that he was taking lessons from his new boss.

Although Kirk was young, his desk and just about every other aspect of the place looked as if it had been locked in a time warp for the past few decades. The old-fashioned filing cabinets, window blinds, and furniture could have qualified as antiques, assuming anyone wanted to collect that kind of shabby stuff.

The computer on the desk was new and so was the phone, but neither was of much use at the moment and maybe not for a long time to come. There was no way to know when the phone and rez-net service would be restored.

The door of the office was open. Harry could hear voices drifting down the hall. There was a fair amount of serious conversation going on among the volunteers who had gathered at the station. While the news of the fire and the arrest of the two young arsonists was of keen interest to the locals, assessing damage and cleaning up after the storm was the first priority this morning.

"You got me there," Kirk said. "But all I can tell you right now is what you already know. According to the ferry ticket stubs and the other info in their pockets, Vince Pritchard and Eric McClain arrived on the island yesterday. Rented one of the Vibe buggies that the tourists use and got a room at Garrison's B&B. Garrison says he didn't see much of them. The kids went out about six o'clock last night and returned with a couple of hamburgers and soft drinks. Ate in their room. He didn't see them leave last night. Didn't even know they were gone until this morning."

"It would have been easy enough for them to take off without anyone noticing after the storm got going," Harry said. "But they must have asked directions to the gate-keeper's cabin. Not like the place is on one of the tourist maps. Only the locals know where it is."

"I'll ask around," Kirk said. He stood behind his desk. "Chief said I was to give you any help I could. But right now, I've got an island to clean up."

"I understand," Harry said. He got to his feet.

Kirk shook his head. "Never seen storms like the ones we've been having lately. Anyhow, sorry I don't have more information for you, Mr. Sebastian. But with the phones and computers down, there's not much I can do. No telling how long we'll be cut off from the mainland."

"I'd like to talk to Pritchard and McClain if you don't mind."

"Sure, help yourself. Myrna can keep an eye on them while you question them."

"Thanks. I'm going to let Rachel sit in on the inter-rogation."

Kirk frowned. "After what happened last night you want her in the same room as those two?"

"No, but she seems to think she might be able to read something useful in their auras."

"Huh." Kirk picked up his cap and positioned it squarely on his head. "I don't know about this aura-reading busi-ness, but Rachel sometimes seems to know things about people."

"Yes," Harry said. "She does."

"Doesn't mean she always knows everything she should about a person, though."

"Are you trying to tell me something, Willis?"

Kirk flushed but he drew himself up to his full height and fixed Harry with a cop stare. Harry had a hunch that Willis had copied the flat, hard look from Slade, along with the brand of sunglasses.

"Rachel is a little different," Kirk said. "Folks say she was raised in some kind of alternative community. One of those places where folks do a lot of meditation and such."

"A Harmonic Environment community, yes, I'm aware of that."

"I don't know much about that kind of thing myself, but Myrna says she got to know Rachel's aunts pretty well when they lived here on the island. The aunts told Myrna that folks—especially men—sometimes get the wrong idea about women who come from HE communities."

"You're trying to warn me not to take advantage of Rachel?" Harry asked politely.

"Doesn't matter where she came from," Kirk said. He was a little red-faced now, but his cold-eyed stare didn't waver. "Rachel's one of us now. We look after our own here on Rainshadow."

"Good to know," Harry said. He suppressed a smile. Willis had definitely been studying Slade's style.

"Right, then, guess that's all that I need to say." Kirk started toward the door. "I'll check back in here at the station in a couple of hours. Good luck with getting something useful out of Pritchard and McClain."

"Thanks," Harry said. "I appreciate it."

He followed Willis down the hall to the entrance of the station, where a small group of people were gathered.

"You've all got your sector assignments from Myrna here, and you know the drill," Kirk said.

"Should know it by now," one of the men in the crowd said. "This is the third or fourth time we've been through it since that first big storm hit a while back."

"You got it, Hank," Kirk said. "Only difference this time is that the chief isn't here, but we'll stick with his plan. Phones are out, so instead of calling in the problems, you'll need to make notes. Check the main roads and the bridges in your assigned sector and note downed trees and other obstructions too heavy for you to move out of the way on your own. Come back in at noon. Earlier if that damn fog gets worse. Don't want to have to go out looking for stragglers in that stuff."

"For sure," someone muttered. "That fog is wicked. Never seen anything like it."

There was a murmur of agreement from the others.

Kirk surveyed the crowd. "Any questions?"

"Heard there was a big fire out at the old gatekeeper's cabin," someone said. "Couple of off-island kids torched the place."

Everyone looked at Harry. He inclined his head politely but stayed silent. This was Willis's show.

"No one was injured and the kids who threw the firebomb are locked up here at the station," Kirk said. "They aren't going to be setting any more fires on Rainshadow. Myrna will keep an eye on them while we're out doing damage control. Right, Myrna?"

The middle-aged blonde at the front desk spoke up briskly. "Don't worry, those two aren't going anywhere."

"That's it, then," Kirk said. "Let's go."

The crowd tromped outside. In spite of the fog, Kirk took his sunglasses out of his pocket and put them on with both hands in a cool, deliberate way that looked very familiar. Harry remembered seeing Slade put his shades on with the same kind of move.

Kirk followed the gaggle of volunteers outside. The door closed behind him.

Harry found himself alone with Myrna. She gave him a cool, speculative look.

"Sounds like you and Rachel had quite the adventure last night," she said.

"Yes," he said.

"Word is that the two of you had to spend the night in your SUV after the cabin got torched."

"Wasn't much choice. Didn't want to risk trying to drive back to town in that storm."

"You seem to be making a habit of getting caught in storms with Rachel and then having to spend the night with her."

"It's only happened twice," Harry said.

"Twice in three days."

"Is this where you give me the lecture on not taking

advantage of naïve, unworldly women from an HE community?"

She narrowed her eyes. "Did someone else already give you the talk?"

"Willis did just a few minutes ago. Couple of days ago I got it from those two retired ghost-hunters at the Kane Gallery, and I believe Levenson, the fishmonger, may have said something along the same lines."

"We look after our own here on Rainshadow."

"I got that message as well."

Myrna turned thoughtful. "Did Slade deliver the same message, by any chance?"

"No. Probably didn't feel it was necessary."

"Maybe. Maybe not. Before he left the island he was pretty focused on meeting Charlotte's family."

"I saw enough of Attridge to know that he takes his responsibilities here on Rainshadow seriously. He wouldn't have hesitated to warn me to stay away from Rachel if he had felt I needed warning."

Myrna pursed her lips and gave that a moment's thought. Then she nodded once, satisfied. "Slade's got good, solid cop intuition. Okay, moving right along, then, Kirk said you wanted to question those two kids we've got locked up in back. When do you want to do that?"

"Now. But I want Rachel with me."

"Why?"

"She suggested it. And since she was there last night when that pair tried to kill us, I think she's got a right."

"Good idea," Myrna said. "Rachel sometimes seems to know things about people."

"So I hear." He started to take out his phone and belatedly remembered again that it wasn't functioning. "I'll go down to the bookshop and get her."

"No rush. I'm not going anywhere and neither is that pair back in the cell."

He started toward the door but stopped halfway across the room. "I've got a question for you, Myrna."

"What?"

"I know people tend to assume that Rachel's a little naïve in the ways of the world because of her upbringing. I get the part about looking after your own. But I'm starting to think that the level of vigilance here is approaching overkill. Mind telling me why you think Rachel needs so much protection?"

"It's not like she has any family here to take care of her," Myrna said. "Now that her aunts have moved away, she's on her own."

"I'll buy that, but only up to a point." He walked back to the desk and stopped in front of it. "There's some other reason you're worried about her, isn't there?"

Myrna picked up a pen and tapped the point on the desk, her expression troubled. But after a while she got to her feet and went to stand looking out the window at the fountain that stood in the town's small main square.

"This is Rachel's business," she said eventually. "I shouldn't be talking about it. But under the circumstances, maybe you should know."

"About what?"

Myrna turned around to face him. "About what happened to Rachel here on the island a while back."

"You're talking about the night she spent inside the Preserve?"

Myrna looked surprised. "She told you about it?"

"Yes."

"About how she can't remember anything about that whole night?"

"She told me about the amnesia, as well."

"It was Calvin Dillard who found her. She walked out of the Preserve right near his place. He brought her back into town that morning. She seemed okay except for the amnesia, but everyone thinks she suffered some kind of psychic trauma from the incident."

"That's why you feel so protective?"

"Probably."

Harry lounged against the desk and folded his arms. "Tell me, Myrna, do you have any theories about what happened to Rachel the night she disappeared into the Preserve?"

Myrna hesitated and then shrugged one shoulder. "It's not the first time someone has managed to blunder through the fence and get inside. But, then, you know that. Until Slade arrived on the island we always had to call Foundation security to conduct a search-and-rescue operation when some drunken boater or drugged-out idiot got through."

"Yes."

"The thing is, most of the people who do crash the fence can't find their own way back out. But Rachel did. Yet she can't remember anything about the experience."

"The energy inside the Preserve affects different people in different ways."

"I'm aware of that," Myrna said evenly. "I've lived here most of my life. I've seen the folks your people have rescued from time to time. They're generally disoriented and usually freaked out of their minds but they don't have amnesia. They remember being terrified. They recall seeing things. They do not forget the whole experience."

"So, because Rachel developed amnesia, you and everyone else in town has concluded that she's emotionally and psychically fragile, is that it?"

"I guess that's one way to put it," Myrna admitted. "But there's another possibility. Maybe what she saw while she was inside was so awful her conscious mind suppressed the memories."

"I'm no doctor but I have to tell you that the woman who ran out of that burning cabin with me last night didn't strike me as fragile. A little too soft-hearted, maybe, but not fragile. I'd be glad to have her at my back in a bar fight any day."

Myrna stared at him, openmouthed.

He opened the door and went out into the foggy street.

Chapter 17

THE FOG WAS GROWING THICKER. THERE WERE NO CUS-tomers and nothing to indicate that customers might materialize in the near future. Rachel sent Lilly home for the rest of the day and hung the *Back in Ten Minutes* sign in the window of the bookshop.

She locked the front door and set off along Waterfront Street with Darwina tucked under one arm and a packet of specially blended herbs in her tote. Darwina clutched Amberella and chortled with anticipation. Rachel smiled.

"Everything's a game to you, isn't it? Just walking down the street is a new adventure."

Darwina chortled again.

"You could give lessons in living in the moment to folks back home in the Community," Rachel said.

It was a short but eerie trek to Looking Glass Antiques. In the pooling fog, Shadow Bay looked like a ghost town locked in another dimension. Lights glowed dimly in a few store windows, but most of the businesses were closed. Her fellow shopkeepers had, by and large, concluded that it was not worth opening for trade today. They were right, Rachel thought. She hadn't made a single sale.

The sidewalks were empty. Ferry and float plane service to the island had been cancelled due to the weather. The upshot was that there were no day-trippers to browse the offerings in the darkened windows. Visitors staying at the local B&Bs and the crowd of people attending the Reflections seminar out at the lodge had wisely decided to remain indoors and sip hot chocolate by a cozy fire.

The memory of the ghostly flicker of awareness that had flashed across her senses when she had picked up the teacup still nagged at her. There was something she needed to remember, and soon.

She opened the door of Looking Glass and stepped inside. The bell over the entrance chimed. Her senses tingled. Darwina made excited little noises.

"I know what you mean," Rachel said.

Charlotte specialized in antiques with a paranormal provenance. The atmosphere was saturated with the energy that leaked out of the old objects displayed for sale. Entering Looking Glass was like walking through a summer shower of effervescent rain.

Darwina wriggled impatiently, demanding to be set free. Rachel put her down on the hardwood floor.

"Okay, but don't get into trouble," Rachel said. "A lot of the stuff in here is seriously valuable."

Darwina ignored her and promptly fluttered out of

sight with Amberella, chattering excitedly. She vanished behind a display of First Generation toys.

Rachel looked at the sales counter. There was no one behind it.

"Jasper?" she called.

"Be right with you, Rachel."

The voice was deep and gruff, perfectly suited to the big, broad-shouldered, bearded man who emerged from the back room. Jasper Gilbert was a retired ghost hunter who had moved to Rainshadow Island with his life partner, Fletcher Kane, several years ago. Jasper was an artist with a talent for riveting landscapes. His work hung on the walls of the Kane Gallery across the street.

Although both men had worked as Guildmen down in the catacombs, they were very different in many ways. While Jasper was big and burly, Fletcher was elegant, lean, silver-haired, and sophisticated, everything one expected from a successful art gallery proprietor. The couple was a fine example of successful matchmaking, Rachel thought, and living proof that opposites really did attract.

Visitors to the island were frequently intrigued by Jasper's color-drenched scenes of the island. He had a true talent for capturing the essence of the eerie atmosphere that had always clung to Rainshadow.

Recently, however, his pictures had undergone an ominous change. Rachel had watched with deepening concern as his paintings had become darker and edgier. She knew she was not the only one who had noticed the transformation. Slade and Charlotte had both commented on it.

Collectors from off-island did not appear to be aware of the subtle shift, but Rachel had seen several of the local residents pause for a long time in front of the windows of the gallery whenever a new painting by Jasper was put on display. When the viewers moved on, they often wore troubled expressions.

The pictures of the familiar local landmarks—the harbor, the picturesque, weather-beaten shops and the waterfront—were still rendered in Jasper's distinctive brushstrokes. The palette was still rich and deep. But the pictures had acquired a new, unsettling sense of atmosphere that put Rachel in mind of the feeling she got just before one of the fierce thunderstorms struck. Lately Jasper's paintings stirred the hair on the back of her neck.

"Heard you were out at the old gatekeeper's cabin with Sebastian when those two kids firebombed the place last night." Jasper went behind the sales counter and regarded her with concern. "You okay?"

"Yes, thanks."

"Must have been damn scary. Like running into a monster ghost down in the tunnels."

"I would not want to repeat the experience," she said. "But I'm fine, Jasper, honest."

He gave her a sympathetic smile. "I'm fussing, aren't I?"

"It's nice of you and everyone else to be so concerned about me but, yes, you are fussing unnecessarily."

"We all worry about you."

"I know you do but there's no need," Rachel said. "Harry took care of things last night. He is in the security business, after all."

"Heard that, too. Everyone is saying that he knew how to handle himself when the ghost-shit came down." Jasper winced. "Sorry about the language."

"No need to apologize. Why do I have to keep telling people that just because I was raised HE, it doesn't follow that I'll faint if I hear a little bad language?"

Jasper gave her an appraising look. "So you and Sebastian ended up spending another night together."

"Uh-huh."

"In a car."

"Uh-huh."

"Seems to be happening regularly."

"This was the first time we had to spend the night in a car." Rachel smiled. "No need to get out the shotgun."

Jasper narrowed his eyes. "You're sure?"

"Positive. I appreciate your concern but I promise you there is nothing to be concerned about."

There was a small, muffled clink from somewhere inside the shop.

"Oops," Rachel said. "I think that might have been Darwina."

Jasper quartered the shop with slightly scrunched up eyes. "I see her. She's on that old dressing table playing with one of the perfume bottles. Better grab her before she gets carried away. Charlotte says some of those bottles are worth a lot of money."

"Perfume?" Rachel started toward the dressing table. "You are such a girly girl, Darwina."

Darwina chortled, put down the bottle she had selected, and scampered out of sight under an old sofa. Rachel abandoned the attempt to distract her and went back to the counter.

Jasper snorted. "From a dust bunny's point of view, this shop is probably just one big toy store filled with bright, shiny objects."

Rachel heard a repetitive creaking sound and turned quickly.

"She found the old rocking horse." Jasper angled his chin toward a dark corner of the shop.

Rachel started cautiously through the crowded space. "Darwina? Where are you?"

The creaking continued, louder and faster. It was accompanied by a great deal of excited chortling.

Rachel rounded a dressing table decorated with intricate inlays of wood and amber and saw the rocking horse. It was exquisitely detailed right down to the elegant bridle and reins. The eyes were made of carved green amber. Darwina was in the saddle with Amberella, bouncing back and forth to keep the rocking action going.

"Stop," Rachel yelped. "That rocking horse is probably worth a fortune."

She rushed forward and scooped Darwina off the toy.

Darwina protested vigorously and scrambled free. She bounded down to the floor and disappeared once more, this time behind a red velvet sofa that looked like it had once graced the reception room of a really tacky pre–Era of Discord brothel.

"Cripes," Rachel said. "I'd better get her out of here fast."

"Let her go," Jasper said. "I doubt she'll do any real harm. She just wants to play. But remind me to check all six paws when the two of you leave to make sure she doesn't take off with anything."

"Probably a wise precaution."

"Where's Sebastian?"

"He's at the police station making arrangements to question the arsonists. I'm going to help him with the interrogation."

"Yeah?" Jasper scowled "How?"

"By analyzing the kids' auras when he talks to them. I'm hoping that I'll be able to see something in their energy fields that will explain why they can't recall what happened last night."

"They're faking. I heard they were locked up most of the night in the woodshed. They had plenty of time to work out a story."

"I'm not so sure," Rachel said. "If you will recall, I'm something of an expert on amnesia."

"I know, but those two young thugs didn't come out of the Preserve the way you did, so they wouldn't have been hit with the energy inside."

"I realize that, but that storm was very violent last night. There was a lot of psi in the atmosphere and a lot of it was unusually hot."

"Probably because the cabin is, or rather, was, close to the fence."

"It wasn't just the energy from the Preserve affecting things," Rachel said. "There were psi currents in the fire that destroyed the cabin. Harry thinks some kind of cutting-edge para-technology was involved."

"Huh." Jasper scowled. "Someone went after you and

Sebastian with a firebomb that used a high-tech para-accelerator?"

"That's what it looked like and also what it felt like. A lot of the fire was burning with ultralight."

Jasper's scowl turned grimly thoughtful. "Does it strike you as passing strange that you happened to be at Sebastian's place last night when someone tried to take him out in the middle of the storm?"

Rachel shivered. "I know where you're going with this, and while we in the HE community don't think much of coincidence we also don't think it's smart to leap to conclusions until all of the evidence is available. My theory is that I've got a stalker who is angry because he thinks I'm involved with Harry. I think he sent someone to murder Harry not realizing that I would also be on the scene."

Jasper shook his head. "This is getting complicated, but I truly do believe that what happened last night is all about the Preserve. Got to be. I've been sensing some bad energy coming down for months, Rachel. It's the same feeling I used to get in the old days when I worked the tunnels with Fletch just before we ran into a really nasty ghost."

"I don't doubt your intuition." She opened her senses a little. The whispery threads of purple and yellow energy in Jasper's aura told her all she needed to know. "Another dream about the Preserve last night?"

Jasper exhaled heavily and folded his arms on the counter. "Yeah. The dreams are getting worse."

"Mine, too." Rachel put the package that she had brought with her on the counter. "I made up another batch of your aura-tea for you."

"Thanks." Jasper picked up the package. "I finished off the last of the old batch this morning. I needed it after last night's dream."

She glanced at his paint-spattered denim shirt. "How's my picture going?"

Jasper straightened away from the counter. "That's what I wanted to show you. Got the easel set up in the backroom. Light's terrible in there but it's not like it's good anywhere else on the island lately. Damn fog."

"Were you able to interpret my dreamscape vision?"

"I'm getting there. Haven't got it all figured out yet but it's getting clearer based on your descriptions. Usually I work with my own dream images. This is the first time I've tried to paint someone else's dreamscape."

"Let's see what you've got."

Jasper came out from behind the counter and started toward the back room.

"I'll tell you one thing for sure," he said. "I know this picture is important. I've got this feeling that I need to hurry up and finish it but I need more input from you."

He walked through the doorway into the crowded back room, stood aside, and gestured toward the easel set up near the window.

"That's what I've got so far," he said. "See if it jogs your memory."

Rachel followed him into the shadowed space. Another heavy wave of psi hit her senses. The room reeked of energy, and not all of it was from the antiques stored in the crates and boxes that were piled everywhere. Charlotte's shop had been the scene of a murder not too long ago. Violent death always left a taint in the atmosphere of a place. It wasn't the kind of stain that you could get rid of with soap and water.

The overhead light fixture cast a weak glow across the array of crates and boxes stacked around the room. The fog was so thick outside that the windows might as well have been draped.

"I see what you mean about the poor light," Rachel said. "I'm amazed you were able to paint anything at all in this gloom."

"Not like I had a choice." Jasper stood in front of the easel, contemplating his unfinished creation. "After the last time we talked about your dream I did some dreaming of my own. Woke up this morning with the feeling that I had to get something down fast. I got here at dawn and started painting."

Rachel moved closer to the easel. She caught her breath when she saw the unfinished canvas. The fierce brushstrokes and the violent palette Jasper was using struck her senses like flashes of lightning—frozen lightning. She did not need the icy, all-too-familiar prickle of awareness on the back of her neck to warn her that the partially finished image was important.

"Oh, Jasper," she whispered.

"Yeah, I know." Jasper eyed his work with a grim expression. "I'm not there yet. But does it feel right? Does it look like anything you're seeing in your dreams?"

"It's a frozen waterfall. I saw it the night I went sleep-walking into the Preserve."

Chapter 18

"YOU'RE SURE YOU HAVE NO IDEA WHERE THAT WATER-fall is located inside the Preserve?" Harry asked.

He stood in the back room of Looking Glass with Rachel, Jasper, and Fletcher Kane. They were gathered around the unfinished painting.

"No," Rachel said. "Judging by where I found my bicycle, I walked into the Preserve at a point not far from my cottage. But all I know for sure is that I was gone for about twelve hours and that I came out near Calvin Dillard's place."

"That narrows it down somewhat," Harry said. "You couldn't have covered a great deal of territory in that span of time because the terrain is too rough." He looked at Jasper and Fletcher. "Slade said that you two are able to get a short distance into the Preserve because of your ghost-hunter talent. Have you ever seen anything like this inside the fence?"

Jasper shook his head. "Not that I remember. But it's a fact that the energy inside the fence sometimes plays tricks on a person's memory."

Fletcher's patrician features tightened in a thoughtful frown. "You didn't forget anything, Jasper. You've never gone into the Preserve alone. It's too damn dangerous. I've always accompanied you. Which means that if you had ever seen this frozen waterfall and forgotten it, so did I. Damn unlikely that we would both forget precisely the same scene."

"I agree." Harry did not take his eyes off the canvas. The currents of psi from several decades' worth of hot antiques swirling in the atmosphere could not mask his intuitive sense that the waterfall was important. "I need to talk to this Calvin Dillard. He's our only witness to the time and place where Rachel emerged from the Preserve. Maybe he can pin things down a little more precisely."

Rachel looked at him. "Do you think this waterfall has something to do with what's going on inside the Preserve?"

"My gut tells me it's important, but I don't know how yet." He glanced at his watch. "I want to question Pritchard and McClain before I talk to Dillard, though."

Jasper looked out the window at the gloom-shrouded day. "Better get moving. The fog is getting heavier. Looks like another storm taking shape over the island."

"Let's go," Rachel said. She raised her voice. "Dar-wina? Where are you? We're leaving."

Darwina appeared in the doorway and fluttered across the floor. She bounced to a stop at Rachel's feet, chortling, and waved Amberella. Rachel scooped her up and plopped her on one shoulder.

Harry went outside with Rachel and Darwina. They walked down the empty street to the police station. The gray sky had lowered in just the brief span of time it had taken him to find Rachel at the antique shop. The fog was so dense now that he could not see the harbor. He could sense the energy of another storm gathering.

"It's going to be another bad one," he said.

"Yes."

"Did you know that most of the town of Shadow Bay thinks you're psychically fragile because of the fugue incident?" he asked.

She winced. "You talked to Myrna, didn't you?"

"Don't blame her. She was just being protective."

"I know." Rachel made a face. "Geez. One little twelve-hour fugue episode and everyone assumes I've been traumatized for life."

"She meant well."

"Of course."

"I told her I was pretty sure that she and everyone else in town is wrong about the condition of your psyche."

Rachel brightened. "Thanks for the vote of confidence."

"However, on the gossip front, it appears you were right. Looks like the entire town assumes that we did not spend last night in separate seats in the SUV."

"Really?" Rachel's smile was smug. "Well, in that case

imagine what they'll say when they find out that you're staying with me tonight."

"I am?"

"You have to sleep somewhere. Your cabin burned down, remember?"

"I could stay at one of the B and Bs."

"Yes," she said. She stopped smiling. "You could do that if you like."

"I'd rather stay at your place."

She smiled again. "Okay, then, it's settled."

He wanted to ask if she intended him to spend the night on her sofa again but he realized he did not want to risk the answer. Better to take the conversation in another direction, he decided.

"Did seeing your dream image of the waterfall on canvas trigger any other memories?" he asked.

"When Jasper showed it to me, I got a flash of another image, a huge icicle suspended overhead like a chandelier. But it was made of hot crystals, not ice."

"Psi-hot crystals?"

"Yes, I'm sure of it. Harry, remember those rainstones in the jar in my kitchen?"

"Yes."

"I told you I thought they were important. Now I think I may know why."

He stopped and turned to face her. "Why?"

"I think the frozen waterfall that Jasper is painting is made of a solid piece of rainstone. But in my dream the stone is energized, it's not cold like the crystals in my kitchen."

Chapter 19

"I'M TELLING YOU, I DON'T REMEMBER WHAT HAPPENED last night." Vince rocked a little in his chair. He watched Harry with a pleading expression. "I don't remember anything after we left the B&B and got into that dumb little rental buggy."

"You ditched the Vibe before you got to the cabin," Harry said. "Remember that?"

"No, I swear it."

Rachel, sitting quietly in a corner of the police station lunchroom, watched uneasily as agitation flared in Vince's aura. It wasn't the wildly gyrating currents of anxiety that worried her—that kind of energy was only to be expected under the circumstances. It didn't indicate guilt, just that Vince was scared.

He had good reason to be nervous, she thought. He was being questioned, after all, and Harry, for all his cool control, or maybe because of that control, was more than a little scary even though he was not using his talent. He faced Vince across the table.

What alarmed Rachel was the glacial blue of a particular band of wavelengths on Vince's spectrum. The currents in that region appeared frozen—not extinguished, but rather in some sort of suspended state. She had never seen anything quite like it.

"I think you remember a little more about what happened after you got into the Vibe," Harry said, calm but relentless. "You remember driving out Gatehouse Road, don't you? How did you find the turnoff?"

Vince's face screwed up in fierce concentration. "I think I remember driving out of the B&B parking lot." He hesitated. "It was night. I do remember that."

"What was the weather like?" Harry prodded.

Vince blinked and then frowned. "It was starting to rain. Wind was gusting. I remember wishing we had some better rain gear. All we had with us were a couple of jackets."

"You had a few other things with you, Vince," Harry said. "You had a device you could use to set a fire and a couple of mag-rez pistols."

"No." Vince slumped in his chair. "I don't remember those things."

"Where did you get the accelerant?"

Vince scowled. "The what?"

"What did you use to torch the cabin?"

"I don't remember."

"You bought the explosive device from someone."

"No."

"Where did you get the guns?"

Vince started to say he could not recall that information, either, but he hesitated, grimacing again. "I think we found them somewhere."

"You just happened to find two very expensive, very illegal mag-rez pistols lying around on the street?" Harry asked as if he were inquiring about the weather.

"No, not on the street." Vince cheered up again, eager to offer hard facts that might placate his questioner. "We found them somewhere else."

"Where?" Harry asked, patient as a specter cat stalking prey.

"I dunno. No, wait, I think they were in a metal box in the trunk of the car."

Harry opened his mouth to ask another question, but Rachel had seen enough. She spoke quietly from the corner.

"Vince?"

Vince stirred and turned his head to look at her. She realized he had forgotten her presence in the room. Harry was looking at her, too. She knew he was sending her a silent reminder that he had told her to stay quiet. She ignored him. Sometime in the past half hour Vince had become a patient who needed her help.

"Was there something else in the box with the pistols?" she asked softly.

Vince started to deny it, but confusion flashed through his aura, disturbing all of the currents except those in the frozen section.

"I think so but I can't remember for sure," he said. He sank deeper into his seat and into his misery.

"I might be able to help you remember," Rachel said.

Harry gave her a hard look but he did not try to silence her.

Vince shrugged. "I don't see how."

"I read auras," Rachel said. "I can see yours now."

"Yeah?" Vince shrugged. "So what do you see?"

"There's a part of your aura that appears to be frozen," she said. "It looks a little like the aura of a person who has undergone hypnosis, but this is not quite the same thing. Hypnotic suggestions usually affect a different section of the spectrum and fade rapidly over time. The iced-over psi in your energy field is in the dreamlight sector and shows no sign of thawing, at least not in the immediate future. It could be weeks or months before your conscious memory of events returns, if ever. But I think the things you saw and did last night will start showing up in your dreams one of these days."

"I don't understand any of that para-psych babble," Vince grumbled. "What does that mean?"

"If I'm right," Rachel said, "someone did more than merely hypnotize you. Whoever put you under went straight to the dreamlight currents of your aura. That takes a very rare kind of talent."

Vince trembled and started to stutter. "H-how do I know y-you're telling me the truth?"

"You can let me try to restore the natural oscillation pattern of the wavelengths in the part of your aura that is now frozen."

Vince did not look convinced. "How do I know I can trust you?"

"All I'm going to do is touch you," she said. "I promise that you will be awake the whole time. If at any point in the process you want me to stop, I will."

Vince took a deep breath. "Okay. Just do it."

Rachel looked at Harry. His jaw tightened. She knew he did not like the idea of her having physical contact with Vince. But Rachel had seen enough of Vince's aura to know that he was no longer a threat. He was just plain scared.

"Trust me," she said to Harry. "It will be okay. Vince isn't going to hurt me. We need answers and this is the only way we're going to get them."

Reluctantly, Harry got to his feet and motioned her to take his place. Then he went to stand directly behind Vince.

"Hands on the table, Vince," he said. "One false move and there will be dreams, all right, the kind of bad dreams you had last night at the cabin."

Vince flinched but he placed his bound wrists on the table.

Rachel sat down across from him and put her fingertips lightly on one of his hands. He was shivering.

"Vince, do you feel ill?" she asked.

"No."

"You're terrified and not just because you've been arrested," she said quietly. "I think that whoever hypnotized you implanted a command intended to keep you from talking about anything you might remember. The command triggers a panic response if someone asks you for the truth about what happened last night, maybe about other things as well."

Vince gritted his teeth. "Just do whatever it is you're going to do and get it over with."

"Right."

She gathered herself, heightened her talent, and focused energy through one of the charms on her bracelet.

Vince's aura was still fundamentally strong. He had the natural vitality of youth and good health on his side. But the ice in his dreamlight was deathly cold.

She studied the frozen wavelengths for a moment, trying to decide how to approach the task. Then she began to pulse gentle, stimulating currents of energy into the paralyzed sectors.

Vince was shaking with fear. There was a wild panic in his eyes. But he did not beg her to stop.

For a moment Rachel worried that nothing was happening and that she could not reset the natural wavelengths of Vince's aura. But gradually the ice-cold hue of the frozen currents began to warm with the familiar colors of healthy dreamlight. The bands of energy started to pulse in what she sensed was Vince's natural pattern.

Vince jerked his hands away from Rachel. He stared at her, shocked. She could almost see his lost memories slamming back into his conscious mind. His mouth dropped open. He sucked in air and tried to come up off the chair, but Harry's hand clamped around his shoulder, forcing him back down.

"What did you do to me?" Horror flashed in his eyes.

"It's just a dream, a nightmare. Eric and I didn't set fire to the old house."

"We were there," Harry said. "We saw both of you."

"We didn't set that fire, didn't try to kill you two." Bewildered, Vince groaned. "Why would we do that? We don't even know you guys."

"Good question," Harry said. "Why did you do it?"

Vince blinked several times as more memories returned. He sank wearily back into his chair. "Because he told us to do it."

"Who?" Harry asked.

"Mr. Cosgrove."

"Who is Mr. Cosgrove?" Harry asked.

Vince shrugged. "I don't know. He just showed up at Second Chance House a couple of days ago and offered us a job."

"What is Second Chance House?" Rachel asked.

"It's this homeless shelter for street kids in Frequency City," Vince said. "Eric and I hang out there."

"Why did Cosgrove send you and Eric to kill Miss Blake and me?" Harry asked.

"Not Miss Blake," Vince said. "Just you. Cosgrove said you were a real bad guy who had killed some people. He said you were going to kill more people if we didn't stop you. He told us to take the ferry to Rainshadow Island and firebomb that old cabin while you were inside."

"But I wasn't the only one inside," Harry said.

Vince gave Rachel a beseeching look. "I swear we didn't know you were in there with him, Miss Blake."

"I understand," Rachel said.

"Where did you get the incendiary device and the two pistols?" Harry asked.

Vince went blank-faced again. "Incendi-what?"

"The device you used to torch the house."

"Oh, that. Mr. Cosgrove gave it to us and showed us how to work it. Then he gave us the pistols and showed us how to use them, too, although we didn't get much practice in before we left Frequency City."

Rachel leaned forward. "Now I have a question for you, Vince."

"Yeah?"

"What is the significance of the tattoo on the back of your hand?"

"Huh? This?" Vince started to raise one hand to glance at it. He stopped when he realized that his wrists were secured together. "You get one when you're accepted into the Circle at Second Chance House."

"What does it take to be accepted?" Rachel asked.

Vince reddened. "I dunno. Mr. Kidwell makes the decision. When he decides you've got what he calls potential, he invites you to join the Circle. There's like this cool ceremony, see? We went down into the catacombs with Mr. Kidwell and we took an oath and swore that we would never reveal the secrets of the Circle and stuff like that. Then we get the tat."

Harry looked at Rachel over the top of Vince's head. "Any ideas here?"

"Yes," Rachel said, thinking about it. "We were right.

Mr. Kidwell and his friend Mr. Cosgrove use Second Chance House to recruit their own private army of street kids."

"An expendable army," Harry said. "Use and toss as needed. No one will notice a few kids who go missing off the street."

Vince looked up at him, alarmed. "What are you talking about?"

"You don't want to know," Harry said.

"One more question," Rachel said. "Did Mr. Kidwell wear any jewelry?"

"Yeah, he's got a ring with a griffin on it. Why?"

"Any other jewelry?"

Vince shrugged. "I dunno. We never see his face. He wears a mask and this big old-fashioned cloak when we meet him down in the tunnels."

Chapter 20

"MR. KIDWELL IS MARCUS LANCASTER," RACHEL SAID. "I'M sure of it."

"We can't be sure of anything yet," Harry said, "but I agree that's a likely possibility."

He leaned back in his chair, stretched his legs out under the small café table, folded his arms, and watched Rachel pace the small space. It was not like her to pace, he thought. Her restlessness said a lot about her mood.

Darwina, perched on the far end of the counter, the Amberella doll clutched tightly in one paw, had picked up on Rachel's tension. The dust bunny was partially sleeked out. Now and again she opened her second set of eyes as if watching for a threat.

Rachel glowered. "I thought we agreed that it is no

coincidence that Vince and Eric are wearing griffin tattoos identical to the one on Lancaster's ring."

"I agree the tats are a link between the three of them, but at the moment, that's all we've got. Keep in mind that it wasn't Kidwell who sent Vince and Eric after me, it was this other guy, Cosgrove. And remember that currently Kidwell is locked up in a para-psych ward at the Chapman Clinic."

"They're working together."

"Sounds like it, yes. But why?"

She opened the glass case that held a selection of chocolate zingers and offered one to Darwina. "Here you go, pal. These cookies won't last another day, and I don't think we're going to get any more from Jilly until the power comes back on."

Darwina appeared to forget about any potential threat in the vicinity. She chortled, dropped Amberella on the counter, and bustled forward to seize the cookie. She settled down to polish off the treat with gusto.

Rachel watched her with affection. "Life is so uncomplicated for a dust bunny. Talk about the ultimate stage of Enlightenment. They truly do live in the now."

"Maybe they have mastered the art of living in the present moment," Harry said, "but I've got a hunch there is a dark side to dust bunny life."

Rachel glanced at him, startled, "Why do you say that?"

"Because they are living creatures and that means they have to work to stay alive. Staying alive always has a dark side."

Rachel blinked "Okay, that's a very yin-yang thing to say. Are you sure you never studied at an HE academy?"

"The HE community isn't the first or the only crowd to seek enlightenment." Harry got to his feet. "Let's go talk to our witness."

"Calvin Dillard? Okay."

She went quickly about the business of closing up the bookshop. When she was finished, she gathered up her tote and Darwina and Amberella and put the Closed sign in the front window. Harry opened the back door, and they all went outside and got into the SUV. Darwina hopped up onto the back of the passenger seat and fluffed up with an air of great expectation, but Harry got the impression she was rather unimpressed when he drove slowly and cautiously through the fog.

"What do you know about Dillard?" he asked.

"Not much but, then, that's not exactly unusual here on Rainshadow. Calvin has never talked about his past. About the only thing I can tell you is that he subscribes to some science journals and that he's a musician."

"Which journals?"

"I can't remember the names. He comes into town to pick up his mail a few times a week and he often stops at my shop for a cup of tea and a package of the tisane I blend for him before he drives back out to his place. A couple of times I've noticed the journals among the items in his mail. I asked him about them once."

"What did he say?"

"Just that they were left over from another life."

"Are they the sort of science magazines that are published for laypeople?" Harry asked.

"No, they were the serious sort that are read by academics and researchers."

"What area of science?"

"Hmm? Oh, biology. I think that once upon a time he did some work in that field. He's a very intelligent man. Brilliant, really."

"You said he was a musician. What does he play?"

"Several instruments. I know for sure he's got a violin and a guitar because he plays them occasionally at local celebrations and get-togethers." She paused. "I think that he was playing a flute the morning I walked out of the Preserve. I remember following the sound of the music. The notes were crystal clear."

"He was playing a flute at dawn?"

"A lot of the locals keep odd hours."

He thought about that. It was true that the residents of Rainshadow were an odd bunch, but something told him that the business with the flute was important.

"One thing we've got in our favor," he said aloud, "is that all forms of communication are down. There's no way Lancaster can know what is going on here. He's stuck in that locked ward at the Chapman Clinic. If he's as deep in this thing as it looks, he must be frustrated and nervous as hell."

"That's a good thing?"

"Yes. Frustrated people tend to get reckless and make mistakes."

"What about this Cosgrove person?" Rachel asked.

"He is now occupying the number-two position on my priority list, right below Calvin Dillard."

"I thought I was Suspect Number One."

His hands tightened on the wheel. "Rachel, I've tried to explain—"

"Never mind. That's Calvin's cottage up ahead."

Chapter 21

IF THE ROAD HADN'T DEAD-ENDED AT THE COTTAGE, IT would have been easy to miss Calvin Dillard's house in the thick fog. As it was, Harry caught only glimpses of the weather-beaten cabin floating in and out of the gray mist.

He shut down the SUV's flash-rock engine, raised his senses a little, and studied the old place. The windows were dark. An ancient pickup truck sat in the weedy drive. He could feel the crackle of psi that leaked out of the nearby Preserve.

"Dillard does live very close to the fence," he said.

"Yes." Rachel grabbed her somewhat battered leather jacket, cracked open the door, and started to get out of the vehicle. Darwina bounded up onto her shoulder and hunkered down with Amberella.

Harry noticed that the dust bunny was not chortling

in her usual enthusiastic way. She had all four eyes open. Probably picking up on Rachel's tension, he thought. Or maybe it was the hot psi swirling out of the Preserve. Or maybe something else.

"Hang on," he said quietly. "I think we need a plan."

Rachel was half in and half out of the front seat. The toe of one boot was on the ground. She turned back to look at him.

"What is there to plan?" she said. "I thought we were just going to ask Calvin a few questions."

"I'm all for questioning him. It was my idea, remember?"

"Your point?"

He considered his point while he slipped the knife out of the ankle sheath and walked around the front of the SUV to join her. He stood for a moment, looking toward the invisible boundary that marked the outer edge of the Preserve. The woods were cloaked in fog, but he could feel the fence and something else, some nameless, formless, impossible-to-describe darkness.

"Something doesn't feel right here," he said.

"Things never feel normal this close to the fence." She started toward the front door of the cottage. "Questioning Calvin is going to be a delicate process. He's very touchy about his privacy. You'd better let me handle it."

"He's all yours."

Harry quartered the fog-drenched landscape one last time, searching for whatever it was that had stirred his intuition. There was nothing to see in the heavy mist, but he couldn't shake the ominous sensation. He held the knife out of sight, alongside his leg.

He thought he'd been slick about the move, but Rachel must have sensed it. She turned to look at him over her shoulder. Her eyes narrowed at the sight of the weapon.

"What is that thing?" she asked.

"It's a knife."

"It doesn't look like a knife. It looks like some sort of medallion."

"Trust me, it's a knife."

Rachel looked dubious. "I've never seen a knife like that."

"It came out of one of the company labs."

"Which company?"

"Sebastian, Inc."

"Well, you won't need that with Calvin. He's harmless, I promise."

"I believe you," Harry said. But he did not sheathe the knife.

Rachel turned back to the door and rapped against it, sharply. Harry did not hear any footsteps on the other side.

Darwina muttered to herself and kept watch with all four eyes as if expecting a predator larger than herself to appear at any moment.

"I don't understand it," Rachel said. She glanced at her watch, winced when she remembered that it had stopped, and eyed the gathering fog. "Calvin's truck is here. He must be home. I wonder if anyone came out to check on him this morning after the storm. Maybe he was injured and can't make it to the door. There was all that lightning last night and this place is so close to the Preserve—"

"I'll take a look," Harry said.

She glanced at him, clearly worried now. He edged her gently but firmly out of the way. He wrapped one hand around the doorknob and opened the door.

Seething currents of dark energy wafted through the opening. Not fresh, he thought, but probably not more than a few hours old. He did not need Darwina's low growl of warning to know that whatever had happened inside the cottage had been of a violent nature. He glanced at the dust bunny. She seemed to be focused on the entrance but she had not gone into full hunting mode.

"Something's wrong, isn't it?" Rachel asked quietly.

"Yes." Harry moved into the shadowed front room of the cottage. "Feels like there was a struggle, but the place is empty now."

"A struggle? Is Calvin—"

"Not dead," Harry said. He moved into the front room. There were muddy boot prints on the floor. "At least he wasn't killed here."

She walked into the cabin. "You're sure?"

"Yes," he said. "I'm sure."

She stopped just inside the room and gave a small cry of anguish. "Dear heaven."

She took in the mute evidence of the struggle that had taken place. A chair was overturned. Pieces of a shattered lamp were strewn across the bare wooden floor. Several aging copies of the *Journal of Marine Biology* were scattered across the floor.

"Someone attacked Calvin," Rachel whispered. "Why would anyone do that?"

"I don't know," Harry said.

"Maybe he *is* dead. Maybe his body is in the bedroom or the kitchen or—"

"No." He put some steel into the word. "I don't know if he's alive or dead but I can tell you that no one was murdered in this cottage."

She eyed him uncertainly. "You can feel that kind of thing?"

He stopped in the middle of the small space and jacked up his senses another notch. "It's an aspect of my talent. I blame my family gene pool. Had a couple of ancestors back on Earth who possessed similar abilities and then there was good old Harry One."

"The pirate?"

"Yes." He did a quick check of the small kitchen.

"And here I thought my sensitivity had a serious downside."

"It does." He glanced back at her as he made his way down a short hall to the bedroom. "I'd say that when it comes to unpleasant talents, being able to see the monsters in our midst ranks right up there with a talent for picking up the psi-residue of violence and murder. But at least your talent has a major upside."

"What?"

"The ability to heal. All I can do is deliver more violence."

She watched him with somber eyes. "So you hunt the monsters."

"It's about all a talent like mine is good for."

"Don't knock it. There's an old saying, one fights fire with fire."

He looked at her again, surprised. "Somehow that doesn't sound very HE."

"Actually it is very HE. People outside the Community have so many—"

"Misconceptions. Yes, you've made that clear."

He took a quick look around the bedroom. The bed was neatly made. An old harmonica sat on the nearby table. A guitar hung on the wall. There was no sign of a disturbance in the small space. Calvin had almost certainly been in the front room when he was taken.

He started back along the hall, pausing to check the tiny bathroom. He heard Rachel speak to Darwina.

"What did you find?" Rachel asked. "Can I see it?"

He arrived in the doorway in time to see Rachel crouched down in front of Darwina. The dust bunny was bouncing up and down excitedly. She still clutched her Amberella doll but she had a crystal cylinder about six inches long in one of her other paws. She graciously gave the cylinder to Rachel and fluttered off to explore the territory beneath the desk.

Rachel got to her feet and studied the gleaming object in her hand.

"What have you got there?" Harry said. "Looks like a miniature flute."

"Yes." She stared at the flute, comprehension heating her eyes.

"More memories?" he asked quietly.

"I remember this flute or one just like it. Calvin wasn't playing it that morning. I was. I brought it with me out of the Preserve. In fact, I used it to find my way out."

"Are you sure?"

"Yes. Listen."

She raised the flute to her lips and blew gently. He felt energy shivering in the atmosphere and knew that she had used some psi to rez the flute.

A delicate note, icy cold and clear as crystal sounded in the small space. It seemed to hang there for a few seconds before it faded. Rachel lowered the flute.

"This was how I navigated the Preserve," she whispered. "How could I forget something like that?"

"Probably because someone helped you forget," Harry said. "Let me see that thing."

She handed it to him without a word. He took it and turned it over in his hand. The design was graceful, almost ethereal, but the crystal flute did not seem at all fragile. There was something ever so slightly off about the feel of the instrument in his fingers, however, as if it had been fashioned for a hand that was not quite human.

"Alien technology," he said quietly.

Rachel's eyes widened. "Yes, of course. That explains a lot. But where did I get it and how did I know how to use it to make my way out of the Preserve?"

"We seem to be piling up more questions than answers."

"What do you think happened here? Where is Calvin?"

"I don't know where Calvin Dillard is," Harry said. "But it's clear that someone took him."

Rachel swung around to stare at him, horrified. "You mean he was kidnapped."

"That's what it looks like."

"But that makes no sense," Rachel said.

Harry hunkered down and jacked up his talent to study the muddy boot prints on the floor of the living room. Darwina scampered toward him to see if he was about to introduce some new game. Together they examined the eddies of hot psi that swirled in the atmosphere around the prints.

"Whoever they are, they came out of the Preserve," Harry said. He rose and went into the kitchen. He opened the back door and looked at the glowing tracks. The fog was so thick he could not see the ground, but the paranormal energy of the tracks glowed in the mist. "They left that way, too, taking their prisoner with them."

Rachel came to join him. She studied the thickening mist. "Why would they take Calvin?"

"I don't have the answer to that but I think it's safe to say that someone did not want me to talk to him."

"Dear heaven," Rachel whispered. "It's because of me."

"I agree there's probably a connection." Harry closed the door and went back into the living room. He opened a drawer in the desk and saw a heap of sheet music. "But why would someone want to kidnap him just because he saw you walk out of the Preserve and gave you a lift home?"

There was a short silence behind him. He looked at Rachel. She was gazing fixedly at the little flute. She raised her head. Her eyes were haunted.

"Maybe it wasn't a coincidence that I emerged from the Preserve here at Calvin's place," she said.

"You think the flute was somehow tuned to this location?" He glanced at the crystal device. "That almost makes sense. But if it's true, it means than Calvin Dillard is involved in this thing up to his neck."

"I don't pretend to understand how or why—my memories are still very foggy—but my intuition tells me that Calvin saved me that night I disappeared into the Preserve. Now he's in trouble. We have to find him."

Chapter 22

"DO YOU REALLY THINK YOU CAN TRACK THE KIDNAPPERS into the Preserve?" Rachel asked.

"Yes," Harry said. "I've done my share of search-and-rescue work inside the fence. The prints are fairly fresh, not more than a few hours old. I should be able to follow them."

They were standing at the rear of the SUV. Harry had the cargo bay door open, and Rachel watched him select items from the emergency kit to go into his daypack. She did not need to view his aura to sense the energy of the hunter whispering in the atmosphere around him.

Darwina was perched on the top of the open door. She burbled encouragingly as if urging Harry to hurry up so that they could get on with whatever adventure he had planned.

"I'm going with you," Rachel said, just to make sure Harry understood.

"Yes," he said. He did not look up from the task of filling the daypack.

"Wow," Rachel said. "You mean you're not going to argue with me about this?"

"Nope."

"Okay, that's good," Rachel said. "Sure glad I wore my leather boots and jacket again today. But can I ask why you're being so reasonable?"

"I don't think you'll be safe if I leave you behind. Whoever got Calvin will probably go after you next. All things considered, you're better off with me."

She took a breath. "Your logic is a little scary and I'm not sure it's solid. Why would whoever took Calvin come after me now? He's more likely to concentrate on trying to kill you. Maybe he has concluded that will be easier to do if he lures you into the Preserve. A lot of people have disappeared inside without a trace."

"I don't have all the answers, Rachel. I'm going with my gut here." Harry zipped up the pack, slung it over one shoulder, and reached up to take Darwina off her perch. She scrambled down onto his shoulder, chortling and waving her Amberella doll.

"Any other reasons for not leaving me behind?" Rachel asked, her voice a little too neutral.

"Yes." He closed the rear door and looked toward the fog-drenched forest. "I sensed almost from the start of this thing that you're the key. Until I find out exactly what lock you can open, I'm not letting you out of my sight."

She winced. "Always nice to feel needed."

His eyes heated a little. "I need you, Rachel. Don't ever doubt that. Ready?"

She flushed and took a deep breath to fortify herself for the senses-rattling job of getting through the psi-fence.

"As ready as I'll ever be," she said.

Harry reached out and took her hand. His fingers closed tightly around hers. "I know you can get through the fence on your own, but it will be easier for you if we have physical contact."

She glanced down at their linked hands. "Can you get anyone in and out this way?"

"Yes, but it's easier taking a strong sensitive through. High-rez talents seem to have some immunity."

"Whoever grabbed Calvin seems to be able to come and go fairly easily from the looks of it."

"Yes," Harry said. "Which raises a lot of interesting questions."

They trekked through the fog toward the invisible fence. Darwina mumbled excitedly. Rachel felt the first ghostly thrills of psi and intuitively heightened her senses in response.

"What if I go blank again?" she asked quietly.

"You won't."

"You sound very certain."

"I am certain. Your amnesia last time was deliberately induced by someone. Whoever it was won't be able to pull that trick again."

She smiled. "Because you've got my back this time."

"Right," Harry said. "Easiest way to go through is with your senses kicked up. Counteracts the force field."

She had done this before, Rachel reminded herself, but the experience of crashing through the psi-fence was never quite the same each time. The unpredictability factor had no doubt been deliberately engineered into the currents of energy that guarded the preserve. But the result was that she could not entirely fortify and prepare her mind, body, and senses for the coming assault.

She summoned up one of the Principles and mumbled it aloud. "Perfection in psychic harmony, as in all else, is not the goal."

"What?" Harry said.

He spoke absently, his full attention on the task of guiding her toward the fence line across the uneven, tree-studded ground.

"Nothing." She tightened her grip on his hand. "Just an old HE saying."

Harry spared her a brief, frowning glance. "I thought the HE philosophy was all about achieving harmony in all things."

"That's another misconception of the philosophy. According to the Principles, perfect harmony would set up a closed-loop system that would make it impossible to adapt to changes in the environment. It would be a recipe for extinction, first of the individual spirit, then of a community, and ultimately of a species."

"Because a true closed-loop system would, in effect, be a machine and all machines are ultimately doomed to fail."

She smiled. "That's very good, Sebastian. What philosophical school are you quoting?"

"The school of common sense."

"An excellent teacher."

She stopped talking then, because she could hear ghosts murmuring in the fog.

Chapter 23

THE WARNINGS OF THE SPECTERS GREW LOUDER AND more urgent. Rachel knew they were auditory hallucinations, but that did not lessen the impact on her nerves. She flinched and intuitively kicked up her senses. The voices faded but she knew they would return.

"It helps to use your talent to deflect some of the fence energy," Harry advised.

"I figured that much out for myself. I told you, I've done this once or twice."

"You and Slade and Charlotte and a couple of kids," Harry said. He did not sound pleased. "No way to know who else has been able to get through the fence lately. So much for the last round of engineering from the Foundation labs."

The voices in the fog got louder and more anguished. Frissons of prickly energy flashed through Rachel. She

knew the sensations would grow stronger and more disturbing until everything inside her would start screaming for her to turn back.

Here there be monsters.

The first vision coalesced in the mist, a shambling
figure summoned up from the depths of one of her own
dark dreams.

"You okay?" Harry asked.

"Yes." She spoke through clenched teeth. "Thought
you said this was going to be easier if I went through with
you."

"Turns out it's not the usual cakewalk for me, either.
This heat inside the Preserve is starting to oscillate with
the fence wavelengths. Not good."

The hallucinations became more realistic and more
horribly detailed. A demonic figure came toward Rachel
through the fog. Its face was a cross between a snake
and a spider. The creature reached for her with a clawed
hand. She pulled harder on her talent. *It's not real.*

The image faded, but other terrible creatures with tentacles and glowing eyes took its place. *Just fragments
from my dreams,* she thought. Whirling storms of energy
threatened to sear her senses. There were disturbing physical sensations as well—hot and cold prickles of panic
shivered through her, triggering a fight-or-flight reaction
that was hard to suppress.

"Interesting," Harry said.

"What's that mean?" Rachel gritted.

"I think that in addition to the energy of the fence, the
fog is acting as an additional barrier."

"Yes." Rachel waved a hand in a futile effort to clear some of the mist. The energy of the fog sent icy shivers through her hand and up her arm. "If it gets any denser we won't be able to see a thing once we're inside. What in the world is going on here?"

"I don't know but it doesn't take a para-engineer to figure out that if the oscillating frequencies get too powerful, things could get a hell of a lot more complicated."

The banshee wailing grew stronger and more unnerving, doomed souls already lost in the fog warning others not to come any closer. Rachel wanted to cover her ears but she knew that wouldn't do any good. The nerve-shattering cries were coming from the paranormal end of the spectrum, not the normal section.

The only one who was unfazed by the frightening energy was Darwina. Evidently thrilled with the new adventure, she chortled and bounded down to the ground. Rachel caught a glimpse of her furry little body and the sparkle of the tiny crystals sewn onto Amberella's gown, and then dust bunny and doll vanished into the mist.

"She'll be okay," Harry said.

"I know. I'm concerned about us. What did you mean when you said things could get more complicated?"

"I'm no engineer or scientist, but because of the nature of my work I've spent a lot of time in tech labs. You hear things. In theory, there's a possibility that if the fence energy becomes too violent, it might become impassable altogether. Worst-case scenario is that no one would be able to get through to stop whatever is happening inside, assuming we can figure out what is happening."

Neither of them spoke for a time after that. Rachel didn't know why Harry stopped talking but she abandoned the attempt at conversation because it required all of her energy, concentration, and willpower just to put one foot in front of the other. Even with Harry's hand clamped around her own, it was all she could do to keep moving forward. The disorienting effects of the seething currents of psi were definitely being exacerbated by the unnatural fog. The only way she could be sure that they were still heading into the Preserve was because with every inch gained, there was additional pressure on her senses to turn around and flee in the opposite direction.

She knew that it took only a few minutes to get through the unnerving barrier but, like a nightmare, the transit seemed endless.

And then, between one footstep and the next, it was over. They were through the fence and inside the uncharted territory of the Preserve. Rachel was surprised to note that the fog was not so dense now. The thick foliage was illuminated with a weak efflorescence. She knew from previous experience that the paranormal radiance infused into the plants and trees would grow stronger and more perceptible as night fell.

Currents of psi still swirled in the atmosphere, but the dreadful hallucinations and the ghostly cries were gone, along with the sense of panic. The relief was overwhelming. Rachel drew the first deep breath she had taken in several minutes and surveyed her surroundings. It was warm, she thought, and not all the heat was from the normal end of the spectrum.

"You were right," she said. "This place actually is getting hotter."

"I told you, if I can't troubleshoot and fix the problem, I'm going to have no choice but to order an evacuation of the island."

"And I warned you, the order won't be very effective. If the Foundation ordered an evacuation without some pretty convincing proof of impending disaster, I think most people here would figure it was a diabolical plot."

"What the hell kind of plot would involve evacuating the island?" Harry asked.

"The assumption would be that something extremely valuable—say a mine of rare amber or some unusual Alien ruins—had been discovered inside the Preserve. The good citizens of Shadow Bay would leap to the conclusion that they were being forced out of their homes so that the Sebastian family business empire could claim the discovery."

"Not to get technical, but my family already owns the Preserve," Harry said dryly. "If there is anything of value here, we've got a rock-solid legal claim to it."

"Doesn't mean it would be any easier to force the citizens of Shadow Bay off the island."

"I'm well aware of that."

Darwina appeared, scurrying out from a small jungle of ferns that were luminous with psi. She waved Amberella, bounced up and down, came to a stop at Rachel's feet, and chittered. Rachel scooped her up and plopped her on one shoulder.

Harry studied the eerie landscape. Rachel felt energy

swirl in the atmosphere and knew that he had raised his talent.

"The tracks go toward that stand of trees," he said. "They've got a few hours' start on us. We'd better get moving."

She fell into step beside him. "You know, maybe your theories about the Preserve are wrong. Maybe the Aliens didn't put up the first psi-fence because there was something dangerous inside. For all we know, Rainshadow was just a big theme park and the fence was installed to make sure no one got inside without buying a ticket."

"Do you really think this place was ever meant to be a fun, safe place for families?"

Rachel watched the ominous darkness pooling in the trees. It seemed to her that shadows moved within the shadows. The hair on the back of her neck stood on end. It was impossible to imagine little children laughing in such a place.

"No," she said. "I don't think the Preserve was designed as a family-oriented theme park. From everything we've learned about them, the Aliens found the atmosphere aboveground poisonous. If they had built a theme park, I think they would have put it down in the Underworld."

"I agree with you," Harry said.

"Maybe Rainshadow was a huge prison, a penal colony. The Aliens probably had criminals in their population, just like we do."

Harry glanced at her, a speculative expression in his eyes. "I hadn't considered that possibility. It's not a bad theory."

He skirted a small, dark pond, giving it a wide berth. Rachel glanced down at the black water. The surface of the little pool gleamed with a chilling luminescence. She shuddered and quickened her steps.

"Or maybe this place is an ancient Alien cemetery," she suggested. "That would account for the old legends of ghosts and specters."

"But not the fence."

"No," Rachel said. "It wouldn't account for the fence."

"Whatever the Aliens kept here in the Preserve, one thing is clear—they were worried as hell that it might be stolen."

"Or that it might escape," Rachel said.

Chapter 24

THEY GOT ONLY A FEW MINUTES' WARNING BEFORE THE storm struck. Rachel noticed that the light was fading more quickly than seemed right for the time of day, and in another moment it dawned on her what that meant.

"It's getting dark and the wind is picking up," she said.

"Another storm," Harry said. "No surprise. We need to find some shelter fast. Shouldn't be too hard. The island is honeycombed with small caves and caverns. I've been keeping an eye on our options. I think I see an option over there at the base of that outcropping that will work."

Thunder rumbled and a jagged bolt of energy flashed in the dark clouds. Darwina chortled, sounding excited by the prospect of getting caught in the storm.

"Everything's a game to you, isn't it?" Rachel said.

"Except when it's not," Harry said. "The dark side of dust bunny life, remember?"

"I'd rather not think about it."

Harry wrapped a hand around her wrist and hauled her forward through the mist. The terrain had changed dramatically in the past hour, the dense woods giving way to more tropical vegetation.

She ran with Harry across a small, iridescent clearing and into a jumble of boulders at the foot of a stony cliff.

"We lucked out," Harry said. "There's a cave. Thought we'd find one here."

She thought she heard the splash of water into a grotto pool somewhere close by, but it was difficult to be sure because the wind was growing louder. Another shaft of lightning briefly lit up the sky.

Harry drew her into an opening in the rocks an instant before the rain hit. She came to a halt beside him and gazed in wonder at the gently glowing interior of the cavern. The walls of stone were faintly luminous with a pale, violet-hued energy. A frisson of memory whispered through her.

Harry released her hand and slipped off the pack. Darwina bounded down to the floor of the cave and bustled about, investigating. Rachel wrapped her arms around herself and studied the glowing walls.

"This is weird," she said.

"No more weird than everything else inside the Preserve," Harry said. He gave the cave a quick, assessing survey. "The rock is some kind of psi-quartz. It probably got hot in response to the storm energy or maybe it just glows naturally."

"That's not the weird part," Rachel said. She looked at

him. "I remember a cave like this, one that was lit with heavy psi. I've been seeing flashes of it in my dreams along with that waterfall."

Harry stilled. "Was it this cave?"

"No." She heightened her senses a little and studied the soft luminescence. Memories came rushing back. "The energy was a lot more intense in the other cave. It came from a darker end of the spectrum. It dazzled my senses. There were massive stalactites and those other things, the ones that come up from the floor of a cave."

"Stalagmites?"

"Right. They were all made of crystals that glittered with ultralight."

"Any idea what you were doing inside the cave in the first place?"

She pulled harder on the fragments of dream memory but they were already fading. She sighed, annoyed with herself. "No."

"Were you lost inside the cave?"

"No, not exactly. That is, I knew how to get out. That wasn't the hard part."

"What was the hard part?"

"Figuring out how to escape without him seeing me."

It was the stunned silence from Harry that alerted her to the fact that she had said something very important. She replayed her own words in her head and caught her breath.

"Without who seeing you?" he asked gently.

"The monster."

Chapter 25

"ALL RIGHT," HARRY SAID. "TAKE IT EASY. YOUR MEMORY is coming back. Let it happen. Don't try to force it or you'll make yourself so tense you'll start blocking the dream again."

"Maybe it's the energy here in the cave," Rachel mused, looking around uneasily. "Maybe it's triggering my memories of that night."

"That's possible," Harry said, trying to sound like he knew what he was talking about—trying to sound positive.

Should have paid more attention in para-psych 101 back in college. But he'd known from his teens that his interest in psychology was limited to the study of the monsters, and that was not the sort of subject you brought up in the classroom. He had not needed a degree to do what he did best. Hunting the bad guys came naturally to him because he could not only track them, he could also think like them. *Always figured I was good at what I did because I had the same damn para-psych profile,* he thought. But Rachel had told him that was not true. And she'd continued to insist on that even after she'd had a close encounter with his dark side.

Now she needed a little positive reinforcement and some helpful understanding and all he could come up with was, *Don't try to force it.*

He pulled a bottle of water out of the pack and settled down on a convenient chunk of rock. Rachel was perched on another bench-sized boulder. She had Darwina in her lap and she absently stroked the dust bunny while she gazed fixedly at the rain falling steadily outside the cave. Her frustration and anxiety were palpable forces in the small space.

He drank some water from the bottle and tried to figure out how to handle the situation. He was no expert on amnesia. He was just the guy who got paid to keep the bad guys out of the Sebastian family's business and out of the Preserve.

"Was the cave bigger than this one?" he asked.

"Yes." She brightened a little. "Much bigger. But the way out was blocked by a crystal chamber. The only way into the chamber was through the waterfall. A second waterfall blocked the far side."

"You're talking about those frozen waterfalls that Jasper Gilbert is painting?"

"Yes, I'm sure of that much now," she said eagerly.

"Lots of caves here in the Preserve," Harry pointed

out. He tried to be gentle about it, but there was no getting around the facts.

She sighed. "I'm not being terribly helpful, am I?"

"We'll get there. Do you remember where you picked up the crystal flute?"

She frowned. "I think that Calvin gave it to me. He's the one who told me how to use it."

"So Dillard was in this big cavern with you?"

"Yes, at least part of the time."

"Is he the monster that chased you?"

"No," she said. "Someone else tried to stop me from escaping. But he couldn't follow me through the frozen waterfall."

"That's how you got out?"

"Yes." Rachel broke off on a long sigh. "Through the waterfall on the opposite side of the chamber. I ran along another tunnel and then I was outside in the night."

"With the flute."

"With the flute," she agreed. She reached into the daypack and took out the crystal flute. "I remember Calvin telling me to play it until I got out of the Preserve. He said that I was to listen carefully to the notes and that I should follow only the clear, pure ones. If the music seemed faint or off-key, it meant I was going in the wrong direction. I walked out of the Preserve playing this flute."

"And good old Calvin Dillard was waiting for you on the other side of the fence. Interesting."

Rachel glared at him. "I don't know what is going on here but I am very certain that Calvin is not the bad guy in this."

"Right." Harry recapped the water bottle.

"Are you always this suspicious?"

"Until proven otherwise, yes."

"I understand." She was quiet for a beat. "Harry, I have this feeling that I need to remember everything, and soon."

"You will," Harry said, going for what he hoped was a soothing tone. "Meanwhile, we've got a job to do."

"Find Calvin."

"When we do find him, we'll get a lot of the answers we need."

"I just hope we're not too late."

"If they had intended to kill him inside the Preserve, they would have done so by now," he said. "But we are following three sets of psi-prints. He's still alive."

SHE AWOKE SOMETIME LATER. THE DARKNESS AT THE mouth of the cave told her that it was still night. The rain continued to fall relentlessly. Harry sat at the entrance, his back braced against the cavern wall. In the shadowy ultralight she could see that he had one leg stretched out. His other leg was bent at a casual angle. He rested one arm on his knee. She knew he had not slept.

She pushed herself up on her elbows, wincing a little at the feel of the unyielding stone beneath the thin plastic emergency blanket. The blanket worked well enough when it came to shielding her from the damp, but it did nothing to soften the hard rock floor.

"Do you think it's necessary to keep watch?" she asked.

Harry turned his head to look at her. "Probably not. I doubt if anything is moving in this storm. I've been doing some thinking."

Rachel looked around. "Where's Darwina?"

"She took off a little while ago. She had the doll with her."

"Good grief. Why would she go out in this rain?"

"She didn't go outside." Harry angled his head toward the back of the cavern. "I think she went hunting inside this cave. There's no telling how far this network of caves and tunnels extends."

Rachel looked toward the rear of the cave. The walls narrowed swiftly, but the tunnel was wide enough for a dust bunny.

"I suppose she knows what she's doing," Rachel said.

"My guess is she does. What woke you? Another dream?"

"Yes." Rachel drew up her knees and hugged them, remembering the images. "Not one of the bad ones, though. I was using the flute to find my way out of the jungle."

"You said Dillard told you how to use the flute."

"Yes."

"Where was he when he instructed you? At his place?"

"No," she shook her head and looked around. "We were in a cavern like this one, only a hundred times brighter. He put the flute in my hand, told me how to use it, and then told me to run. That's what I did."

"Through the prehistoric sea where the monsters swam?"

"And through a waterfall of stone," she concluded. She groaned. "But that's all I've got for now."

Harry uncoiled to his feet and walked to where she sat hunched on the emergency blanket. He sank down beside her and cradled her against his shoulder.

"You'll have it all soon," he said.

"Yes, I think so. Harry?"

"Yeah?

"What if I don't like the truth when I finally recover my memories?"

"You're afraid that you'll find out that you've been wrong about Calvin Dillard?"

"Maybe. But there's a worst-case scenario."

He tightened his hold on her. "You're afraid you'll discover that maybe you're more involved in this mess than you realized? That maybe you bear some responsibility for what is happening here in the Preserve?"

"Yes."

"Doesn't matter."

She raised her head so quickly she almost collided with his jaw. He moved in the nick of time.

"What do you mean, it doesn't matter?" she demanded.

He turned her in his arms and caught her face between his hands. "Intent is what matters, at least as far as I'm concerned. Maybe we'll find out that you made a mistake or that someone suckered you into getting involved in something you should not have gotten yourself involved in. But one thing I know for sure, we will not discover that you deliberately set out to hurt anyone or do something illegal for the purpose of personal gain. Whatever your involvement in this thing, your intentions were honorable."

She tightened her fingers in his shirt. "You know this, how?"

His smile came and went in the shadows. "Maybe because I'm psychic?"

"Harry, I'm serious."

"So am I. Don't ever forget that, Rachel."

His mouth closed over hers, silencing any protest she might have made. A person could drive herself crazy worrying about the future, she thought. She had something very special right in front of her—a chance to lose herself in Harry's arms again. She would be a fool not to seize the moment.

She gave herself up to the embrace, longing and need twisting through her.

"Harry."

She gripped his shoulders tightly and opened her mouth to him. He eased her slowly onto her back and came down alongside her. Gently, deliberately, he opened her shirt and found her bare breasts. His palm was warm and firm and incredibly tender on her sensitive skin.

He kissed her throat, her ears, and then her nipples. She felt his hand glide downward over her stomach. He paused long enough to unfasten her trousers and tug the garment down to her ankles and off altogether. Her panties followed and then his hand was between her legs.

She lowered the zipper of his pants and he thrust into her waiting hand. He groaned when she encircled him.

He caressed her until she was full and tight and desperate; until she was pulling him to her, demanding that he give her what she craved.

And then he was inside her, filling her until she could not stand it any longer. She wrapped her arms around him and clung to him. He rode her until her release broke through her in throbbing waves that reached far out onto the spectrum.

He followed her over the edge, his climax powering through him. She opened her senses and watched his aura flare—not the graveyard-cold energy that he used to cloak himself in shadows and terrify his prey—but a hot, wild, masculine fire that resonated fiercely with the currents of her own aura.

"Rachel, Rachel, Rachel."

He said her name as if it were a charm to hold against the darkness.

Rachel heard the gentle, silvery music of her bracelet. The small crystals cast an ultralight rainbow against the wall of the cave.

Outside the storm raged on, but inside the energy felt good, Rachel thought. It felt right.

Chapter 26

SHE AWOKE TO THE REALIZATION THAT THE RAIN HAD stopped. The low light of another cloud-shrouded dawn illuminated the entrance of the cave. She sat up on the emergency blanket, wincing a little.

She looked around and discovered that she was alone. There was no sign of Darwina or Harry. She pushed herself to her feet and used her fingers to rake the hair out of her eyes.

The interior of the cave was still illuminated, but the glow was fainter now that the storm had subsided and morning, weak as it was, had arrived. She stretched and went to the entrance to search for Harry and Darwina.

There was no sign of Harry, but she saw Darwina perched on the edge of a grotto pool. Darwina waved the Amberella doll and chortled a greeting.

"Good morning to you, too," Rachel said. She crossed

the rough ground to the edge of the pool and took a closer look at Amberella. The doll had evidently taken a swim in the pool. The bright red hair and pretty gown were soaked.

"Good thing she's hollow inside," Rachel said. "At least she floats. What did you do? Throw her into the pool to see if she could swim?"

As if in answer, Darwina chittered gleefully, leaned precariously out over the edge of the pool, and dropped Amberella into the water. Rachel smiled when she saw the gently swirling currents of the pool carry the doll into a slow, graceful circle and then under the falls. The cascading water pushed the doll down out of sight, but she popped back to the surface a short time later and continued on her serene journey.

Darwina waited attentively, hind paws gripping the ledge, to grab the doll out of the water when she came back around.

"That looks like fun," Rachel said. She looked around. "Where's Harry? Did you toss him into the pool, too?"

"Over here," Harry said. He emerged from the darkness of the trees, walked across the clearing, and rinsed his hands in the grotto pool. "Ready for breakfast?"

"Starving. Where did you go?"

"I was making use of the amenities," he said.

She felt like an idiot. "Oh, yes. I need to do the same."

"Go ahead but don't wander off. Stay within visual range of the cave."

"Trust me, the last thing I want to do is get lost." She glanced at the pool. "Is the water safe to drink?"

"It's salt water, not fresh," Harry said over his shoulder. "I tried a sample earlier."

"Really? How did salt water get this far inland on the island?"

"That grotto pool must be linked to some of the flooded caves on the island."

She made her way toward a palm adorned with huge fan-shaped fronds that promised some privacy. When she had finished with her personal business, she went back out into the small clearing. She paused by the grotto pool to rinse her hands. She shook her fingers vigorously to dry them.

Amberella had almost completed another circuit of the pool.

When the doll glided out from under the waterfall, Darwina gripped the rocky rim with her hind paws and leaned forward, preparing to snatch the toy.

"Time for breakfast," Rachel said. She turned to head back to the cave. "Catch Amberella and we'll go chow down on some yummy energy bars."

Darwina chortled.

The chortle turned into a hissing growl.

Rachel spun around in time to see that Darwina had sleeked out into full hunting mode, her fur flat against her small body, all four eyes glowing. Her fangs were showing. Not a good sign, Rachel thought.

Amberella had vanished. The water started to ripple and churn.

Darwina growled furiously and leaped into the pool.

A long tentacle appeared. It was wrapped around Amber-ella. A second tentacle reached out for Darwina.

"Darwina, no," Rachel shouted. She raced toward the grotto pool. "Come back."

But it was too late. The tentacle snaked out and caught Darwina. The dust bunny screamed. That was the only way Rachel could describe the terrible, high-pitched sound Darwina made.

Rachel reached the edge of the pool. Terrified that the creature would drag Darwina under, she did the only thing she could think of. She grabbed one tentacle in both hands and hauled mightily in a desperate attempt to drag the water beast out of the pool and onto dry land.

"Harry!" she shouted.

The tentacle was slimy and so slippery Rachel was afraid she would not be able to hang on to it. But the crea-ture seemed intent on snagging her as well. Two of its writhing limbs coiled around her upper arms and the struggle became a tug-of-war. The beast was heavy and powerful, but it was trying to hold on to three different prizes, two of which were struggling mightily.

More of the creature was visible now. A bulbous body appeared. The dome-shaped head was covered with doz-ens of slender, bobbing stalks. Each stalk was topped with what looked like a tiny eye. The dancing eyes glowed with paranormal energy. And then Rachel saw the beak that was the thing's mouth.

She pulled hard, trying to use her weight as leverage, and wound up landing hard on her butt. The relentless

tug of the beast was strong. She was being dragged forward by inches. The heels of her boots gouged grooves
in the damp ground.

"Damn it, Harry, where are you?"

Darwina gnawed furiously on the tentacle that shack-
led her small body. Dark blood spurted. Evidently the
wound annoyed the beast and it flung its prey clear. Darwina sailed a short distance through the air and landed
with a soft thud. She bounced back to her six paws and
charged toward the nearest flailing tentacle.

The water beast was half out of the pool, clinging to
the rocks while it fought to hang on to Rachel. The myriad eyes jiggled wildly.

Rachel saw a small, silvery disc arc through the air
and slice effortlessly through one of the tentacles wrapped
around her arm. Dark blood gushed from the wound. The
beast jerked violently in response.

The severed tentacle fell to the ground near Rachel
and twitched wildly. An instant later, the other tentacle
unwound itself from her arm. She was free.

Evidently sensing that it had taken on more than it
could swallow, the water beast flung its remaining prey
aside. Amberella flew across the clearing, the jeweled
skirts of her Restoration Ball gown sparkling in the weak
daylight, and landed in some green foliage.

The creature started to scramble back into the pond,
but Harry got there first. He had a stout tree branch in
one hand and swung it like a baseball bat. The branch
connected with the bulbous body, knocking the bizarre
animal off the rocks and onto the ground.

Rachel watched, horrified, as the creature flopped about frantically, gills heaving, for what seemed forever before it grew weaker and went limp. The psi-light winked out of the bizarre eyes, and the unmistakable aura of death silenced the atmosphere.

"Monster," Rachel whispered. "Just like the ones I see in my dreams."

Chapter 27

HARRY DROPPED THE TREE BRANCH AND RETRIEVED THE disc-shaped knife. The adrenaline and psi were still heating his blood. He was going to have nightmares about this in the future, he decided. It had been a near thing.

He looked at Rachel. She watched him, dazed and maybe numb from the shock of battle. She was trying to catch her breath and steady her nerves.

"Are you all right?" he asked.

"Yes." She inhaled deeply. "Yes, I think so."

Darwina appeared from a clump of bushes. She was once again fully fluffed. She chortled in triumph, waved Amberella, and scurried across the clearing to show Rachel her prize.

"You know," Rachel said, "all things considered, it would have been easier to just buy you a new Amberella."

Harry crouched and used some damp grass to wipe

the black blood off the gleaming blade. He would clean it properly later. When he was finished, he pulsed a little energy into the disc. The razor-sharp cutting edges retracted into the medallion.

He sheathed the knife, straightened, and crossed quickly to where Rachel still sat on the ground. There was a lot of mud on her pants, and he knew she would be bruised where the tentacles had gripped her arm, but she looked unhurt.

He reached down. She took his hand and allowed him to pull her to her feet. She slapped some of the mud off her pants.

"I told my parents that Amberella was an excellent role model," she said.

"She's not the only kick-ass female in the vicinity," Harry said. "Is mud-wrestling with creatures from the Obsidian Lagoon a popular sport in the HE community?"

"Not that I recall." She brushed off her hands. "I see that knife of yours functions in a heavy psi environment. Most high-end technology doesn't."

"One of our labs is dedicated to producing useful gadgets that ghost hunters, Underworld exploration teams, and guys like me can carry into places where the fancy gadgets don't work."

"Is there a lot of money in that sort of thing?"

He smiled. "Oh, yeah."

"You've had some experience throwing that thing," she said neutrally.

"Yes."

She raised her brows. "You managed to sever one

tentacle without accidentally amputating my arm in the process. That's precision work."

"Practice, practice, practice."

A knowing look illuminated her eyes. "Your ability to handle that knife is linked to your talent, isn't it?"

"Yes."

They walked to where the dead water creature lay on the ground.

"What is that thing?" Rachel asked. "I've seen monsters like it in my dreams, the ones where I'm running through the prehistoric sea to escape the human monster."

Harry studied the dead creature. It looked smaller in death but no less weird.

"In the past two hundred years since the First Generation colonists arrived on Harmony we've barely begun to catalogue the flora and fauna of the planet, not to mention the underground rain forest," he said. "There's no telling what's waiting for us in the oceans."

"I know." Rachel's expression tightened into a troubled frown. "But this creature feels somehow wrong."

"It definitely qualifies as strange. Looks like some kind of cross between a decopus and a Siren-fish."

"All those eyes," Rachel said. "When the creature was alive, they were all lit up with psilike tiny lanterns."

"They aren't real eyes. As I recall, Siren-fish generate a tiny current of energy through those eyelike appendages. It's how they attract their prey."

"I know. I saw one once in an aquarium," she said. "But this isn't a Siren-fish and it's not a decopus, although it has characteristics of both species. This poor thing feels unnatural."

"That poor thing just tried to drag you down into the grotto pool and eat you."

"Yes, well, everything has to eat."

"Another HE saying?"

"Fact of life." Rachel looked at him. "There have always been tales of monsters and demons prowling the Preserve."

"Legends and myths but no hard evidence. And this thing wasn't prowling the Preserve, it was living in a flooded cave."

"You and others from the Foundation have spent more time, all told, inside the Preserve than anyone else and you've got records that go back to Harry One. Have there been any reports of severe mutations aside from the psi-infused flora?"

"As far as the experts know, there isn't a lot of wildlife in the Preserve. What there is of it seems normal enough and it comes and goes easily through the fence."

They both looked at Darwina. Aware that she was the object of their attention, she preened.

"Like dust bunnies," Rachel said.

"Like dust bunnies," Harry agreed. "Also plenty of standard-issue birds, insects, rodents, and other small animals."

"But nothing like this?"

"No," Harry said "Nothing like this." He looked at the dark woods that crowded the edge of the clearing. "But most of the Preserve is still unexplored and unmapped.

Same goes for the cave system. This place is like the deep ocean trenches as far as the biologists are concerned. Unknown territory."

"The question is, where did I encounter other beasts like this one?" Rachel asked. "I'm no expert on marine biology, but—"

She stopped and looked mutely at the dead creature.

"You're thinking what I'm thinking, aren't you?" Harry asked quietly. "You're not an expert on marine biology but you know someone who might be—Calvin Dillard."

Chapter 28

HARRY SAT ON ONE OF THE BENCH-WIDE BRANCHES OF AN Umbrella Tree, his legs hanging over the edge some fifteen feet off the ground. He studied the faintly glowing psi-prints below. The three sets of tracks disappeared into a cave that was faintly illuminated with psi.

"They went inside a couple of hours ago," Harry said. "The storm delayed them, just like it did us."

"Without the complications of the storm, this place would have been about half a day's hike from the perimeter fence," Rachel said.

She was perched on the branch beside him, her booted feet dangling over the side. Darwina crouched between them with Amberella. The dust bunny was fully fluffed, but all four eyes were open. She seemed to sense that this was not a game. Nothing like having a scary sea monster try to steal your doll to make you take the situation seriously, Harry thought.

He estimated that the massive canopy of the Umbrella Tree covered about two acres. The extensive network of wide branches—two and three feet across in many cases—was supported by sturdy pillars of aerial roots that had originally descended to the jungle floor in clusters. In time the root strands had grown together and taken hold in the ground, forming thick columns that sustained the tree and allowed it to spread farther.

Beneath the tree an entire ecosystem thrived—vast fairylands of mushrooms, veils of spectacular orchids, and miniature fern forests. All of it glowed with psi even though it was mid-morning. The dense ceiling of leaves overhead created a perpetual twilight that today was deepened by the cloud cover.

"It's true this cave is only about half a day's trek from the boundary," Harry said, "but only for someone who knows exactly where he's going—someone who can also navigate the Preserve. That's not a common talent."

"Obviously the people who kidnapped Calvin knew where they were going and were able to find their way," Rachel said. "Which probably means they've got one or more of those crystal flutes."

"They might also have someone like me with them, a hunter-talent who can track psi-prints."

He meditated briefly on the entrance of the cave. "We know that at least three people went in there—Calvin and the two guys who grabbed him. But I can make out another set of prints, too. Figure a total of at least four inside."

"But Calvin is a prisoner, so that means there are only three bad guys."

"Ever the optimist when it comes to human nature," Harry said. "It's touching."

Rachel ignored him. "You'd think there would be more people involved in whatever is going on down there."

"First, we don't know what is going on down there. Second, bringing in a lot of staff would be a hell of a lot easier said than done, not to mention very high-risk."

"What do you mean?"

"The job requirements for anyone working here are fairly strict. Among other things, you'd need people who can handle the heavy psi inside the Preserve. This place isn't nearly as accessible as the catacombs or the rain forest. Just getting people through the fence is a huge issue. Once inside, most folks get extremely disoriented very quickly."

"Unless they know how to use one of the flutes," she reminded him.

"Maybe," he conceded. "But navigation problems aside, there are other, pragmatic considerations."

"Like what?"

"Feeding your crew comes to mind."

"Feeding them?"

"Living off the land here in Rainshadow is doable but not very practical. A large group of people would need to spend the majority of their time hunting and foraging in order to survive. Realistically, if you wanted to station even a small crowd here, you'd have to find a way to bring in provisions."

"Ah, got it. That wouldn't work well over time. Sooner or later someone in town would be bound to notice."

"Rainshadow is a natural fortress with only one little harbor and a few small pocket beaches. Anyone who tried to purchase a serious quantity of supplies in town on a regular basis would draw attention. Same goes for trying to bring stuff in by boat."

Rachel gave him a look that was equal parts amusement and admiration. "You've really thought this through, haven't you?"

"It's what I do. I can think like the bad—"

She held up one hand. "Don't say it. You don't think like the bad guys, you think strategically. That's different."

He smiled. "If you say so. I'm going to take a look inside that cave while you wait here with Darwina."

Rachel pondered that briefly and shook her head. "No, I need to go with you."

"I'll just do a quick recon," he said. "I'll be back in a few minutes."

"You're going to need me."

She sounded very serious. Energy whispered in the atmosphere. When he raised his talent, he saw that her eyes were a little hot. He knew without being told that more of her memories were coming back.

"Why am I going to need you?" he asked.

"Because I've been inside that cave." She did not take her eyes off the entrance. "Or one very much like it."

"What do you remember?"

"The color of the ultralight that is illuminating the entrance, among other things. The night I disappeared into the Preserve I woke up inside a cavern lit with that same kind of bronzy-gold energy. What's more, I'm almost certain now that the creatures with the tentacles are inside that cave."

"But they would be in water, not in a cave."

"They're in there, Harry. I don't know how that's possible, but they are inside that cave, I promise you."

The charms on Rachel's bracelet chimed softly.

"All right, I believe you," he said. "But that's not a good reason for taking you inside."

"How about this reason? I may be the only one who can get you out."

He contemplated the entrance of the cave. "You're thinking about that frozen waterfall of rainstone, aren't you?"

"It's important."

"You were running from someone when you went through the waterfall. Do you remember what he looked like?"

"No. I just remember Calvin waking me up and putting the flute in my hand."

"Calvin had to wake you up?"

She touched one of the stones of her bracelet, seemingly unaware of the small action. He felt energy whisper in the atmosphere.

"Yes," she said. "I'm sure of that much now. I need to go in there with you, Harry."

*   *   *

THERE WERE NO UNPLEASANT SURPRISES WAITING INSIDE
the entrance of the glowing cavern. No traps closed. No
nets dropped. No guards appeared.

Harry glanced up, automatically checking for cam-
eras even though he didn't expect to see any. There were
none. High-tech audio and visual monitoring devices
were as useless in a heavy psi environment as most other
hardware and software.

The radiance from the walls cast an eerie glow on the
scene. But it was the colonnade of massive, glittering stalactites that hung from the ceiling and the wonderland of
sparkling stalagmites rising from the floor that dazzled
the senses. The crystal formations glowed like great jewels, creating a paranormal rainbow composed of ultralight colors.

"This is incredible," Rachel whispered.

"Do you remember this cave?" he asked.

"No," she said.

Darwina was hunkered down on Rachel's shoulder,
partially sleeked out, all four eyes open. The little beast
was not treating this venture as a game—she was ready
to hunt. *Like me,* Harry thought. *We were both born for
this. What the hell does Rachel see in either of us?* At
least Darwina had the virtue of being totally cute when
she was not in attack mode.

He studied the shadowy psi-prints on the floor of the
cave.

"They came this way," he said. He kept his voice low

and put his mouth very close to Rachel's ear. "There are a lot of other prints but they're too old and murky to make out clearly. I'd say people have been coming and going through here for quite a while."

The whispering was probably unnecessary. The heavy energy in the vicinity had a dampening, distorting effect on sound waves, so voices could not carry far, but there was no point taking chances. A strong hunter-talent or someone with some version of an audio-clairvoyant sensitivity might be able to hear a pair of intruders.

They followed the three sets of tracks deeper, weaving a path through the glittering crystal formations. When they rounded one corner, the tunnel through which they were moving became abruptly regular in shape; the rocky surface of the floor, roof, and walls smoothed as if they had been bored by a huge machine, one that could function in a paranormal environment.

"Damn," he said very softly. "This explains a few things."

He heard Rachel's sharp intake of breath and knew she had been hit with the same realization.

"This tunnel sure wasn't constructed by humans," she said. "Looks like you were right about the Preserve. The Aliens were here first."

"But that still leaves the big question unanswered. What the hell were they guarding?"

"One thing at a time. First we find Calvin."

He glanced at her. "I'm not the only one who knows how to set priorities."

Her lips parted on a retort, but he raised one hand

slightly to signal silence. She closed her mouth very quickly. Then she went still, her eyes widening a little. He knew that she had felt the subtle shift in the atmosphere. The hair on the back of his neck stirred, and his intuition went to high-alert status. Even Darwina seemed to get the message. She sleeked out fully but she did not growl.

Harry urged Rachel to the side of the cave. She flattened herself against the luminous rock, making as small a target of herself as possible. Evidently sensing that the action was going to be with Harry, Darwina gave Amberella to Rachel and then bounded up onto his shoulder.

He felt the tiny claws of her two hind paws sink into the leather of his jacket. When this was over, he thought, the jacket was going to have a few more souvenir scratches.

He motioned Rachel to stay put. She nodded once to show she had received the message. She looked anxious, but he knew she was a lot more worried about him than she was about her own safety.

He rezzed a little energy into the medallion and caught the frequency that gave him control of the blade. The deadly, serrated edges appeared.

He glanced back once and knew from the stubbornly determined expression on Rachel's face that she had caught some of the backwash of his talent. But she angled her chin, letting him know that she was okay.

Cloaked in darkness, he and Darwina were not truly invisible, but he knew that to the normal eye they would appear only as shadows. The question was whether one or more of the kidnappers possessed some form of paranormal vision. A strong hunter-talent would be able to detect them. As a precaution he hugged the wall when he turned into the branching cave.

He found himself at the entrance to a crystal tunnel through a sea that glowed with paranormal energy. The psi-hot ocean surrounded the transparent tube in which he stood.

Monsters swam through the radiant water. Tentacles writhed, iridescent scales glistened, oddly shaped fins rippled lazily in the currents. And everywhere, cold, pitiless eyes stared at him through the transparent walls of the tunnel.

The creatures came in a myriad of varieties, many so bizarre-looking that it would have been easy to believe that they had been transported from another world. *And in a sense, they had,* he thought. That other world comprised the unknown depths of Harmony's oceans.

This was the prehistoric sea of Rachel's nightmares. In reality, it was a vast aquarium, one that could only have been bioengineered by the Aliens.

Two men entered the tube from the opposite end. Harry knew from the way they moved that they were both hunter-talents. He could also see that they were young, about the same age as Pritchard and McClain.

Darwina rumbled a low warning and tensed, ready to spring. Harry raised a hand and touched her, trying to convey a silent message not to blow their cover. She trembled and bared her teeth but she stayed on his shoulder.

The two hunters appeared oblivious to the sea monsters on the other side of the crystal tunnel. They were talking in low, urgent tones. There was a tension in their manner that made it plain they were not happy campers. As they moved closer Harry caught snippets of the conversation.

". . . He's flat-out crazy, I tell you. This lab is too damn dangerous. The money's good, but I've had it with this job. I want off this damned island."

"Forget it. You saw what happened to Tom when he tried to leave. He ended up as fish food. The bastard killed him."

"All the more reason for us to get out of here while we can."

"How the hell do you think you're going to do that? It's not like he'll let us get anywhere near one of the flutes. No way to make it out of the Preserve without one."

"Then we hold a knife to the SOB's throat and make him get us out of here."

"You can't get close to him as long as he's got that Alien gadget."

The pair drew closer to where Harry waited.

"Tom's mistake was that he got caught trying to steal a flute," the first man said. "He tried to go it alone. But if you and I work together—"

The man stopped in midsentence. He stared hard at the wall. "Do you see that?"

"What?"

"Something over there near the wall."

The second man tensed and swung around, searching for the source of the threat. "I don't see anything."

"Shadows. There shouldn't be any shadows there."

Harry moved forward, pushing the shock wave of his talent ahead.

"There's something here," the first man said. His voice rose in fear. "Can't you feel it?"

"Shit," the second man looked around. The heat of panic burned in the atmosphere around him. "What's going on? Maybe one of the monsters got out of a tank in the lab room."

"None of those weird things can live long out of water."

"How do we know what they can do? You heard the doc. He says he hasn't even begun to figure out the secrets in this lab."

"There's something here," the first man screamed.

He whirled and started to run back toward the far end of the tunnel. Harry jacked up his talent and touched the kid on the back of his neck. His mouth opened on a silent cry of horror. He dropped, unconscious, to the floor.

"Gil?" The second man stared at his companion. "*Gil*, get up."

Harry tapped him on the shoulder and pulsed a little more energy.

The young man collapsed without even a groan.

Harry dropped the shadow cloak. He had burned a lot of energy in the past few minutes and the ambient psi in the aquarium chamber was playing havoc with his control. He needed to conserve his talent.

Darwina bounced enthusiastically and started to chortle.

The chortle ended in a warning rumble. Darwina

sleeked. Her claws tightened on Harry's shoulder as she prepared to spring.

Harry spun around and saw Rachel walk slowly into the crystal tunnel. She was not alone. A rumpled, middle-aged man with shaggy gray hair and an unkempt beard was with her. He wore a pair of black-framed glasses.

A second man followed behind Rachel and her companion. He kept what was either a respectful or very cautious few steps to the rear. Harry was pretty sure it was caution that made the newcomer keep some distance between himself and the other two.

"Control your silly pet and your boyfriend, Rachel," he said. "Or I'll kill them both, starting with Sebastian. He's the bigger target."

"Darwina, run," Rachel said quietly. "Hide with Amberella."

Darwina seemed to get the message. She vaulted off Harry's shoulder and dashed away toward the far end of the aquarium chamber.

Harry looked at the rumpled man with the glasses. "Calvin Dillard?"

"I'm sorry about this," Calvin said. He shook his head in a forlorn, world-weary manner. "I never meant for things to end this way."

"You never had any say at all in how this would end," the second man said.

"Who the hell are you?" Harry asked.

Rachel wrinkled her nose. "His name is Nathan Grant. He's on the staff at the Reflections retreat operation out at the old lake lodge. Turns out he was the human monster I was trying to remember. It was his energy I picked up on the cup at the tea-tasting event."

"I knew you were going to be trouble, Sebastian," Grant said. "But I must admit, I'm surprised that you got this far, this fast. How did you manage to figure out that Rachel was the key?"

"I knew that as soon as I heard about her little fugue episode and the convenient amnesia that followed it," Harry said.

"I was his chief suspect," Rachel said grimly.

"I just knew that you were the key to the lock that had to be opened," Harry said.

"I was suspect number one on your list, admit it."

"Only at the beginning," Harry said, trying to project a calming tone. He really did not have time for this.

But Rachel was not in a mood to be placated. "That first night you wound up on my doorstep in the middle of the storm—"

"I don't have time for this," Grant snarled.

"My thoughts exactly," Harry said.

"How did you get her to recover her memories?" Grant demanded. "The amnesia was for real. She didn't fake it. That was obvious when she failed to connect Dillard to what happened to her."

Chapter 29

FURY FLASHED THROUGH RACHEL. SHE'D HAD ENOUGH. Harry and Nathan were talking about her as if she wasn't even there.

"My memory has been coming back for the past few weeks," she announced. "What's more, the memories of those two kids you sent to firebomb the old gatekeeper's cabin would have eventually returned as well. Whatever you used to implant the hypnotic suggestions is not one hundred percent effective, not by a long shot."

Nathan shrugged. "Dillard's amnesia drug works well enough. But the good news is that this little device works even better. Just ask the doc. He saw me demonstrate it."

Harry glanced at the oddly shaped weapon. Then he quirked a brow at Calvin.

"That right, Doctor?"

"I'm afraid so," Calvin said. "He used it to murder

one of the young guards a while back. He found out the kid was planning to try to get away from this place."

Rachel tightened her hands into fists at her side. Her charms clashed lightly, ominously, but none of the men appeared to notice. She looked at Nathan.

"I remember everything now," she said. "I was riding my bike home to my cottage that afternoon. I saw you standing at the side of the road next to your car. It looked as if you were having car trouble. I asked if you wanted me to go back to town to alert Brett at the service station. You said thanks, that you had already called him and then you aimed that device at me."

Nathan glanced briefly at the black weapon. "On the lowest setting, it induces unconsciousness. Take it higher and it kills. You have to have a sufficient amount of talent to rez it, but I've got more than enough."

"When I woke up, I was in this place," Rachel said.

"But you managed to escape," Nathan said. "I know you had some help from Dillard, here, but we won't go into that now. What fascinated me was the manner in which you got out of the aquarium complex. I picked you up initially because—"

"You mean you kidnapped her," Harry said.

"Semantics," Nathan said.

"And a little matter of twenty-five years to life in prison," Rachel said. "Why am I so important to you?"

Calvin shook his head. "Don't you understand, Rachel? The only reason you and I are still alive is because he needs both of us. He'll kill all of us when this is over."

Harry watched Nathan with the unblinking gaze of a predator waiting to strike. "Why do you need them?"

"At this point, Dillard is the only one who can tune the navigational flutes," Nathan said. "The instruments are necessary to chart a course through the heavy psi of the Preserve. As for Rachel, I've got a little problem with some crystal. I think she can resolve it for me."

"The rainstone waterfall," Rachel said. "You want me to unfreeze it for you so that you can get into that crystal chamber."

"What's inside the chamber?" Harry asked.

"An incredible trove of Alien artifacts," Calvin said. "Most of it appears to be of a technological nature."

Harry whistled softly. "Alien technology. Worth a fortune on the black market."

"You are so bloody right," Nathan said. "But I can't get at the artifacts because of the damn rainstone."

"How did you know I could work rainstone?" Rachel asked.

Calvin exhaled heavily. "That's my fault, too. I made the mistake of telling him that I had watched you energize some of the small rainstones that the kids found on the island."

"It wasn't proof that you could open the chamber, but I thought it was worth running a test," Nathan said. "That's why I brought you here. But the next thing I knew, you were awake and running away through this chamber, straight toward the crystal vault that contains the artifacts. I saw you go through the solid rainstone as if it were liquid. You did it again on the other side of the vault."

Calvin looked at Rachel. "He chased you that night. So did the guards. But they were too late. The waterfalls at both ends of the vault froze solid right after you went through them. And then you were gone."

"I was pissed, to say the least," Nathan said. "But I figured you'd never survive the Preserve. Thought I'd have to waste a lot of time trying to locate another talent who could do what you had done."

"He didn't know at first that I had given you one of the flutes," Calvin said.

"Imagine my surprise when you showed up alive and well the next day," Nathan said. "The only reason Dillard here is still alive is because he assured me that he had given you the hypno-drug and a command to forget everything that had happened."

"What is this amnesia drug you keep talking about?" Harry asked.

"I designed it years ago," Calvin said wearily. "It's a long story that doesn't end well."

Rachel looked at Nathan. "Once you knew I was alive, you started plotting a way to kidnap me again, didn't you? But you had to be very careful because if I went missing a second time inside the Preserve, the local police were certain to call in Foundation security, to say nothing of what my family would have done. My father would have been here in a heartbeat, demanding answers."

"I couldn't risk that," Nathan said. "Before I could figure out my next move, you had returned to Frequency City. I notified my business partner there immediately and told him to keep an eye on you from a distance."

"Marcus Lancaster," Rachel said. "So that's how he became obsessed with me. He was spying on me."

"I told him not to get too close. I didn't want any more mistakes. He found you working in that low-rent tearoom easily enough, but the next thing we knew, you had joined the staff at the Chapman Clinic."

"That was when you discovered what a real wacko Lancaster actually is," Rachel said. "He checked himself into the clinic just to get close to me."

"I'll admit I didn't see that coming," Nathan said. "Your diagnosis is correct. Lancaster is bat-shit crazy, at least when it comes to you."

"If you had asked me, I could have told you he fit the profile of a psychic stalker," Rachel said crisply.

Nathan smiled. "What a colorful way of expressing his little instability problem. But in fairness, I have become rather obsessed with you, myself."

"Seems to me you've miscalculated a lot in the course of this project," Harry said. "Must have come as a shock when you discovered that the town of Shadow Bay had just hired a new chief of police and that he was ex-FBPI. Then you found out that Slade Attridge could track inside the Preserve. Before you could adjust to that problem, you discovered that Attridge had called in Foundation security to investigate the trouble inside the fence."

Rachel clicked her teeth, tut-tutting. "Things got bad for you, Nathan, and then things got worse. I thought it was Lancaster who sent those kids to firebomb the gatekeeper's cabin, but it was you. You're the one who got desperate and brought the boys in from Frequency City.

You programmed them to set the fire while Harry was inside but you had no way of knowing I'd be there at the same time."

"Everything that could go wrong, went wrong," Nathan growled.

"What did you expect?" Harry asked. "You used a pair of street kids, not trained assassins."

"It's not like reliable professionals are easy to come by," Nathan said. "And pros are dangerous. If I'd gone with a professional and he had figured out what I was hiding here in the Preserve, I wouldn't have survived any longer than it took to pay him. The pros will sell you out in a heartbeat."

"It's harder to get rid of the professionals, too," Harry said. "You used the kids from the Second Chance House because you thought no one would notice later when you made them disappear."

"And also because I knew they had some degree of talent," Nathan said smoothly. "That's the purpose of the Second Chance operation, you see. It's a big net that we use to pull in a lot of street people that no one cares about. We feed them, give them a place to sleep, and assess them for paranormal talent. We keep the useful ones and throw the others back out into the street."

"When the firebombing plan didn't work, you decided to try to lure me into the Preserve where I could conveniently disappear," Harry said. "You grabbed Dillard, knowing that I would follow his psi-prints."

"It didn't occur to me that Rachel would be with you when you finally got here," Nathan said. "But that turns out to be a piece of luck. About time. This will save me having to figure out how to grab her again." Nathan motioned with the Alien weapon. "Enough chit-chat. Move, all of you."

"Where are we going?" Rachel asked.

"You know where," Nathan said. "You're going to unlock that vault for me. I'm going to grab as many of those artifacts as I can carry out of here in a backpack and then I'm going to get the hell off this damn island. Move. You first, Sebastian."

Harry turned and walked along the crystal tunnel through the indoor sea. Rachel and Calvin fell into step behind him.

"I'm sorry," Calvin whispered again. "So damn sorry."

"It's all right," she said quietly.

"No, it's not all right," he muttered.

"Shut up, both of you," Nathan barked.

Harry did not appear to be paying any attention to what was going on behind him, but Rachel sensed that he was just waiting for an opening. She cast a quick, covert glance around and was relieved when she saw no sign of Darwina.

"You do know why the Foundation is focusing on Rainshadow, don't you, Nathan?" Harry said almost casually.

"You're here because that bastard, Attridge, contacted you," Nathan said.

"The reason he called us in is because something is happening here on Rainshadow," Harry said. "The Preserve is getting hotter. Or maybe you hadn't noticed?"

"I noticed," Calvin offered uneasily.

"Not my problem," Nathan said. "But it is just one more reason for getting out of here as soon as possible."

Rachel locked eyes with one of the bizarre creatures on the other side of the crystal wall. Its tentacles writhed as though it was aware of her interest and was sizing her up for lunch. She could have sworn that she felt a pulse of raw, inhuman energy through the transparent barrier.

She jerked her gaze away from the monster and looked at Calvin.

"At least one of those escaped recently, didn't it?" she said.

Calvin gave her an uneasy look. "How did you know about the accident?"

"What accident?"

"Several of the tunnels that lead to the main aquarium chamber contain smaller aquariums," Calvin explained. "The entire complex is linked to the sea via a network of caves that flood at high tide. There is a series of floodgates. The system has been functioning for centuries without any problem, but this genius"—Calvin jerked a thumb at Nathan, who ignored him—"tried to test fire one of the gadgets he found here in the complex. There was some damage to one of the gates. It failed to close when the tide came in. A lab tunnel flooded. After the tide receded we discovered that two of the small aquariums had shattered. The specimens escaped. I had hoped that they were all swept out to sea."

"Why?" Rachel asked.

"Because they won't last long in the wild. They have

all been genetically bioengineered for a heavy psi environment. I ran some experiments with some of the small specimens. They don't survive under normal psi conditions. But if some of them got into the cave system here in the Preserve, they may do very well because of the high levels of paranormal radiation throughout the island."

They walked out of the crystal chamber into what appeared to be a lab. The walls were lit with an eerie ultralight. An array of workbenches and tables—none of which were quite the right height for humans—marched down the center of the hall. The furnishings were constructed out of the familiar green quartz that the Aliens had used to build their cities and the catacombs.

Smaller aquariums lined the walls. More hideous examples of the Aliens' experiments swam in the glowing waters. Sensing the presence of potential prey, the bizarre creatures came close to the crystal windows of their tanks, jaws and beaks open, tentacles and fins twitching.

Rachel turned away from the cold eyes, shuddering.

"You ran through this room and straight into that vault at the other end," Nathan said.

She looked at the crystal vault at the far end of the chamber. The last of the misty images from her dreams coalesced into solid memories.

The transparent room was sealed with what looked like a solid wall of rain that had been flash-frozen into a crystalline form. But unlike the cold stones in the jar in her kitchen, the huge rainstone waterfall was infused with a chilling energy. Currents of ominous power swirled in the atmosphere. The far side of the chamber was blocked by another, identical door of stone. Beyond that, a glowing tunnel extended into the distance. It was the route she had used to escape.

A vast number of crystal and quartz objects—some smaller than a human hand, others as large as a rez-screen—were stored inside the vault. The Alien devices were neatly arranged on a series of green quartz shelves that were stacked to the ceiling of the tunnel. One shelf contained several of the small flute-shaped devices that she had used to find her way out of the Preserve.

On the floor in the center of the vault was a murky gray crystal that did not resemble any of the other artifacts. It was just a chunk of stone, not a precision-engineered object. And it glowed psi-hot.

Harry looked at the hot crystal.

"Well, hell," he said very softly.

"I've tried everything I've found in this place on that rainstone," Nathan said. "Nothing has worked. Now you see why I need you so badly. Those relics inside that vault are hotter than a mine of ruby amber."

"Probably in more ways than one," Harry said. "You do realize that the Aliens may have had some good reasons for locking up those devices?"

"I don't doubt for a minute that they're dangerous," Nathan said. He grinned humorlessly. "That's what makes them so valuable on the black market. Don't worry; I'm not going to try to take all of them. I'm just going to grab some of the small stuff. I had plans to haul everything out of here, but that's not possible now. I can only take what will fit in my pack, but that should be more than enough to set me up for life."

"Something tells me that may not be the way it goes down," Harry said.

"What are you talking about?" Nathan demanded.

"The potential customers for those gadgets will be just as dangerous as the artifacts. Think about it. The only people who will want to buy Alien technology will be those who can sense the power in the relics, folks who have enough talent to rez them."

Nathan narrowed his eyes. "So?"

"High-end talents who deal in the black market tend to be a tough crowd," Harry said. "They like to keep a low profile. And they like to keep their secrets."

"Not a problem," Nathan said. "I've been doing business with customers like that for a long time. I know the players." He gestured with the device in his hand. "Open the chamber, Rachel, or I'll start showing you what this thing can do. Dillard will provide the first demonstration. If that doesn't impress you, I'll use it on Sebastian."

"All right," she said.

She did not look at Harry but she sensed the readiness in him. He would know what to do when the time came, she thought.

She raised her talent and waded through the ice-and-fire currents of energy until she stood directly in front of the frozen rainstone. She flattened her hand on the surface of the crystal. Energy stirred in response to her touch, thrilling her senses. The charms on her bracelet clashed. The small stones glowed hot.

She got a fix on the latent energy locked in the rainstone and generated a counterpoint through her charms. It was no more difficult than the little magic tricks she did for Devon and his buddies when they brought rainstones to her.

The rainstone unfroze with astonishing speed. Suddenly a cascade of shifting energy filled the doorway of the vault. She walked through the shimmering torrent of liquid crystal. There was a tingling sensation, but she felt no ill effects.

She moved into the chamber and turned to look at Nathan.

"Like walking through a waterfall," she said. "But you don't get wet."

"Son of a bitch," Nathan said. "You do it with the charms, don't you? Figured that out yesterday at the teatasting. Throw the bracelet out here, now. I'm not going to give you a chance to refreeze that stone."

She tossed the bracelet through the liquid crystal doorway. It landed on the floor a few feet outside the chamber. She heard Darwina squeak from somewhere close by.

Nathan moved toward the doorway of the vault, careful to keep the Alien weapon aimed at Rachel. She looked at Harry and knew from the heat in his eyes that he understood that she was about to give him the opening he needed.

"Darwina," she said quietly. "Come here, sweetie. Bring Amberella to me, please."

There was a low growl from beneath one of the quartz lab benches. Darwina, sleeked and in full combat mode, Amberella clutched in one paw, dashed across the floor. She zipped past an unheeding Nathan, and through the doorway. She bounded up onto Rachel's shoulder.

"Keep the rat under control or I'll kill it," Nathan threatened.

But he was not paying any attention to Darwina. He stood in the entrance of the vault, the liquid crystal flowing around him and stared in wonder at the objects on the quartz shelves.

"So many relics," he whispered. "So much power."

Rachel reached up as though to pet Darwina. Her fingers brushed Amberella's crystal-studded ball gown. The energy in the tiny gems whispered through her. She touched the edge of the doorway.

Nathan was so distracted by the wonders of the vault that he did not realize immediately that the waterfall in which he stood was starting to harden into its crystalline state.

"Shit."

He yelped in rage and panic, dropped the weapon, and scrambled backward out of the vault. He barely managed to yank his leg out of the doorway a split second before the waterfall refroze.

"Damn bitch," he shouted.

Rachel knew the exact instant when Harry sent the full weight of his coffin-cold talent slashing across

Nathan's senses. She could feel the ice even through the now-solid rainstone.

Nathan screamed. He stared at Rachel with horror-filled eyes. He fell to his knees and continued to scream until he went limp.

Harry looked at Rachel. "You can come out now."

She heard him clearly through the crystal. She unfroze the waterfall and emerged from the storage chamber. She rushed out to retrieve her bracelet.

"Are you all right, Harry?" she asked, securing the bracelet around her wrist.

"Yes," he said. He went past her into the vault. "You?"

"I'm okay." She turned to Calvin. "What about you? Are you all right, Calvin?"

"I'm not hurt," Calvin said. He was not looking at her. His attention was on Harry. "What are you doing?"

"Retrieving an old family heirloom," Harry said.

He walked out of the vault with the murky gray crystal in one hand.

"What is that?" Calvin asked.

"I'll explain later," Harry said. "We need to move now. Something happened when Grant dropped the Alien weapon inside the vault. Take a look."

Rachel turned quickly and saw that the artifact was glowing with paranormal fire.

"What's going on?" she asked.

"Grant probably rezzed the artifact with the energy of his panic," Calvin said. "There's a tremendous amount of psi-heat in raw fear, but it's terribly chaotic and unpredictable. I think that a moment ago when the relic came in contact with the overheated atmosphere inside that vault it set off a chain reaction. All of the relics are starting to overheat."

Several of the relics inside the vault were now glowing with various shades of paranormal fire.

"You're right, Harry, this is not good," she said.

"Let's get the kids and get the hell out of here," he said.

"Can you wake them up?" Rachel asked.

"Yes, but they'll be groggy. Calvin, you handle one, I'll take the other."

"I've got a better idea," Calvin said. "Wake them up. I'll be right back."

"Where are you going?" Rachel called after him.

"There's a small utility sled in one of the side tunnels," he shouted over his shoulder. "The same kind of vehicle that they use down in the catacombs. It can function in this heavy psi. I brought it in piece by piece a few months ago. We won't be able to use it to get through the Preserve because it wasn't designed for rough terrain, but it will get us out of the aquarium complex."

"Get it," Harry said.

Rachel looked back at the unconscious figure of Nathan Grant.

"What about him?" she asked.

"Can't save everyone, Rachel, you should know that by now."

"We can't leave him here."

"Give me one good reason why we should save that bastard?"

"You know the reason," Rachel said. "We're the good guys."

"I hate it when you pull that HE philosophy crap."

"Okay, here's another reason," she said. "When this is over, we're going to need answers and he's got some of them."

"Good point."

He went back to where Nathan lay sprawled on the floor and did something that made Nathan stir. Harry got him to his feet and hauled him forward into the crystal tunnel.

Rachel heard the faint whine of a simple, amber-based motor. A few seconds later a small, open-sided utility sled emerged from the tunnel. Calvin was at the wheel.

Rachel ran toward the sled, Darwina clinging to her shoulder.

Harry pushed the half-conscious Grant into the rear of the sled. Then he roused the two youths and dumped them in with Grant. Rachel hopped up onto one of the bench seats.

"I'll drive," Harry said.

Calvin didn't argue. He shifted to the far side of the front seat.

Harry got behind the wheel, put his foot down hard on the pedal, and drove back toward the entrance to the cave.

Nathan levered himself to a sitting position in the rear of the sled.

"What's going on?" he asked, his voice slurred.

"You ignited the contents of that vault, you damn fool," Harry said.

"The para-radiation levels are getting too high," Calvin said. "I think the vault's going to blow and it will probably take most of this complex with it."

"But the artifacts," Nathan said.

"If you want to go back for them, feel free to do so," Harry said. "Hauling your ass out of here was not my first inclination."

Rachel glanced back toward the far end of the crystal tunnel and saw that the lab room was now glowing with a fierce paranormal radiance.

They were almost through the crystal tunnel now. The creatures on the other side of the transparent wall seemed more agitated than they had been a short time ago. They twisted and turned in the glowing waters.

"They sense the heightened energy in the atmosphere," Calvin said.

"Poor things," Rachel said.

"Any one of those poor things would just as soon eat you as look at you," Calvin said.

"I know. But they aren't responsible for what they are."

"I think they are all the products of some experiments that the Aliens conducted centuries ago," Calvin said. "They survived for the same reason the underground rain forest did. The Aliens were clearly brilliant bioengineers."

"Not brilliant enough to survive here on Harmony, apparently," Harry said.

A sharp, ominous crack echoed through the transparent tunnel. Rachel turned quickly in her seat and saw a jagged fracture line appear in the crystal. It grew longer with startling speed. A spidery web of smaller cracks developed on either side of the original fissure.

"It's the fire in the vault," Calvin shouted. "It's generating so much energy it's starting to affect the crystal aquarium."

Harry powered the sled out of the crystal tunnel and along the corridor that had been machine-bored centuries ago by the Aliens. When he reached the raw cave with its glittering stalactite and stalagmite forest, he slammed on the brakes.

"This is it," he said. "Can't take the sled through that maze of rocks. Everybody out who wants to get out."

Gil and his pal were paying attention now. They stumbled out of the sled with the others and looked to Harry for direction.

"Outside," Harry said. "Into the Umbrella Tree. If that aquarium goes, the whole complex will flood and the water is going to pour out of this entrance. Getting into the branches of the tree is our best bet."

They ran toward the entrance of the cave, dodging the brilliant natural jewels in their path.

Outside, Rachel led the way to the tiers of branches that offered a ladder up into the huge, sprawling tree. Calvin, Harry, and the two teens followed.

Nathan Grant, however, fled straight ahead and disappeared from sight in the undergrowth.

"I knew going back for him was a waste of time," Harry said.

A muffled explosion reverberated deep inside the cave complex.

"The vault," said Calvin, clambering up onto a massive branch beside Rachel and the guards. "It just blew. I think that the aquarium walls will give way any second now. Some of the water will flow into the side tunnels, but Sebastian is right, a lot of it will take the path of least resistance and come out the same way we did."

Rachel studied the cave entrance. The roof of the opening was a few feet below their perch.

"This branch should be high enough off the ground to keep us all safe," she said.

"This tree has withstood a lot of major storms," Harry said. "And this section is not in the direct path of the water. But we're going to feel the impact." He reached out and took Rachel's hand. "Hang on tight, everyone."

There was another muffled explosion.

"The aquarium," Calvin said softly.

The gushing wave of water sounded like rolling thunder as it swept through the cave. The ground shook. A moment later the deluge surged furiously through the entrance. Rachel thought she saw some dark forms twitching and twisting in the crashing waves.

The Umbrella Tree shuddered. Several of the smaller, newer root systems tore free of their moorings, but the ancient pillars that supported the section in which she and the others crouched held fast.

Darwina clung to Rachel's shoulder and chortled with excitement.

"Little adrenaline junkie," Rachel said.

After clearing the narrow entrance of the cave system, the water spread out across the jungle floor, its energy dissipating rapidly.

The rushing waters surged for what seemed an eternity before gradually slowing to a river, a stream, and finally, a small creek.

An eerie silence fell.

Then the screaming started.

"Grant," Harry said. "Sounds like he made it, after all."

THEY FOUND NATHAN A SHORT TIME LATER. HE WAS ALIVE but he was pinned against one of the root pillars by the weight of a dying sea monster. The creature's tentacles were wrapped tightly around him.

He continued to scream until Harry and Calvin and the two teens hacked away the last of the tentacles.

Chapter 30

"SO YOU'RE THE ONE WHO ERASED MY MEMORIES OF GET-ting kidnapped and waking up inside the aquarium complex," Rachel said.

"You probably won't believe this," Calvin said, "but I was trying to protect you."

"I believe you," she said gently.

They were sitting in Rachel's kitchen. She had prepared a tisane to harmonize her inner energies and special brews for Harry and Calvin as well. She figured they could all do with some therapeutic aura balancing.

Darwina showed no ill effects from the adventure. She was perched on the refrigerator, munching pretzels. She had Amberella at her side. The doll, amazingly, looked only a little the worse for wear. A tribute to modern plastics and synthetics and her mother's sewing skills, Rachel thought.

"Grant planned to kill you after you opened the vault room for him," Calvin explained. "When you escaped, he was furious but he thought his secret was safe because he was sure that you would never survive the Preserve."

Harry drank some of his tisane and lowered the cup. "He didn't know that you had given Rachel one of the crystal flutes and told her how to use it."

"Not at first," Calvin said. "I was fairly certain that anyone with as much talent as you possess, Rachel, could use the flute. But if you did get out, I had to make sure that I got to you before Nathan did."

"He would have tried to murder me to keep me quiet," Rachel said.

"Without a moment's hesitation. The flute was tuned to the location of my cottage," Calvin said. "I knew that if you did find your way out of the Preserve, you would emerge there. I was waiting for you. I slipped some of my hypno-drug into that tea I served you and told you to forget the whole damn night and most especially Nathan Grant's aura. I told you that if you saw Grant again, you would not be able to get a clear fix on his aura."

"Which was why his aura was murky when I did see him at the tea-tasting."

"I also planted the suggestion that it would be a really good idea to head back to Frequency City as soon as possible. Later I explained to Grant that you were not a threat."

"He was content with that because he didn't want to have to kill Rachel until he could figure out how to replace her or get her back to the island to open the vault," Harry said.

Rachel winced. "I'm that easy to hypnotize, Calvin? And here I thought I was immune."

"You probably are immune to psychic hypnosis," Calvin said. "But the stuff I developed is a powerful drug. No one is immune. I made the mistake of demonstrating it to Grant. He and Marcus Lancaster saw the possibilities immediately and started experimenting with the stuff on the street kids that were filtering through Second Chance House."

Harry looked at him. "When did you develop the drug?"

"Years ago in another life I was Doctor Calvin Dillard, director of research at a high-flying pharmaceutical lab in Resonance City. My specialty was marine biology. I derived the hypnotic drug from the glands of a certain species of fish."

"What happened?" Rachel asked. "How did you end up on Rainshadow?"

"I succeeded in destroying my own career," Calvin said. "Pharmaceutical research is tremendously competitive. In my rush to beat the competition, I released the results of some research done in my lab that was later proven to have been falsified by two of my assistants."

"But you were in charge, so you took the hit," Harry said.

"It was my fault. I knew there was something a little too good to be true about the results, but getting the edge on the competition was the top priority. In the end the scandal made a train wreck out of my career. I lost the respect of my peers, my friends turned against me, and my wife ended our MC. There was nothing left but my music. So I moved to Rainshadow."

"Where did you find the flutes?" Rachel asked.

Calvin smiled faintly. "You could say they found me. My talent for music extends into the paranormal range. I can hear notes generated beyond the normal spectrum. About a year ago I noticed that during severe storms I could hear music coming from somewhere inside the Preserve. I thought at first that my loneliness combined with the energy leaking out of the fence was creating audio hallucinations."

"The music called to you," Rachel said gently.

"Like a siren song. Once, during a violent thunderstorm, I decided I had nothing left to lose. I managed to get through the fence and into the Preserve. Once inside, I just kept walking, following the paranormal music. I swear, at the time, I didn't care if I ever got back out."

Harry watched him with cold interest. "The music led you to the cave system that housed the Alien aquarium and the associated labs."

"It was, to put it mildly, the discovery of a lifetime," Calvin said.

"Wait, I don't understand," Rachel interrupted. "Who was playing the music?"

Calvin grimaced. "Not Alien ghosts, I can assure you of that. I found the flutes in that crystal tunnel that ran through the aquarium. There were seven of them. They were stacked very neatly in a triangle-shaped container. I'm sure they had been there for centuries. I suppose that it was the energy of the storms that occasionally stirred up the latent power in the flutes and caused them to resonate in a harmonic fashion. With my talent and my proximity to the Preserve, I was able to hear the music occasionally."

Harry looked at the chunk of murky crystal sitting on the kitchen table. "Over the years people have occasionally claimed to hear ghostly music coming from inside the Preserve during heavy storms. But you've lived near the fence for nearly a decade and you didn't hear the music until last year?"

"Sometimes I picked up a note or two during very violent storms," Calvin said, "But never any sustained music that was clear and strong enough to follow—not until last year."

"Then some new factor was involved," Harry said.

They all looked at the crystal that he had retrieved from the vault.

"You think the energy of that stone ignited the flutes?" Calvin asked.

"We don't know much about the three crystals that my ancestors brought with them from Earth," Harry said, "but what little we do know indicates that under certain circumstances they can resonate strongly with the natural geothermal currents generated at nexus and vortex points. The Sebastians kept the rocks stored in a kind of high-tech obsidian chest. The obsidian dampened the natural energy of the crystals. But sometime in the past eighteen months the crystals were removed from the storage container."

Calvin's eyes heated with comprehension. "You found one of them inside that crystal vault."

"I think it's probably been sitting in there for a while, gradually heating up the atmosphere and the other artifacts, including those flutes," Harry said.

Rachel turned back to Calvin. "I understand how important the discovery of the aquarium was to you, but how in the world did you get involved with a couple of criminals like Nathan Grant and Marcus Lancaster?"

Calvin exhaled wearily. "You haven't figured out that part yet?"

"For pete's sake, you're not the criminal type. You're a *scientist*," Rachel said.

Harry regarded Calvin with a knowing expression. "A scientist who had made an incredible find and knew that he was going to need cash in order to pursue his research, a lot of cash."

"Yes," Calvin said.

Rachel winced. "Oh, I see."

Calvin looked at her. "Marcus Lancaster's obsession with you pales in comparison to my obsession with the secrets locked in that lab complex. I was afraid to tell anyone about what I had found because I knew the Foundation would step in and take control."

"True," Harry said.

Calvin turned back to him. "Your family not only commands enormous resources, it owns the Preserve and would have a proprietary interest in reaping the profits of any discoveries made inside. Given my past, I wouldn't have been invited to step foot inside the aquarium, let alone conduct any research there."

"But you needed money to outfit a proper marine biology lab," Harry said. "You knew that some of the Alien relics scattered around the complex would be worth a fortune on the black market. So you decided to try to sell them."

"It was a world I knew nothing about." Calvin picked up his cup. "I went to Frequency City and started asking around at the various antiquities shops. The next thing I knew, Grant and Lancaster came around offering a partnership. It seemed like the answer to my dreams. But all they cared about were the relics. And when they discovered that vault, they could not rest until they had figured out how to open it."

"The only reason you're still alive," Harry said, "is because the flutes are similar to most crystal and amber-based technology. They have to be retuned frequently."

"And you were the only one with the kind of psychic talent required to do the tuning," Rachel said.

"I'm sorry," Calvin said. "I know that's not enough, but I am truly sorry. I almost got you killed."

"You know," Rachel said, "this sad tale about doing a deal with the devil—or devils, in this case—in exchange for knowledge has a familiar ring to it."

Harry and Calvin looked at her.

"What?" she said. "Haven't either of you ever heard of the story of Dr. Faustus?"

"No," Harry said.

Calvin's brow furrowed in a puzzled expression. "Is he a biologist?"

Rachel smiled. "It's an Old World legend about a guy who trades his soul to Lucifer in exchange for all the secrets of science, which he never gets, of course, because the devil can't be trusted. It was one of my favorite bedtime stories."

"Huh," Harry said. "I used to read *Creature from the Obsidian Lagoon* comics under the covers at night."

"I had a subscription to the *Journal of Paranormal Biology*," Calvin said. "I usually took the latest issue to bed with me every night. Still do, come to think of it."

"Moving right along," Rachel said crisply. "Upon reflection, my analogy to the Faust legend does not apply here because, unlike the doc in that story, you redeemed yourself, Calvin. You risked your own life to save mine the night I was kidnapped and you did your best to keep me safe by blanking my memory."

Calvin grimaced. "I doubt that will matter a whole lot to the powers that be at the Foundation or the FBPI. What with being sort of an accessory to kidnapping and dealing in illegal Alien artifacts I expect I'll be spending the next few years in prison. I wonder if they'll let me have my violin?"

"As it happens," Harry said, "I'm the one who decides what legal actions will be taken. I've made an executive decision. We need both your biological expertise and your unique musical skills here on Rainshadow in order to proceed with the investigation."

Calvin stared at him. "There's nothing left to investigate. The aquarium complex and the artifacts in the vault were destroyed by the explosion."

"We have to assume a lot of those marine specimens made it into the flooded cave system and will probably survive," Harry said. "Got a feeling that there will be plenty of the monsters to catch and study. I'm putting you in charge of that aspect of the investigation."

"Me?" Calvin was dumbfounded.

"You've obviously got more experience in Preserve marine life than anyone else in the vicinity. You'll have access to the full resources of the Foundation labs."

"I don't know what to say," Calvin whispered. "I'm . . . stunned."

"Get over it fast," Harry said. "We don't have time for you to sit around being stunned."

Rachel raised her brows. "Don't get me wrong, I think putting Calvin in charge of locating and studying some of the escaped aquarium creatures is an excellent idea, but why the rush?"

"I'm now convinced that my original theory is correct. The problems in the Preserve were caused by the theft of the three stones that Harry One concealed here on the island. To date we have recovered only one of those damn rocks. With luck, removing it from the aquarium complex will bring down the psi-temp inside or at least slow the heating process and buy us a little time. But that leaves two more stones unaccounted for."

"It also leaves the thief unaccounted for," Rachel said.

"Yes," Harry said. "It does."

"I think I know where you're going with this," Calvin said. He gestured toward the gray crystal on the table. "You don't believe that first stone wound up in the aquarium by accident, do you?"

"No," Harry said. "I think whoever stole the three stones understood something of their power. The thief placed one of those damn rocks in the aquarium complex for some reason."

"You're wondering what he did with the other two slabs," Rachel said.

"We need to find them," Harry said. "I think that the territory we call the Preserve was in reality the Alien's version of a biological laboratory, a place where they could carry out dangerous paranormal experiments in a desperate effort to bioengineer the surface of the planet so that they could survive. In the end it didn't work. They were forced to go underground."

Rachel drew in a sharp breath. Calvin's expression was grim.

"In other words, you think that the aquarium complex wasn't the only lab on the island," Rachel said.

"I've got a feeling that there are other experimental labs deep inside the Preserve," Harry said.

"It makes sense," Calvin said. He nodded slowly. "What better location for labs engaged in dangerous parabiological research than a remote island in the Amber Sea?"

"It would go a long ways toward explaining the legends and myths that have developed about Rainshadow," Rachel said. "But it doesn't explain why the paranormal radiation levels inside the Preserve have started to rise recently."

"No." Harry looked at the quartz stone sitting on the table. "But the missing quartz stones would explain it."

"Maybe they were also inside the aquarium," Calvin said. "Either in that vault or elsewhere. There's a lot of crystal in that network of labs."

"If that's the case, the explosion may have taken care of the problem," Harry said. "But I don't think it's going to be that easy. It's far more likely that the thief was trying to use the three crystals to enhance a natural geothermal power grid. That means that the rocks are placed far apart in a carefully calculated arrangement."

"But why would anyone want to do such a thing inside a dangerous nexus like the Preserve?" Rachel asked.

Calvin snorted. "Do you have to ask that after knowing what I did? I'm an example of just how far some people will go to discover the secrets of the para-biological world. The answers hold the promise of curing disease, enhancing psychical powers, and increasing longevity. Trust me, the prospect of making those kinds of discoveries is more than enough to cause a man to do a deal with the devil."

Rachel reached out and touched his hand. "It's okay. You canceled that contract."

Calvin smiled. "Thanks to you."

"One way or another," Harry said, "we have to locate the two missing stones because it looks like those old explorers' maps are right about Rainshadow. *Here there be monsters.*"

Chapter 31

HARRY'S PHONE RANG, SHATTERING THE PLEASANT MORN-
ing routine of the sunny kitchen. Rachel gave a small start
of surprise. Darwina, perched on top of the refrigerator,
chortled and took another bite of the freshly baked biscuit that Rachel had just given her.

Harry reached for the phone. "Looks like we're back
in contact with civilization. He glanced at the incoming
code. "My brother." He clicked the key to take the call.
"Good timing. We got power back an hour ago. Figured
phone service wouldn't be far behind. I've got an update
on the missing crystals."

"I'm listening," Drake said.

"We found one. And you're not going to believe what
else we stumbled onto inside the Preserve."

He ran through the litany of recent events. By the time
he was finished, Rachel was placing a plate of golden

yellow scrambled eggs that had been laced with herbs and cheese in front of him. She went back to the counter for the bowl of berries and cream and the platter of biscuits that she had just removed from the oven.

"It looks like the psi-heat in the Preserve is no longer rising as fast as it was when I got here," Harry said. "I think it's safe to assume that we were correct about the source of the problem."

"Those damn crystals," Drake said.

"Right. Taking one out of the Alien aquarium quieted things down, but it doesn't fix the problem. We need to find the other two. Meanwhile, there's no way to know what's waiting for us inside the fence."

"You don't think that the Aliens fenced off that much territory just to protect that aquarium, do you?" Drake said.

"No. I think we're in for a few more surprises before this is over. Any luck on your end?"

"I found North's great-granddaughter," Drake said. The cold satisfaction of the hunter edged his voice.

The familiar frisson of intuition heated Harry's senses. "She's alive?"

"I think so, although I can't absolutely confirm it yet. Looks like she's living under an assumed name and a new identity."

"Working? Married?"

"Not married, at least not any longer. She was in an MC, but the husband died under mysterious circumstances. She's working as a magician's assistant in a low-rent magic act in the Old Quarter of Crystal City. She went to a hell of a lot of trouble to make herself disappear."

"The question is, why go to so much trouble to hide?"

"The family of the dead husband has always believed that she murdered him."

"Was there an investigation?"

"Yes, but no proof was found, so no charges were brought," Drake said. "That didn't satisfy the family of the deceased, however. The Whitcombs are very powerful in Resonance City. They never did approve of the marriage. Even if they couldn't get the widow charged with murder they made it clear that they wanted revenge. They made life miserable for her. It's not like she has any family of her own to protect her."

Harry munched on a bite of the biscuit he had just buttered while he considered that information.

"Are you eating?" Drake asked.

"Breakfast." Harry swallowed. "Scrambled eggs and biscuits."

"You don't cook stuff like biscuits. Don't think I've ever seen you whip up a batch of scrambled eggs, either."

"Cooking's not my thing. But I'm good at eating."

"Can I assume that the cooking was done by Rachel Blake?"

Harry met Rachel's eyes as she sat down across from him. He smiled. She smiled back. And then she wiggled her fingers.

"Tell your brother I said good morning," she said.

"Rachel says to tell you good morning," he said into the phone.

"Same to her." There was a short pause. Drake cleared his throat. "Is this breakfast together in the morning a special occasion or is it going to be a routine event?"

Harry locked eyes again with Rachel. "Routine, as in lifelong."

Drake cleared his throat. "Does she, uh, know about . . . ?"

"My sordid past? Oh, yeah. But Rachel was raised in a Harmonic Enlightenment community. They take an enlightened view on stuff like that. Tell me more about the Whitcomb family. Did they come up with a motive to explain why the widow might have whacked her husband?"

"Sure. That's the interesting part, at least as far as we're concerned. They think she seduced him into an MC because she needed him to help her find something valuable."

"The dead husband was a talent?"

"Yes and apparently quite powerful, but the exact nature of his abilities is unclear," Drake said. "All I can tell you for certain is that he had a degree in para-archaeology. He was on the staff at a private museum."

"In other words, Whitcomb was the kind of talent who might have been useful when it came to locating a cache of Old World artifacts inside the Preserve."

"Right," Drake said. "Even if the widow had an old amber-psi map like the one you used to find the slabs a few years ago, it's doubtful that she would have risked going inside the fence alone."

"In addition, she may have concluded that she might need a guy who was good with Old World relics."

"The Whitcomb family's theory is that after the son and heir helped his bride find whatever it was she was looking for, she offed him and did the disappearing act."

"They may have been right. Except that she obviously did not make it out of the Preserve with the crystals or, apparently, anything else that was valuable. If she had, she wouldn't be working in a low-rent magic show."

"You've only confirmed that one of the stones was still inside the Preserve," Drake said. "It's possible that she got out with the other two."

"No," Harry said. "The other two are still in there. It's true the psi-temp isn't rising as fast as it was, but there's still a lot of heat inside the fence."

"Okay, I'm not arguing with you. When it comes to this kind of thing, your intuition is solid. Looks like the next step is to track down the widow and see what she knows."

"Yes," Harry said. "Go do that and do it as soon as possible. When you find her, bring her here to Rainshadow. Something tells me we're going to need her."

"Uh, what if she doesn't want to go to Rainshadow?"

"That's your problem. I'm putting you in charge of that end of the investigation. I don't care how you do it, just make sure you bring her here as soon as possible."

"You know, there are laws about forcible abduction. . . ."

"I'm going back to my breakfast now," Harry said. "Call me when you have her. Good-bye."

Chapter 32

"DAMN IT, SEBASTIAN, I GO AWAY FOR A WEEK AND YOU start blowing up things on my island." Slade Attridge's ancient desk chair squeaked when he lounged back in it. "And then there's the little matter of a firebombing and a report of some mutant sea monsters that escaped into the flooded caves of the Preserve. Not to mention the discovery of a couple of bad guys who were trafficking in illegal relics that they found inside an Alien lab."

"It's been busy here on Rainshadow," Harry said. "How did your week go?"

"How do you think it went? Charlotte has a huge family and I must have met every single one of her relatives. I endured a grilling by her father, who made it clear that if I didn't treat his little girl right I would disappear permanently into the catacombs."

"He could make that happen?"

"Evidently he has connections in the local Hunter's Guild," Slade said. "After that I made the mistake of accepting an invitation from Charlotte's brother to go out for beer and a few rounds of rez-pool at a no-name tavern in the Quarter."

Harry smiled. "What could go wrong?"

"My memories are foggy, but I think there may have been some intoxicated ghost hunters and a few broken bottles involved. I vaguely remember calling an old friend to bail us out of jail. Luckily, said friend was able to exert some influence to get all charges dropped, an act of kindness that puts me squarely in his debt."

Harry raised his brows. "Your old friend must have some excellent connections."

"He does. His name is Winters."

"As in Adam Winters, the boss of the Frequency Guild?"

"One and the same. I will not go into the trauma of the big family reception at the hotel the night before last." Slade's chair squeaked again when he sat forward. "Let's just say that I was more than ready to come home to my quiet little island and resume my small-town lifestyle. Instead, I find nothing but trouble, and it all seems to be revolving around the Preserve."

"Yes," Harry said, "it does."

"What do you plan to do about it?"

"Funny you should ask. I've spent a lot of time lately developing a strategy to fix the problem."

"Any good ideas short of evacuating Shadow Bay? Because I'll tell you right now, an evacuation won't work very well. The locals aren't going to pull up stakes and leave just because the Foundation thinks the Preserve has gotten more dangerous. They'll start inventing conspiracy theories instead."

"Rachel warned me about that," Harry said. "But the good news is that I think we've got some time. The psi-temp appears to have stabilized, at least temporarily, because we pulled one of the crystals out of the aquarium cave. Got to locate the other two stones."

"How?"

"We start by finding the person who evidently stole them."

"Got a name?" Slade asked.

"There was one other individual besides my great-grandfather who knew where the rocks were hidden—his pirate-hunting associate, Nicholas North. According to my great-grandfather, they both made psi-maps of the location."

"North has been dead for decades."

"That's a fact," Harry said. "And unlike my great-grandfather, North wasn't very prolific. But there is one direct descendant of Nick North alive today, a great-granddaughter."

"So? I've heard that the only person who can read a psi-map is the person who made it."

Harry smiled slowly. "Or a blood relative who just happens to inherit a version of the mapmaker's talent and, therefore, a similar para-psych profile. Psychic genetics is unpredictable. I'm the first person in the Sebastian family who was able to interpret my great-grandfather's map."

"Now you're wondering if maybe North's great-granddaughter got hold of his map and was able to decipher the psi-code?"

"It's a place to start looking. My brother Drake is tracking her down now."

"What if she isn't cooperative?"

"She's Drake's problem."

Chapter 33

JILLY WAS STILL NOT ANSWERING HER PHONE.

Rachel drummed her fingers on the sales counter. She contemplated the empty bookshop and café. The Closed sign hung in the window. It was not quite nine, so, technically speaking, Jilly was not yet late. But Jilly was always early.

Rachel looked at Darwina, who was sitting on the window ledge with Amberella and playing with the tassel of the pull cord that was attached to the shade.

"I'm getting worried about Jilly," Rachel said.

Darwina chortled and batted the tassel. Rachel opened her phone and punched in Harry's number. She smiled to herself when he answered halfway through the first ring.

"What's wrong?" he asked.

"You know, that's not a very harmonically balanced way to answer the phone. It assumes a negative."

"I'll have to remember that. What's wrong?"

"Nothing, at least I don't think there's anything wrong. But I'm a little worried about Jilly. She hasn't come in yet today and she isn't answering her phone. She's all alone out there on Cliff Road. If she's ill or had an accident, she might not be able to call for help. I'm going to borrow a Vibe from Brett and go see if she's okay. I didn't want you to worry if you happened to notice that the shop was still closed."

"Thanks, because I sure as hell would have worried if you had disappeared on me. Are you taking Darwina?"

"Naturally." Rachel crossed the room as she spoke. She collected Darwina and Amberella off the window ledge. Darwina made enthusiastic little noises. "You know how she loves riding in cars."

"A Vibe is a rezzed-up golf cart, not a car. Call me when you find out what's up with Jilly."

"Will do. Any news on your end?"

"Slade is a little annoyed because he missed all the excitement. But we had a long chat with Grant, who is talking as fast as he can before the FBPI agents arrive. He told us all about the Second Chance operation and he even offered to provide evidence that Lancaster murdered his wife. That's the good news."

"What's the bad news?" Rachel asked.

"Now who's being negative? The bad news is that because of the information about the murder, the authorities in Frequency City have opened an investigation. Evidently one of the detectives there was suspicious all along. He went to the Chapman Clinic an hour ago to take Lancaster into custody."

"Why is that bad news?"

"Because the FBPI and the Frequency City cops are fighting over who has jurisdiction in this case. As the representative of Foundation security, I don't have any clout. For all intents and purposes I'm just a private investigator. But Slade is working his connections at the Bureau. He thinks he can get me in to question Lancaster."

"I suppose a murder investigation does take precedence."

"Don't worry, one way or another, we're going to have a chat with Lancaster and soon."

Rachel tucked Darwina under one arm, slung her tote over her shoulder, and let herself out the back door of the shop. "If Lancaster finds out that you're trying to get at him, expect more delays. He's a very, very talented con artist."

"I'm not in the mood for delays. I want answers."

"So do I. Bye for now. I'll check in as soon as I make sure Jilly is okay."

"Do that."

THE NARROW ROAD ALONG THE TOP OF THE CLIFFS HAD been mostly cleared of downed tree limbs and other storm debris. Rachel reached the turnoff to Jilly's cottage in good time and drove cautiously into the muddy, rutted lane that wound through the forest.

She stopped in the drive in front of Jilly's weather-beaten cottage and climbed out from behind the wheel. Darwina fluttered up onto her shoulder.

Rachel left the tote sitting on the passenger seat of the Vibe. Smash-and-grab robberies were not a big problem on Rainshadow. The low crime rate was one of the pleasures of small-town life, she thought. The only things folks had to worry about on the island were the monsters— human and nonhuman—lurking in the Preserve.

"But every neighborhood has a few drawbacks," Rachel explained to Darwina.

They went up the three wooden steps and crossed the front porch. Rachel rapped loudly on the door.

Her charms clashed lightly. Icy energy kicked up her pulse.

"Jilly? It's Rachel. I got a little worried about you when you didn't show up early for work today. Everything all right?"

Footsteps sounded on the other side of the hall. A few seconds later the door opened. Jilly stared at Rachel through the screen door. Her gray eyes were stark with fear. Darwina gave a low, rumbling growl and sleeked out into full hunting mode.

"Rachel," Jilly whispered. She clutched the lapels of a faded pink robe to her throat with one hand. "Lancaster's here. It's a trap. For God's sake, get away. Run."

"I'm not leaving you alone with him. If I do, he'll kill you now. You know too much. Besides, it's me he wants." Rachel raised her voice a little. "Isn't that right, Marcus?"

A figure moved in the hallway behind Jilly. The weak light glinted on the mag-rez in his hand.

"You know me so well, my love," Lancaster said. "Just as I know you. I told Ms. Finch that you would come out here to check on her when she did not show up at work today. It was exactly the sort of move that a concerned employer would make."

Darwina growled again. Rachel reached up to touch her.

"No, Darwina," she said quietly. "Not yet."

Darwina shivered but she obeyed.

"What the hell is that thing on your shoulder?" Lancaster asked, amused. "It looks like a rat. Is that a doll she's holding?"

Rachel ignored the question. "I'm impressed, Marcus. You took a big risk coming here to get me."

"You left me no choice. I tried to make you understand that you belonged to me, but you insisted on trying to run. The next thing I know you're fucking that bastard, Sebastian. You can't expect me to allow that. I blame Sebastian for seducing you, but there's no going back. You are damaged goods now, Rachel. Such a shame."

"When did you arrive on the island?" Rachel asked.

"This morning. I took the ferry to Thursday Harbor and hired a local fisherman to bring me here to Rainshadow. I knew everything I needed to know about the local situation, including the fact that Ms. Finch worked for you."

"Because Nathan Grant kept you informed. You do realize he's currently sitting in the local jail waiting to be picked up by FBPI agents? I'm told he's chatting quite freely about your Second Chance House operation and he even offered to provide proof that you murdered your wife."

"It doesn't matter. I'll be gone before anyone even knows I'm not in Frequency City. I kept some of Dr. Dillard's hypnotic drug with me at all times while I was in the clinic in case I needed it. I used it on one of the orderlies this morning when I discovered that I was going to be transferred to the custody of the police. As far as the orderly is concerned, I suffered a seizure during the night and was transported to Frequency City General. There will be mass confusion before anyone realizes that I disappeared."

"Are you going to use the drug on Jilly, too, so that she won't remember that you were here?"

"Sadly, I used the last of my supply of the drug on the orderly," Lancaster said "I'm afraid Ms. Finch will not survive the day. Neither will you."

"I can promise you that Harry Sebastian and Chief Attridge won't stop until they find you."

"But they won't find me, Rachel. Not ever. When I leave here today, I will vanish. Believe me, when it comes to disappearing, I'm the best. Got a talent for it, you see."

She moved her wrist slightly. The silvery charms jangled. One of them, a tiny dagger set with a small black stone, caught the light and brightened. Distracted, Lancaster glanced at the bracelet and then looked away. His brow furrowed and his eyes tightened as though he was having trouble concentrating.

"You should never have run from me," he said. "You

are mine. I truly did believe that we were destined to be together but I see now that I was wrong about you."

She pulsed a little more energy into the charms. The miniature dagger grew hotter. Lancaster looked at the bracelet again, scowling. He jerked his glance away with a visible effort of will and shook his head, as though to clear his senses.

"I was wrong about you, too, Marcus," Rachel said, keeping her voice calm and even. "I can't believe I made the mistake of telling Dr. Oakford that you were one of the smart monsters. You aren't, are you? You're just a low-end con man and that's all you'll ever be."

Rage flared in Lancaster's eyes. "Shut up, you stupid whore. I would have given you everything."

"But there's the problem. You see, you have nothing I want. Absolutely nothing."

The charms clashed and jangled; louder now. Currents of energy swirled in the atmosphere. Jilly stood frozen. She stared at Rachel, obviously aware that something was happening. The growing energy of the charms was not aimed at her, but she was catching some of the backwash.

Lancaster's eyes heated with a red tide of uncontrolled fury. He looked at the dancing, dazzling charms and this time he could not look away.

"Stop it," he shouted.

He shoved Jilly out of the way, took two long steps forward, and seized the wrist on which Rachel wore the bracelet. Darwina hissed.

"No, Darwina," Rachel whispered.

She sent every ounce of energy she possessed surging through the stones of the charms. The dagger flashed sun-hot. The tiny pinpoint of energy lit up the room.

Lancaster spasmed violently. His mouth opened on a scream that was cut off almost before it began. He started to shake violently. The gun fell from his fingers and landed with a thud.

Jilly rushed forward to retrieve the weapon.

Incredibly Lancaster managed to stay on his feet, Rachel's wrist clamped in one hand. His eyes burned with panic and rage.

"What have you done to me?" he screamed.

He tried to pull her closer so that he could grab her by the throat. She went with the flow of his violent energy, turning toward him. Using the leverage of her hip and the force of his own momentum, she swept him off balance.

He crashed to the floor. Darwina pounced, going for his throat.

Lancaster screamed again.

"It's all right, Darwina," Rachel said. "Let him go."

Darwina retreated but she kept her attention focused on Lancaster, ready to spring at him in an instant.

"Don't move or I'll let Darwina tear your throat out," Rachel said.

"You can't do this," Lancaster gasped. He put a hand to his throat and then stared at his bloodstained fingers, shocked. "It bit me."

"She missed your jugular," Rachel said. "You'll be all right. Sort of. But you have no idea how much meditation I'm going to have to do tonight to harmonize my senses. It's not like I don't have better things to do with my evenings these days, you know." She turned to Jilly. "Are you okay?"

"I will be after I've had a few drinks," Jilly said. "What did you just do to him?"

"I extinguished his talent. He's still Marcus Lancaster but he won't be quite the super salesman he was once upon a time."

"Oh, geez," Jilly said. "And here I thought you were just real good at brewing tea and reading auras."

"I can do those things, too."

The muffled roar of a big flash-rock engine sounded in the drive. The heavy vehicle slammed to a stop in front of the cottage. Boots pounded on the steps and an instant later Harry came through the door riding a dark wave of fierce energy. His eyes burned.

Slade Attridge was right behind him, gun at the ready. Rex raced through the doorway with the men, all four eyes and plenty of teeth showing. There was no clutch purse in sight. He had come ready for battle, Rachel thought.

But Rex seemed to register almost immediately that there was no longer a threat. He fluffed up, closed his hunting eyes, and scurried over to greet Darwina. She, too, went into full drier-lint mode and chortled coyly.

Harry looked at Lancaster, who was moaning on the floor. Then he switched his attention to Rachel.

"Are you okay?" he asked a little roughly.

She gave him a wan smile. "It seems like you've asked me that question a lot lately."

"What's the answer?"

"I'm okay."

He pulled her into his arms and hugged her tight. "Don't ever, ever scare the hell out of me like that again."

"Okay," she mumbled into his shirt front. "How did you know that he was on the island?"

"When I realized that there had been some kind of bureaucratic snafu, I called your old boss, Ian Oakford. He told me he had a feeling that the paperwork mix-up at the clinic had been engineered by Lancaster. Said to tell you that he thinks you were right about him all along. He also said that the bastard's obsession with you was real—the only thing that Lancaster didn't fake. Said that if Lancaster had managed to slip away, he would go after you immediately."

Rachel raised her head. "Dr. Oakford said that I was right in my diagnosis?"

"I think he said something about telling you that you could have your old job back, but by that time I wasn't listening. Slade and I were heading for the door."

"Lancaster is going to be a problem," Slade said quietly. "If we send him back to the Frequency City cops, he'll use his talent to slip away again, just like he did this time."

"I know," Harry said.

The cold, hard edge on his words made Rachel lift her head from his shoulder. She looked at Harry and then she looked at Slade. She knew what both men were thinking. It would be so easy and so convenient to make Lancaster disappear into the Preserve.

"That won't be necessary," she said briskly. "If he gets out of jail, it won't be because of his talent."

"What did you do to him?" Harry asked.

"You could say I charmed him."

Chapter 34

"WHEN I GENERATE THE RIGHT AMOUNT OF ENERGY through the charms on my bracelet, they create a psychic dissonance. It's very disturbing to those in the vicinity but it doesn't do any real damage unless I focus on an individual's aura," Rachel said. She wrapped both hands around her teacup. "When I do that, each charm becomes a small paranormal mirror. I can aim those mirrors at any place on an individual's spectrum, but I need physical contact and a clear target. When Lancaster flew into a rage, he automatically rezzed his talent."

"Which provided you with the psychic target you needed," Harry said. "I understand."

They were sitting in the kitchen. Dinner was over but the table had not yet been cleared. The last slice of the enormous takeout pizza that Harry had picked up earlier was sitting in a box. The bottle of wine next to the box was almost empty. Instead of dessert, Rachel had brewed some harmony tea for both of them.

Darwina was on the windowsill munching a chocolate zinger. She had Amberella with her. Doll and dust bunny looked out into the night as if expecting company.

"Technically speaking," Rachel said, "I didn't destroy that section of his aura but I threw the wavelengths into what will probably be a permanent state of disharmony. He won't be able to focus his psychic talent clearly again."

"Serves the bastard right."

"Lancaster is still one of the monsters." Rachel picked up her tisane, took a sip, and lowered the cup. "Like I told Dr. Oakford, some things can't be fixed, at least not with the para-psych knowledge that we have now."

Harry set down his cup, reached across the table, and captured her face in one hand. "Have you considered Oakford's offer to return to the clinic?"

She smiled, enjoying the power and tenderness of his hand. "Nope."

"Not even for a moment?"

"I knew the day I was fired that I was not cut out for the mainstream world."

"I don't seem to be cut out for that world, either."

"Where does that leave you?" she asked.

"Here on Rainshadow Island with you."

"You won't be going back to Frequency City?"

"Not to live," he said. "My work is here on Rainshadow, at least for now."

"Yes," she said. "You're needed here."

"I need to be here but not because of the Preserve. I could handle the logistics of the investigation from off-island. I need to be here because this is where you are. I loved you from the first moment I saw you, Rachel."

"Ha. You had me at the top of your suspect list."

"What's that got to do with it?" He seemed genuinely confused.

"Are you serious? How could you fall in love with someone you thought was up to no good inside the Preserve?"

"You expect me to answer a question like that?" Harry asked. "You're the one trained in Harmonic Enlightenment philosophy."

"All right, maybe you were sexually attracted to me from the start," she suggested.

"Maybe?"

"That's okay. I was attracted to you, too. Sexual attraction can sometimes be a starting point for a deeper, more enduring relationship."

Harry smiled his pirate smile. "Honey, I'm a guy. I know all about sexual attraction and how fast it works."

"Oh, right."

"There was definitely a lot of heat between us right from the start. But here's a little insight into my personal psyche. I wouldn't set out to rescue a female suspect from whatever mess she had landed in just because I was sexually attracted to her."

Rachel was overwhelmed with emotion. Tears gathered in her eyes. "You wanted to rescue me? Even though you thought I might be guilty? That is so—"

"Irrational? Crazy? Unenlightened?"

"No." She sniffed and grabbed a napkin to blot her eyes. "That is so romantic."

"First I'm a gentleman for taking the fall in my divorce and now I'm a romantic because I fell in love with a suspect." He shook his head. "Mind telling me what herbs you put in the aura tea blend that you brew for yourself?"

She ignored that. "What would you have done if it turned out I was guilty of stealing those three stones?"

"I knew that you weren't exactly the cold, calculating criminal type. I figured that, if you were involved, it was because you had been lured into trouble and gotten in way over your head."

"Gee, thanks. You think I'm that naïve?"

"Worst-case scenario was that you had allowed misplaced loyalty to a friend to get you into trouble," Harry assured her.

"Like my loyalty to Calvin Dillard? Because I don't consider that misplaced."

"Neither do I," Harry said. He captured her hand, rose, and pulled her to her feet. "It's part of who you are. I'm good with that. In my family we understand loyalty, even when it's misplaced. Marry me, Rachel. I want a full Covenant Marriage with all the trappings."

"Again?"

He smiled. "I'm willing to risk it if you are."

"Are you sure that's what you want?" she asked uneasily. "You'd have to meet my family, and there will be an additional Harmonic Enlightenment ceremony to go through. We have our own set of traditions in the Community."

His eyes burned with the heat of love. He drew her into his arms.

"Lately you and I survived a firebombing, an encounter with a sea monster, and some bad guys who wanted to kill us. Not to mention the escape from an exploding Alien laboratory full of hot artifacts and the results of some paranormal biology experiments. As long as I have you at my side, I can deal with your family and an HE wedding ceremony."

She smiled and wrapped her arms around his neck. "Of course you can. You're the great-grandson of a pirate and you're a shadow-aura. You're a real-life legend. You can handle anything."

Harry kissed her. She kissed him back.

After a while he picked her up in his arms and started to carry her out of the kitchen.

Darwina grabbed Amberella and another chocolate zinger. She hopped down from the windowsill and bustled to the door, chortling.

"I think she's expecting a hot date," Rachel said. "I'd better open the door for her."

"We may have to install a dust bunny door," Harry said.

He carried Rachel across the kitchen. She reached down and opened the door. Warm, balmy night air wafted into the room.

"No storm tonight," Harry said. "That's a good sign."

Darwina dashed outside onto the darkened porch with Amberella and vaulted up onto the railing.

"Have fun," Rachel said. "But no riding around in fast cars with guys."

Darwina chortled.

Rachel closed the door and locked it. Then she de-rezzed the lights. After all, Harry did not need artificial illumination to find his way to the bedroom.

At the top of the stairs Rachel heard the delicate, musical clash of her charms and then she forgot everything except the sweet, hot fire of love that burned in the atmosphere.

REX APPEARED OUT OF THE NIGHT, HIS CRYSTAL-STUDDED clutch purse glittering in the moonlight. He fluttered across the yard and bounded up onto the railing, chortling a romantic greeting. Darwina was waiting, with Amberella clutched in one paw. She gave him half the chocolate zinger.

They perched there together for a while, savoring the evening and the chocolate zinger. When the moon rose, they bounced down to the ground and slipped away into the darkness. A wonderland lit with sparkling crystal waterfalls and flowers that glowed in shades of ultralight beckoned. It was a fine night to go hunting.

TURN THE PAGE FOR A LOOK AT

Dream Eyes

by Jayne Ann Krentz

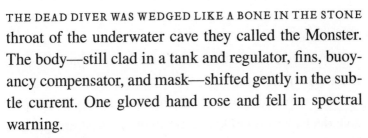

THE DEAD DIVER WAS WEDGED LIKE A BONE IN THE STONE throat of the underwater cave they called the Monster. The body—still clad in a tank and regulator, fins, buoyancy compensator, and mask—shifted gently in the subtle current. One gloved hand rose and fell in spectral warning.

Turn back.

But for Judson Coppersmith there was no going back.

The locals on the island claimed that the flooded cave beast swallowed divers whole. The adrenaline junkies who were foolish enough to ignore the signs outside at the entrance never got far inside the uncharted labyrinth of underwater passages. The smart ones turned back in time. But the explosion in the dry section of the cavern had sealed the aboveground exit and canceled that option. His only hope was to try to swim out to the sea through the Monster.

There was no darkness as dense and relentless as that of the interior of an underwater cave. But the clarity of the water was surreal. The beam of the flashlight sliced through the deep night like a laser, pinning the body.

He swam closer and took stock of the dead man's equipment. Relief swept through him when he saw that the killers had not bothered to drain the victim's air tank. He stripped it off the bloated body, tucked it under one arm, and helped himself to the diver's flashlight as well. Throughout the process the dead eyes stared at him reproachfully through the mask.

Sorry, pal, but your gear is of no use to you now. Not sure it will do me any good, either, but it will buy me a little time.

He eased past the body and focused the sharp light on the twisted rock passage. The urge to swim forward as quickly as possible was almost overwhelming. But impulsive decisions would kill him as surely as running out of air. He forced himself to drift for a few seconds

There it was, the faint but steady pull of the current. It would either be his lifeline or the false lure that drew him to his death. He slipped into the stream of the ultra-clear water and allowed it to guide him deeper into the maze.

The islanders claimed that there was an exit to the sea. That had been proven years ago by a simple dye test. A coloring agent poured into the cavern pool had emerged a short distance offshore. But the island was riddled with caves, and no one had been able to find the underwater exit point. Divers had died trying.

It was getting hard to breathe off the first tank of air, the one he had grabbed when he had been forced into the water. It was almost empty. He took it off and set it down on a rocky ledge with great care. The last thing he needed now was to stir up the sediment on the floor of the cave. If that happened, he would be forced to waste precious time waiting for the current to clear out the storm of debris. Time meant air usage. He had none to spare. There was, in fact, a staggeringly high probability that he would not have enough air regardless of how carefully he managed the one commodity that meant life or death.

He slipped into the dead man's tank and waited a beat, drifting upward a little. Sometimes in a flooded cave the current was stronger toward the roof of the tunnel.

Once again he sensed it, the faint, invisible tug that urged him deeper into the flooded labyrinth.

Some time later—he refused to look at his watch because there was no point—the flashlight began to go dark. He used it as long as possible, but the beam faded rapidly. The endless night closed in around him. Until now he had never had a problem with darkness. His paranormal night vision allowed him to navigate without the aid of normal light. In other circumstances, the natural para-radiation in the rocks would have been sufficient to illuminate his surroundings. But the strange aurora that had appeared in the cavern and the explosion that had followed had seared his senses, rendering him psychi-

cally blind. There was no way to know if the effects
would be permanent, and not much point in worrying
about it now. The loss of his talent would not matter if he
did not make it out of the flooded catacombs alive.

He fumbled with the flashlight that he had taken off
the body, nearly dropping it in the process of switching
it on. The chill of the water was making him clumsy.
The thin suit he wore provided only limited protection.
Although the island was in the Caribbean, he was in
fresh water here in the cave and the temperature at this
depth was unpleasantly cold.

Ten minutes later he rounded a bend and saw that the
rocky corridor through which he was swimming narrowed drastically. He was forced to take off his tank and
push it into and beyond the choke point. He barely managed to squeeze through after it. The nightmare scenario
of getting stuck—unable to go forward or back—sent
his heart rate climbing. He was suddenly using air at an
even faster rate.

And then he was on the other side. The passage widened once more. Gradually he got his breathing back
under control. But the damage had been done. He had
used up a lot of air.

He got the first clue that the current was guiding him
in the right direction when he noticed that the once
crystal-clear water was starting to become somewhat
murky. It was an indication that he had reached the point
where the fresh water of the underground river was con-
verging with seawater. That still left a lot of room for
things to go wrong. It was entirely possible that he would

discover the exit only to find out that he could not fit through it. If that happened, he would spend his last minutes as a condemned man gazing upward through the stone bars of his cell at the summer sunlight filtering through the tropical sea.

The second flashlight slowly died, plunging him into absolute darkness. Instinctively he tried to heighten his talent. Nothing happened. He was still psi-blind.

All he could do now was try to follow the current. He swam slowly, his hands outstretched in an attempt to ward off a close encounter with the rocky walls of the cave.

At one point, to keep his spirits up more than anything else, he took the regulator out of his mouth long enough to taste the water. It was unmistakably salty. He was now in a sea cave.

When he perceived the first faint glow infusing the endless realm of night, he considered the possibility that he was hallucinating. It was a reasonable assumption, given the sensory disorientation created by the absolute darkness and the fact that he knew he was sucking up the last of his air. Maybe this was the mysterious bright light that those who had survived near-death experiences described. In his case, it would be followed by for-real death.

One thing was certain. If he survived, he would never again take the light of a summer day for granted.

The pale glow brightened steadily. He swam faster. Nothing to lose.